To Catherine

With all best
happy reading !

# Everybody
## has a past

# Everybody
## has a past

## Peter Holmes

*Everybody has a past*
Peter Holmes

Published by Aspect Design 2012
Malvern, Worcestershire, United Kingdom.

Designed and Printed by Aspect Design
89 Newtown Road, Malvern, Worcs. WR14 1PD
United Kingdom
Tel: 01684 561567
E-mail: books@aspect-design.net
Website: www.aspect-design.net

Cover Design Copyright © 2012 Aspect Design

ISBN: 978-1-908832-26-9

*Acknowledgements*

Many, many thanks to my wife Hilary for all her support - unlike *This is Not a Love Story* she was allowed to read this one, and gave her approval. Very many thanks again to Jane Garfield and Karen Watson for reading earlier drafts, and offering positive comments. I am very grateful to Edward Gillespie, Managing Director of Cheltenham Racecourse, for showing me behind the scenes. Thanks also to Jas Karmil at the Chittening Industrial Estate - I apologise for having you stabbed! And thanks again to Allan and Sue Smith at Aspect Design, and this time I promise to turn up at a book signing.

*Chapter 1*

The sun rose above the horizon into a salmon pink dawn. The night had been still, so all the dust had settled. There was not a cloud in the sky. In the clear and relatively cool air the hills at the far side of the plain were perfectly visible, and looked much closer than they actually were. This heavenly period would be short-lived. In half an hour the sun would be a glaring bright yellow ball. And the wind would start to lift the dust kicked up by the morning traffic, so that soon the hills would have completely vanished.

A hyena edged its way forward. It knew what its nose was telling it, but the proximity of the road made it very nervous. It would have preferred to find this feast in the dark. But there was no traffic this early in the morning, so slowly it made its way up to the edge of the road. A zebra was lying dead, stiffening already with rigor mortis. Now in place, fear was replaced by hunger, and the hyena tore in to the zebra's belly.

Already in the sky the vultures had seen it. Within minutes they were arriving, ones and twos to start with, but then in rapidly increasing numbers. The hyena had to divide its time between eating and bird scaring. Then a second hyena arrived, and a jackal circled nervously.

One vulture, maybe realising the competition would be fierce, circled again. In doing this it picked out the second, smaller body. No other scavengers had found this one yet, so here was the chance for a few gulps before something more dominant turned up. It landed a few yards away, and waddled up to the carcase. A quick look, turning its head backwards and forwards to decide the best point of attack, then a quick prod with its beak. Go for the eye first. But just as it was about to do that, a car approached.

The vulture wasn't going to abandon this meal, so it just flapped off about twenty yards or so, to wait till the car had gone. But the movement caught the driver's eye, and in turning his head, he glimpsed the body. He braked sharply, and then reversed back.

No attempt had been made to hide the body. He looked at it through his open window, scanning round for anything else of significance. Slowly he got out, and walked carefully up to it, checking where he trod in case there was any evidence lying in the dust. Then he stopped and thought.

If the body had been that of a black man, it probably wouldn't even make a footnote in the local paper, except in the unlikely chance it was someone famous. With the still simmering ethnic and political tensions (as if ethnic and political were in any way separate in Kenya, and tensions were ever not simmering), dead black men turned up with monotonous regularity.

A dead black woman then? Even less interest. Probably just one of the prostitutes from the edge of Nairobi, who'd chosen the wrong customer. But a white man? Now that would be interesting. It would certainly shake a few people out of headquarters.

But it wasn't a white man. It was a white woman. And, despite the bullet wound in the head, clearly a very attractive woman. Very smartly dressed, so not a prostitute, or a tourist. This was someone who was going to be missed, and quickly.

He looked closely. There was no blood on the ground, so she hadn't died here. She must have been shot somewhere else, and just dumped here. Why?

This is going to be a shitload of trouble, he thought. Some of his colleagues he knew would have speedily dragged the body out into the bush. Very quickly it would just be a dispersed set of whitened bones, which when, or if, found would be bagged up and taken away. Identification, if it happened at all, would be much later.

But Daniel Kipruto was a very conscientious officer. Such a thought never crossed his mind. Quite the opposite. He had aspirations to be a detective, and this was a glorious opportunity.

Without further ado he walked back to his car to radio it in. But then he became aware of the mass of vultures ahead. Fearing something much worse, a massacre maybe, he jumped into his car and drove on, maybe three hundred yards. He was relieved to see, as his car dispersed the scavengers, that it was only a zebra. Already the hyenas and vultures had attacked the carcase so much it would have been difficult to see how it had died. But Officer Kipruto could work out how without getting out, not that he would get out with the hyenas there.

Was it just a coincidence the two bodies were so close? He thought not. Having dumped the woman the vehicle sped off, and ran straight into the zebra. The vehicle couldn't have been a car, because if it had it would still be there, a wreck, and probably with dead or injured people inside. You don't come away lightly damaged from a collision that kills a zebra, even a yearling like this one.

A truck then, or a wagon. Even that would have been badly damaged. The glass on the road presumably came from the lights. But the vehicle had clearly still been drivable, since it was no longer there, so had at least limped away. How far? It was more than ten miles to Salama, but there was nowhere closer in the Mombasa direction. And back towards Nairobi, nothing of significance before Kyumvi.

Although the zebra was evidence, he could only guard one body. He reversed his car back down the road. The persistent vulture was back, in position to start eating. And he now had friends coming to join him. Hyenas would be here soon, and possibly even lions, which were as partial to carrion as everything else. This was going to be dangerous.

So he parked his car as close as he could to the body. He mostly closed the window, so nothing could reach in, and got out his gun. Then he reached for the radio. It was starting to get hot. They'd better be quick, he thought.

*Chapter 2*

Four fifty four. The second hand seemed almost not to be moving. Slowly it dragged its way round. Ten seconds, five, two. Four fifty five. Now even slower.

"Are you all right, Baz?"

The question was half joking, half concerned. Barry shook himself, and tore his eyes away from the clock "Sorry, Linda. I was miles away."

"Doesn't matter how hard you watch it, it'll still take the same time to get to five. Look Baz, if you've got the time I've got the Morrison account ready, and if you sign it off I could get it in the post tonight."

"Pass it here then." Barry no more than glanced at it, then signed the bottom.

"Is that all the checking you do?"

"When was the last time you got something wrong?"

Linda smiled. "One day I'll put in a deliberate mistake. Maybe add a nought or two."

"No you won't." Barry looked at the clock again. Four fifty nine. Close enough. He looked round the room. As well as him and Linda there were seven others, all seemingly hard at work. "Come on you lot. Time to go. We're not paying overtime you know." There was some movement, but Barry was already almost out of the door.

Linda was looking after him. "Why does he go so quickly?" she asked, to no-one in particular. "He never used to. It's not as if he's got any reason to get home."

Barry walked briskly down the corridor, and out of the front door. It was five minutes to the bus stop, and the bus left at nine minutes past. He'd be there on time, as he had been most evenings for the last eight weeks. But would she be on it?

The Park and Ride stop was on the Promenade, right outside Whittards of Chelsea – very useful if the bus was late and you were short of tea. Barry never had been.

He joined the end of the queue. She wasn't in it. The bus came, and the queue all shuffled on. Barry got his usual seat, a group of four, where he had room to spread out if the bus wasn't full. Her seat was already occupied; maybe she'd have to sit next to him, though she never had yet. And he'd never sat next to her.

The door closed, and then opened again. Just in time, she got on. Same light blue coat as always. Same black trousers. She walked up the aisle, and sat next to a woman three seats in front of Barry. She didn't look at him, and he didn't stare at her.

Barry had never spoken to her. It wasn't that he was shy, just that he'd never really had the opportunity. Or anything to say. And he was considerably older than her. And she was wearing a very chunky, and rather tacky, wedding ring.

At the car park she was off before him. He walked to his car, which he parked in the opposite direction from hers; subconsciously he probably realised that otherwise he might be moving into stalker territory. Her car was as conspicuous as she was, a bright yellow Seat. Barry saw it some way in front, heading down the Gloucester road.

And that was it. The highlight of his day. There was nothing else to look forward to. An empty house. Something from the fridge. Perhaps watch a film on television. Then alone in bed. More than two years of being alone in bed.

Suddenly he just couldn't face it. Instead of turning right to head up the motorway to Worcester, on a whim he turned left, to Bristol.

The Victoria Bar was, not surprisingly, on Victoria Street. Since it was a Tuesday he parked relatively easily. How long was it since he was last here? Maybe over a year. He'd not consciously been avoiding coming; in fact he had rung only a couple of weeks ago. Or was it longer?

The first thing he noticed was that the place was almost empty. Six o'clock on a Tuesday was never going to be busy, which was a pity. The second thing was that he didn't recognise the girl behind the bar. She seemed very young. Student, Barry surmised.

"What can I get you?"

"Pint of Carlsberg, please. Is Nick around?"

"He went out about an hour ago. Chris had some sort of domestic crisis. But I don't reckon he'll be long. Do you want to see him?"

"If he gets back soon. I'll sit over in the corner."

In a strange way sitting alone in the corner of the familiar bar was not as bad as sitting alone in his familiar house. That was probably because the house was a place of shared memories, but this was his own place, before he'd met her. He had even thought of throwing everything up and coming back here. But he didn't have the courage for that.

A man soon joined the barmaid, having come in from the back. She spoke to him, and pointed to the corner. Steve noted the look of surprise on Nick's face when he saw who was in the corner, and immediately he came over to join Barry.

"Mr Clark, isn't it?"

"Hi, Nick. Good to see you."

"And you, Barry." Nick wasn't one to push. He knew he wasn't the reason Barry had stayed away. He could only guess at the emotions Barry had gone through, but two years was a long time to not start moving on. But there had been no blame in his jibe.

"Do you want to talk?

"I don't think so, but thanks Nick."

"You just really don't want to think."

"That's about it."

"Happy to sit with you anyway. It's a long time to not see a friend." He called to the barmaid. "Bring me over a red wine, Jude."

"How's Chris?" Barry asked, genuinely interested and not just to make conversation.

"He's fine. We've just had a bit of a plumbing crisis, but it's under control now. You'll remember he's not the best at practical stuff." Nick paused for a couple of seconds, then continued. "You know, we'll have been together twenty years this year. There's going to be a party, and we're hoping you'll come. After all, I've known you nearly that long as well."

Christ, was it really that long? Well, nearly. He remembered that day so clearly. How old had he been? Just over twenty? No, a bit older. Twenty two. When he arrived at the Victoria Bar he'd been quite surprised. He had expected something a bit rougher. But he had dressed smartly anyway. Ten o'clock in the morning, so the bar wasn't open. The door was unlocked, and he went in.

He had never had an interview in his life. He had no idea what to expect. Maybe some people behind a desk. Him sitting on a chair, like Mastermind, answering (and deliberately not answering) questions on his specialist subject – himself.

But Niklaus Papandopoulos didn't value that sort of interview. He knew himself to be the best judge of a person. And the best way to do that was just to talk. Hiring an employee was like hiring a member of your family, or, in a small business like this, more like a spouse. Someone you would spend long hours with, and whose company would not become irksome. So they sat down, and Barry was easily persuaded to take off his jacket and tie.

Nick was looking for a doorman. It was clear that physically Barry was well equipped for this role. But he had no certification, and the City Council was clamping down hard on unlicensed bouncers. But Nick also needed a barman, and a barman who could look after himself if things turned nasty would be a real bonus.

The first thing that Nick decided about Barry was that he liked him. He seemed pretty decent, and bright. But it was also clear that a past, and a recent past at that, was not being revealed. That wouldn't necessarily be a problem, and he wasn't going to pry. But it was subject to one question. "Are you wanted by the police?"

"No."

"OK then. So, if I employ you, how long will you be around?"

"I don't expect to be going anywhere soon. I want to enrol at college and get some qualifications. But before that I need to get some money, so I'm looking to work some long hours to start with."

"And when could you start?"

"Today, if you want me to."

He'd worked at the Victoria Bar for five years, give or take. They were five very happy years. But not as happy as ones to come. And Nick was undoubtedly his best friend. When Barry's life had gone in a new direction, it wasn't the way he had expected. But he certainly wasn't complaining. Now so much had now come to an end, and he felt hollow. Would he ever be able to move on? He couldn't see how. But there was that woman on the bus.

And he wasn't going to tell Nick about her.

*Chapter 3*

Calm was suddenly restored to the house. The children had left. Late, as always. But they'd still managed to just catch the bus.

Steve put the paper on the kitchen table, and half looked at the front page. "What time's your flight?" he asked.

"Not till four. But I'll call in to the department first. What are you doing today?"

"I've got to do a bit of research. Then I'm on the radio at two thirty, and again at five. But I'm hoping to fit in some writing around those. Anything's better than looking through Meyer's report again."

"Is it bad?"

"It's excellent work. But whereas Jim Wilkins could make paint drying a riveting page-turner, poor old Hans would stop you reading the Charge of the Light Brigade after the first paragraph."

"Well, you chose him. It's your panel."

"I know. Anyway Prof, when's your presentation?"

"Tomorrow morning. First thing. But I've also got to open the conference tonight, after dinner. You know, I just can't get used to the 'Professor' bit yet. It's all shiny and new, and I just can't believe it belongs to me."

"But it does Debs, and you thoroughly deserve it. And I get the fun of shagging my professor."

"Technically I'm not your professor. And I've had no offers from the more attractive students attempting to inflate their grades."

"Not yet. What about from the less attractive ones?"

"Those days have long gone. Do you remember Lucy Martin was doing that? Given how little work she did, that upper second was a surprise, for those who didn't know."

Steve didn't reply. "Surely you remember Lucy? Redhead, lovely smile, swore more than me."

Still no reply. Steve was clearly engrossed in something in the paper. Deborah walked across, and peered over his shoulder. "What's more interesting than me?"

Steve was looking at a photo of a woman. "So now you're lusting after women in the paper?" She read a few words. "And dead ones, at that. Mind you, she was a stunner."

To her amazement, she saw a drop of water hit the paper. "Fuck, Steve. I am sorry. Did you know her?"

"Yes."

"Well?"

"I couldn't have known her much better."

The implication of that hit her. "Before you knew me?"

"Yes. Of course."

"I'm sorry, but I had to ask."

"I know."

Deborah read a bit more. "Sylvia Murungaru? She doesn't look like a 'Murungaru' to me."

"She was plain Sylvia Jones when I knew her. The second last time I saw her she lent me a bottle of aspirin, which I never returned. The last time was at our college reunion, before I joined you in Peru. She was single again then."

"Single again?"

"She had a tosser of a boyfriend. I was a bit of distraction during one of their bad patches. Later she married him. But she divorced him soon after, because he was sleeping with a colleague, or maybe his secretary, or possible both. She admitted it was hypocritical of her, but I knew them both and she was the decent one. Maybe a touch over-sexed, but that's not a crime."

"So after that she married a Mr Murungaru. You get the impression from this he was an up and coming chap in Kenyan politics."

"You've seen this bit at the end? He's missing, along with their kids. I wonder if he killed her. I find that unlikely. No-one who knew Sylv would want to kill her. I bet this is political. Kenya gives me the impression of being a pretty unstable place these days."

"This is going to be the end of your research today, isn't it? But don't forget your interviews."

"They will be ringing me, so that won't be a problem. But you're right. I'm going to see what I can find out. I feel I owe it to her."

As soon as Deborah left, Steve was on the internet. First he looked up Patrick Murungaru. He'd studied at King's College, Cambridge, from where he graduated with a first in economics. Currently Minister of Trade in the Kenyan government. A picture showed him to be a very handsome man, athletically built. Steve felt a pang of jealousy; brilliant, and good looking with it. No wonder Sylvia had taken to him.

A bit more digging found that they'd met at a conference on trade relations between Africa and Britain. They had two young children. With their genes, they should have a bright future!

The Kenyan papers had some more information. Murungaru was described as a rising star in the Kenyan government. As Trade Minister, he had expressed concern about the effects of political instability on the country's wildlife. Steve grunted his approval of the environmental credentials; perhaps Sylvia had a soft spot for environmentalists as well. Poaching had hugely increased, and there was evidence that ivory was being shipped abroad.

There were a few suggestions of what might have been behind Sylvia's murder, but none seemed particularly plausible. The Minister had disappeared with his two children. Family and friends had been interviewed, but none could cast any light on that.

The *Daily Nation* had a few more details. She'd been found by the side of the Nairobi to Mombasa road, outside a place called Salama. No cause of death was given. Steve called up Google Earth. The search did not find Salama. So he moved to Nairobi and zoomed out till he picked up Mombasa. The A109 joined the two. The implication from the paper was that Salama was the Nairobi end, so he zoomed back in along the road until he found it, about fifty miles south-east of Nairobi. On both sides of the town the road seemed to pass through a large featureless area, which Steve assumed was bush.

How old would Sylvia have been? His age, of course. Just over forty. That was cruelly young to be killed. And with young children too, although their fate was clearly in doubt. He wondered how thorough an investigation the Kenyan police would carry out. Their general record was not good.

He shook himself. It wasn't his job to investigate. He'd better get back to publicising his report.

*Chapter 4*

Barry was deep in thought walking to the bus. It had been quite a bad day. Laura had made a serious error on the Paterson account. Fortunately he had picked it up in time, and had been able to appease Patersons.

But Laura had been very upset. Whilst it was her error, Barry had known she was quite inexperienced. He should have kept a closer eye on what she was doing. Maybe it was just her name that made him really upset, but in any case he hated to see one of his team in tears.

He got on the bus and sat in his usual seat, mind still lost in thought. The bus filled up. A young couple sat opposite him, the young man loud and arrogant, posing to his girlfriend. He put his feet up on the seat next to Barry. Barry despised such ignorant, loutish behaviour, but he held his tongue. The youth's foot knocked against Barry. Restraint was becoming very difficult indeed. Fortunately traffic was light, and the journey was quick.

The bus pulled in to the car park. People started to stand up as it pulled to a stop. Barry was kicked again. Something snapped. He swept the offending feet off the seat. Surprise spread across the youth's face. As they caught each other's eyes, they both jumped to their feet.

Barry half expected what happened next. He was back many years, but this time he didn't shout 'Knife!'. Instead he took half a step backwards. A woman screamed. Barry kept a steady look into the young man's eyes, but his anger burnt deep. "So, what are you going to do now, big boy?" he taunted.

"Fuck you, mate. I'm going to stick you."

"Really? That would be smart. So you'd kill me. For all you know, I could be dying already. Maybe I've just been diagnosed with cancer.

Six months to live. You'd be doing me a favour. What about you? Life imprisonment. Maybe serve ten years. By the time you come out you'd have been so many people's girlfriend, you'll have to wear a nappy. And she'll have three kids with your best friend, and will have forgotten what you look like."

"The police won't touch me, fucker. You don't know who you're talking to. I'll take my chance." He lunged forward with the knife.

But he also didn't know who he was talking to. Barry sidestepped, deflected the knife-wielding arm with his left hand. His right hand moved behind the youth's head, and smashed his face into the upright bar. There was an unpleasant crunching noise, and blood spurted out. With a scream the boy sunk to the floor, dropping the knife.

The bus door was open, and most people had left already. But Barry was surprised to see the blue-coated woman looking at him, mouth agape. He hadn't seen her, possibly because she wasn't blue coated today, but wearing a very smart brown jacket. As he caught her eye, she turned and got off. Barry followed, but, as he passed the driver, said, "Sorry about that, mate." But he had no intention of waiting for the police to arrive.

Back in his car, Barry took a couple of deep breaths. He reflected on how calm he'd been. Maybe violence was like riding a bike – you never forget about how to do it.

As he turned on to the Gloucester road he saw that there was only a single car between him and the yellow Seat. What would she have thought of what he'd done? He hadn't even noticed her get on, he'd been so engrossed in his thoughts. But why, of all people, had she stopped to stare at what was happening?

As always, everyone was accelerating hard on the long straight. A dark blue Mondeo shot past on the outside, but then, no doubt having misjudged the distance to the motorway turn, cut in sharply. Barry saw immediately the danger, but it all happened too quickly. The Mondeo just clipped the front wing of the Seat. It was only a small impact, but it was enough to push the yellow car to the left. The front wheel of the Seat caught the kerb.

Barry could not believe what happened next. The Seat flipped into the air. It rolled over sideways, but at the same time its nose dipped so that when it hit the verge it flipped over lengthways as well. Even this may not have been too serious, since both rolls had taken it back upright, but it smashed into a tree and came to a dead stop.

Brakes screeched all around. There was a small series of minor collisions as drivers watched what was happening, rather than the road. Barry had mounted the verge, and had avoided all of this, but he raced from his car to the wreck of the Seat.

Amazingly, the girl was just sitting in her seat. There were no airbags, but her seatbelt seemed to have done the trick. Barry tried to open the door, but it was too damaged to open. The passenger side was better, and he pulled it open and leant over. The girl's eyes were open.

"Are you OK?"

She turned her head towards him, but her expression was blank. Not surprisingly she was in shock, but at least she was alive.

He tried again. "Are you hurt?"

No answer. But she looked unhurt. But as Barry scanned down, his heart missed a beat. A large red pool was forming on the floor. It seemed to be coming through the black trousers.

A hand pulled at his shoulder. He turned. The man behind said, "Are you a first aider?"

"No," Barry admitted. "But she's got a bad injury on her leg. She's losing a lot of blood. Let's get her out."

"No, it's too dangerous to move her. Let me look, and you check that the ambulance has been called. And take her bag so we can find out who she is."

Barry pulled the bag off the seat, and stepped back. There was a loud hissing coming from the front of the car. Presumably from the radiator, he thought. But then he noticed the strong smell of petrol. Before he could shout a warning, with a loud 'woof' the engine compartment burst into flames.

"Shit!" he shouted. He threw the bag away from the car. Then he pulled the first-aider away back out of the car and pushed him to one side. It may cause her more damage, he thought, but he wasn't going to let her burn alive.

The heat was already close to unbearable, and the tank could explode at any moment. He reached in and undid the seatbelt. Then, roughly grabbing her under the armpits, he used his strength to pull her out of the car. He dragged her back about thirty yards before his strength gave out, and he collapsed on the ground. There was a loud bang, and the whole car was suddenly alight. He had just been in time.

The first-aider reappeared, rather shaken. "Thanks mate," he said. "But we're going to have to stop this bleeding. What's your name?"

"Barry."

"I'm Tom. Right, we need to tear her trousers to see what's going on."

The blood was coming, and coming fast, from above her right knee. Using a small tear, Barry used his strength to rip a substantial length off the trouser leg. He wasn't prepared for what he saw. Blood was pumping out, and there appeared to be the end of a bone sticking through the skin. He turned to one side, and retched.

"Come on, Barry. She needs you to be better than that. We need to stop this bleeding pretty damn quick." Tom quickly took the torn length of trouser, folded it and pressed it to the wound. This only partly reduced the bleeding. "Can you get the first aid kit from my car?"

Before Barry could move, a hand stretched out from the crowd. "Here, use mine."

"Thanks," said Tom. "Barry, take over here. Just keep pressing."

Barry was scared he would hurt the girl, but looking at her face he could see she was already unconscious. Loss of blood was taking its toll.

Tom worked quickly, padding the wound, and, with Barry's help, bandaging it. But blood still kept coming, although more slowly.

And then the ambulance arrived, and now Barry was superfluous. As the professionals took over, Barry left Tom to report what had happened, and what they'd done. The car was still burning furiously, but Barry needed to approach a bit to retrieve the handbag. Retreating again, he opened it. He pulled out a purse, and in that found her driving licence. Michelle Young.

The police were now on the scene. They were moving the onlookers back to a safe distance. The road was closed. A fire engine arrived, coming up the wrong side of the now empty carriageway from the motorway roundabout. Very quickly the car was extinguished, but all that was left was a smoking wreck.

Michelle was on a stretcher. There was urgency about the actions now, so Barry realised her life was in danger. A policeman started to push Barry back, but he resisted. "I'm with her," he said. "Her name's Michelle. I want to go to the hospital with her."

"You can't go in the ambulance. I'll take you in my car."

"Mine's over there. It's not damaged."

"I thought you said you were with her."

"I work with her." Barry thought it easier to lie.

"OK." The ambulance pulled away. "Follow me. I'll ask some questions when we get there."

Barry took the bag, and jumped in his car. The police car pulled away, lights and siren both on.

The ambulance arrived at Cheltenham General just before them. The policeman led Barry through into A&E. But Michelle wasn't there. She'd been taken straight to surgery. There was nothing Barry could do. Exhausted, dirty and dishevelled, and with Michelle's blood all over him, he collapsed in a chair.

The policeman sat next to him. "I'll get you a drink." He brought back two cups, one with water, the other with some sweet tea.

"Thanks." Barry knocked the water back, and then sipped at the tea.

"Wait here for a bit, Sir. I've got to report in."

"OK." Barry finished the tea. Then he opened Michelle's bag again. He rummaged through all the standard female items, and pulled out a mobile phone. This was promising. It was still on. Naughty, thought Barry, it should be off while you're driving.

He scrolled through the contacts. Lots of names. 'Dad' was promising, but he carried on through, and was pleased to come to 'ICE'. He dialled the number.

"Hello, Shell." A man's voice.

"Sorry, it's not Michelle. I'm using her phone. I'm afraid she's had an accident. She's in Cheltenham Hospital."

"Who are you, mate?" The voice was aggressive, and, Barry thought, more suspicious than concerned.

"My name's Barry. Who am I speaking to?"

"I'm Justin. She's my wife. What happened?"

"She crashed her car. She's in the operating theatre now. I'm in the A&E. I'll wait here till you get here."

"OK, mate. I'll be there soonest." Less aggressive now.

Barry put the phone back in the bag, just before the policeman returned. "Right, Sir. I'm going to have to get some details from you. The car's registered to a company called Gloucester Imports. Is that who you both work for?" There was an odd tone as he asked this.

"She probably does. I don't"

"I thought you said you worked together."

"I did. That seemed the easiest thing to say. We just see each other on the bus." This was also still a stretching of the truth, but it was notionally correct. "Her name's Michelle Young. I've rung her husband, Justin, and he's on his way."

The policeman's eyes narrowed. "You know Justin Young?"

Alarm bells were ringing loudly in Barry's head. He could feel he was digging a hole, but he couldn't work out why. "No. I just see Michelle on the bus."

"So, if you don't mind me asking, what is the nature of your relationship with Mrs Young?"

"I don't have a relationship with her. I just see her on the bus."

"Have you ever spoken to her?"

"No. Not till tonight."

"I see." And Barry could see that he did indeed see. A middle-aged man lusting after an attractive younger woman. Possibly even a stalker. Well, Barry couldn't stop him thinking that, and it wasn't so far from the truth.

But whatever he was thinking, the policeman had a job to do. He got his notebook out. "I'll need you to tell me what happened tonight. Can you give me your name and address please."

Just as Barry was finishing, Justin Young arrived. Barry had no doubt who it was. He was mid twenties, thick set and with tattooed arms. But it wasn't that that gave him away. It was the policeman standing up and saying sarcastically, "Mr Young. How pleased to see you."

Justin barely glanced at Barry. "What's the plod doing here then? I want to see my wife."

"She's in theatre. I suggest you sit with Mr Clark here till there's some news. I expect he'll be waiting. Goodnight." And he was off.

Barry had stood up, and now Justin gave him some more attention. He looked him up and down. Barry could see that he was being appraised. He wasn't sure of the outcome, but he suspected Justin decided that Barry wasn't someone to mix it with, unless absolutely necessary. "OK mate, tell me what happened."

So Barry explained again. While he was doing this, a much older man quietly, almost meekly, sat down next to Justin. Justin glanced at him and gave an off-hand greeting. "Evening, Derek." And to Barry, "Her dad." The older man nodded, and then coughed alarmingly.

They sat in silence for a good half hour, before Barry went to ask at reception if there was any word.

"Sorry, no. She's still in theatre. We've had no word on how she's doing."

Barry gave it another half hour, but then decided that he might as well go. There was nothing to be gained from waiting here; it would only fuel some sort of suspicion. Before going he asked, "Will it be OK if I call to see how she is later?"

Justin did give him a half suspicious look, but just said, "Up to you, mate. If you want to."

"Thanks." Barry headed out the door, but if he thought his evening was over, he was sadly mistaken.

"Mr Clark. Can I have a word please?"

Despite the lack of uniform, Barry was certain this was another policeman. How come he knew Barry's name? But he decided to act innocent. "Who are you?"

"Detective Inspector Simon Howell. My car will be a good place to talk."

"What about?"

"I have a few questions about your relationship with Justin Young. And about an earlier incident on a Park & Ride bus."

Barry decided his best interest would lie in a degree of co-operation. "OK."

"So," DI Howell began, "how long have you known Justin Young?"

"About an hour."

"Really?"

"Yes. I know his wife by sight from the bus. I just came in to see if there was anything useful I could do."

"But according to PC Harrison you claimed you worked with her."

"Yes. That was on the spur of the moment. I didn't think I'd be allowed to come in otherwise."

"But why would you want to, since you only know her by sight? You'd done your bit at the scene."

Barry didn't answer.

"So, you see this good looking woman on the bus, and you fancy her. Bit of a fantasist maybe. And here's the opportunity to get to know her."

"I'm not entirely sure what I've done to deserve this sort of abuse."

"Well, I'm not entirely sure I believe you about not knowing Justin Young. But you'd be a brave man, no, not brave, foolhardy, to fancy his wife."

"Thanks for the warning."

"But there is the matter of the fight on the bus."

"What fight was that?" Barry asked.

"A couple of witnesses have said you were involved in a brawl. But the injured party has made no complaint."

"He just had an accident. Slipped."

"Of course he did. Stood up too soon, while the bus was still moving."

"That would be it."

"OK Mr Clark. I can see you aren't going to say anything about that. But I have to say that, if it wasn't an accident, you appear to know how to look after yourself. So, on the off chance, before I came out I did a bit of a search through our records, to see if you had any form. There was nothing in the Gloucestershire force area. And nothing in West Mercia either. Not even a speeding ticket.

But given PC Harrison told me about your accent, I though I'd phone one of my West Midlands colleagues. Got talking to an old chap there. And bingo. They certainly know about you."

"I have no criminal record." Barry just stated that. It wasn't a protest.

"No. Not exactly. But not through lack of trying. And then for fifteen years you dropped completely off their radar. So, do you see much of Mr and Mrs Adams these days?"

"No."

"Well, I'm not surprised. I don't expect they'd have much to say to you."

Barry had had enough. "Since you don't appear to be charging me with anything, I'm going to go home." He opened the door.

"Before you go Mr Clark, a word of warning. I've decided I believe you when you say you don't know Justin Young. That means you don't know the sort of people you're mixing with. You may be able to look after yourself, but not against these people. You drive to Cheltenham every day from Worcester?"

"Yes."

"Why, when there's a perfectly good train? Have you never heard of global warming?"

"I just like to listen to music on the way in."

"That may be so. But I strongly recommend that for the foreseeable future you leave your car in the garage. You can guess what I mean by that. After all, Michelle Young won't be on the bus to lust after."

"I may take your advice."

"Do." D.I. Howell's tone softened. "Look, Mr Clark. Everybody has a past. But sometimes it can come back to haunt them. And according to other witnesses it was a brave thing you did there. You saved her life, for which I'm sure she'll be grateful. And maybe even Justin Young will be as well." He rummaged in his pocket, and produced a card. "Take my number. If you run in to difficulties with these people, give me a call. Don't just think you can sort things out yourself."

"OK." Barry took the card, put it in his wallet, and without another word went back to his car and drove home.

## Chapter 5

Barry rang the hospital from work the next day. Michelle was in Intensive Care. They would not give details, but Barry got the impression she was seriously ill. She would not be allowed visitors except for close family. It was recommended that he waited till after the weekend before ringing again.

The days passed slowly. This gave Barry far too much time to think. He thought about how this girl, who before had just been some sort of fantasy, although fantasy wasn't really the right word, had now somehow become part of his reality. He thought about the police, and the things they had asked about her husband. Since Michelle was just a fantasy, he'd be best waking up from it. But he was like a moth drawn to a candle.

So it was barely first thing on Monday morning that he phoned, although he did this with real trepidation. After all, she might be dead.

But she wasn't. She was out of Intensive Care, but still in the High Dependency Unit. She was still heavily sedated, and still not able to receive visitors except close family. Barry decided it was time to lie, and claimed to be her brother. This ploy was surprisingly successful, and he was allowed to call at six o'clock.

It was spot on six when Barry entered the Department of Critical Care. He had the sense not to bring flowers, and he was thorough in his use of the alcohol cleaner. He had been told that Michelle was only allowed two visitors at a time, and that nothing must be done to disturb her.

There was one other visitor present. Barry was relieved to see it wasn't Justin, but her father, Derek. Derek turned as he entered, and a surprised expression crossed his face. "I'm her brother," Barry said. "The son you forgot about."

Despite the circumstances, a half smile crossed Derek's face. Barry thought it was the type of face that smiles rarely crossed. Derek was probably no more than fifty, but he could pass for seventy easily. He seemed to have the weight of the world on his shoulders. And the condition of his daughter was probably only part of the reason for this.

Barry sat down. Michelle was asleep, drugged sleep. She seemed to be breathing normally. Her face was peaceful, and Barry thought how attractive she looked. "Justin not here then?" he asked.

"No." There was a strange tone to this 'no'. It wasn't 'no, but he'll be in later' or 'no, he's just gone'. It was more like 'no, why would he be here?'

Derek was clearly not going to talk. But he sat silently quite easily, and Barry got the impression he just didn't say much, rather than he just didn't want to talk to Barry. That was fine with Barry. He was happy to just sit.

Twenty minutes passed in silent watching, apart from occasional coughs from Derek. In that time Michelle barely stirred. No medical staff came in, but Barry was sure they would have looked frequently through the glass. Although he could have stayed much longer, Barry felt he didn't want to intrude. So he stood up to go.

"You off then?" That made four words Derek had spoken.

"Yes. I don't want to be in the way. And if she wakes up she'll want to talk to you, not me."

"You'll come again?" It wasn't a question. It was more of a plea. Barry was really surprised.

"Won't Justin be here with her?"

"I doubt it."

This was getting very odd. Barry wanted to ask a lot of questions, but didn't feel this was the time.

"I'll come again. Tomorrow, same time."

"Thanks. Stay longer though."

As he walked back to the car Barry's mind was racing. He couldn't work out what this all meant. Why wouldn't Justin be with his wife at this time? Was it because he couldn't bear to see her ill? Did he have a hospital phobia – unlikely, since he'd happily come in on the day of the accident. Of one thing Barry was certain, more would become clear as time went on, and he was determined to be around to find out.

At five to six the following day, Barry was heading back into St Luke's Block, towards the Department of Critical Care. What he didn't expect after the previous night's conversation was to walk straight into Justin Young.

"You back then, mate?" It was a funny sort of greeting. Not particularly aggressive, unlike what Barry would have expected. Just matter of fact.

"I thought I'd just call and see how she is."

"Not sure how you blagged your way in, mate, since you're not a relative. But she's through that way. Her dad's there."

"Since she's only allowed two visitors at a time, I'll come back another time."

"Don't worry, mate, I'm not stopping."

"No? Why not"

"Why would I want to stop with her? She's a cripple."

"What?" Barry wasn't sure he'd heard this correctly.

"She's a cripple, mate. They took her leg off. Couldn't save it apparently. Well, I don't want to spend my life with a fucking cripple. Imagine sleeping with that. No mate, I'm out of here. Tell you what though. You seem to like her, so you can have her." And with that he turned, and walked off.

Barry stood, frozen in place. He had never been so lost for words in his life. He was so incredibly angry it was like a physical pain. He wanted to run after Justin, and beat him to a pulp. He just couldn't believe what he had heard. His anger completely overwhelmed the actual news he'd received. But as his breathing started to calm, he realised the enormity of Michelle's position. She was to spend the rest of her life severely disabled, and her husband's response was to dump her like a soiled hanky.

He had to be calm before he went in. So he stood there, just breathing, for a full five minutes. Only when he felt fully back in control did he enter the unit.

Derek was by the bed. As Barry sat down, Derek nodded, the said "Did you pass Justin?"

"Yes." It was Barry's turn to say little.

"Did he tell you?"

"Yes." Barry looked at Michelle, still asleep, lying peacefully on her back. And he couldn't stop himself imagining what was under, or, more appropriately, what was not under the covers.

"Justin won't be back." Again Derek was just matter of fact.

"How can he abandon her?" Despite his control, the anger was clearly in Barry's voice.

"That's the way he is. I knew he would."

"How can you be so calm about it?" Barry was in danger of redirecting his anger towards Derek, who seemed not to be sufficiently protective of his daughter.

"What choice have I got? You don't know them."

"No, I don't. And the people who do seem to suggest I need to keep it that way. What will she do when she gets out of here?"

"That's a long way off."

They sat in silence for some time, each lost in thought while looking at the peaceful, apparently untroubled face in front of them. Barry was thinking what future lay in store for Michelle? There would be a long period of rehabilitation. No doubt she would be fitted with a prosthesis. But how would that rehabilitation go, in the light of the unbelievable cruelty of her husband?

Both their thoughts were interrupted by movement in front of them. Michelle's eyes fluttered. They didn't actually open, but she formed her lips as though speaking. Derek got out of his chair and bent down to listen. But it was clear that he couldn't make out any words. So he pulled his chair closer, and sat holding her hand.

Barry thought she'd lapsed back into sleep, but maybe five minutes later the lips moved again, and this time it was clearly a word. "Dad."

I'm here, Micky." Did no-one call her by her proper name?

"Dad. My leg hurts."

There was a sob from Derek. It was the first real emotion he'd shown, although Barry had been sure that it was always there. Unlike in Justin.

"Is Justin here?"

"No, Micky. He was here, but he left while you were still asleep."

With what seemed a tremendous effort she opened her eyes. "Thanks for being here Dad."

Without letting go of her hand, Derek moved back a bit to let her see more. Her eyes gazed straight ahead for some time, as if having to adjust to the shock of being open. They then moved slightly from side to side. Barry knew immediately when they had focussed on him. He sat, almost fearful of what her reaction would be, that's if she recognised him at all. But her expression didn't change. Barry almost started to think she wasn't really looking at him, but was just gazing into the distance.

Then she spoke again. Just one word. "Hello."

"Hello Michelle. Nice to see you awake."

She didn't answer for a bit. Barry wasn't sure if this was because each word was a struggle, or because she was thinking over what to say.

"What's your name?"

"Barry."

"It's good of you to come. You were there, weren't you?"

"Yes."

There was another long pause.

"You've always wanted to talk to me, haven't you?"

Barry was sure he'd gone bright red. But he might as well be honest. "Yes."

To Barry's great relief a nurse came in, at least temporarily saving him from further embarrassment. "Good," she said, "you're awake. I'll get the doctor."

Barry decided this was his opportunity to make his escape. He stood up and said, "Goodbye Michelle. I hope you get better soon." He hoped it didn't sound as trite to her as it did to him. Derek gave him a bit of a look, but said nothing.

"I'll get better quicker if you come and talk to me. Come back tomorrow."

There was no way he could resist that instruction. "OK. I'll be back at six."

He walked slowly back to his car, pondering all that had transpired that evening. He could see that this could be a pivotal point in his life. But he also realised that whatever his feelings were, they were suffused with a heavy feeling of guilt. He toyed with the idea of going back to the Victoria Bar and talking to Nick, but realised that he would have to spend his own time thinking this through before having that conversation.

*Chapter 6*

It was now very hot. The traffic was heavy on the road, and, even though this wasn't one of the unmade sections, dust was everywhere. It was over two hours since Officer Kipruto had radioed in his report. Within half an hour the other two Salama based constables, twin brothers Samuel and Joseph Amakobe, had arrived. The three of them had secured the scene, screening the body from the road and reducing the number of rubberneckers.

The zebra carcass was a problem. It was in the road and an obstruction to traffic. But it was also evidence. After a long discussion, they agreed to move it. So, with Daniel guarding the human body, Samuel and Joseph tied a rope to the legs of the already much reduced remains, and hauled it out into the bush.

Daniel's instructions had been just to wait for the forensics team to arrive from Nairobi. They clearly weren't in much of a hurry. Daniel was in need of a drink, and he had not had any breakfast. Joseph volunteered to head back into town to pick up some supplies.

He had been gone half an hour when two smart black cars and an ambulance sped up and skidded to a halt. As though carefully choreographed, all eight doors of the cars seemed to open at once, and eight suited men stepped out. All were wearing expensive looking sunglasses, and the suits did not appear cheap.

"You talk to them," Samuel whispered to Daniel, and then retreated. Joseph pulled up next to Samuel in the car, and he got in.

Daniel walked up to the group, who hadn't till that point in any way acknowledged the presence of the two uniformed officers. One of the group stopped him, not with a word but just with a raised hand. "Yes?" he said, with disdain.

"Officer Daniel Kipruto, Sir."

"And what do you want?"

"To make my report Sir. I was first on the scene."

"I assume the body's behind there?" He motioned at the screening.

"Yes Sir."

"OK. You've made your report. Now leave this to real policemen."

Officer Kipruto was outraged. He knew the city detectives had a reputation for arrogance, but this was beyond belief. He believed he had crucial information for the investigation, and had to pass this over. "With respect Sir, I have made detailed notes of the situation on my arrival, which I think will be........"

"I'm not in the slightest bit interested in your amateur scribblings. Do you think you will have found things we would miss? I just hope you haven't contaminated the scene with your interfering. Now just piss off back to your village. Haven't you got some traffic to direct somewhere?" And with that he turned back to the rest of his group.

Daniel initially just stared after him, seething with rage. He stood there, perhaps thinking that this was some sort of morbid joke, and that they would come back for his report. But not a glance came his way. So he went back to join the brothers.

"So, they didn't want help from the great local detective?" Daniel had made no secret of his desire to move out of uniform, and Samuel in particular ribbed him about it.

"No. Pass me a drink Joseph." They ate and drank in silence, watching the Nairobi detectives start to work. Despite their arrogance, Daniel thought he might learn something, so watched attentively. After a fairly elongated discussion, three of the group walked up to the screening. Instead of carefully parting it, one just pulled it apart. The other two crossed inside, and, to Daniel's horror, took an arm each of the body and dragged it towards the ambulance.

"That's not right," Daniel shouted, and reached for the door handle.

Joseph realised the danger. "No, Daniel. He grabbed Daniel's left arm, holding him in the car. But the door swung open, attracting the attention of the group. One walked briskly towards them. What he was proposing to do or say, however, was quickly forgotten. There was a splintering crash, as two lorries ran into each other, almost head on. The sight of a group of suited, sunglass-wearing men dragging a white woman's body out of the bush was clearly too distracting for one driver.

The advancing man, having instinctively leapt back as the crash occurred, took one last look at the three policemen in the car, and then turned back. With a screech of wheels, the doors slamming with the cars already moving, the three vehicles headed back towards Nairobi, neatly avoiding the traffic chaos they had left behind.

The three policemen ran to the scene of the accident. The impact had damaged the offside wheel of both vehicles, and neither looked like it would drive. But both drivers were out, and uninjured enough to be starting a fight. Nairobi traffic was trying to move past, but the Mombasa traffic was also trying to force its way in. So, for a time they would indeed be traffic policemen.

It was two o'clock before any semblance of normality was restored. Joseph and Samuel sped back towards Salama. But Daniel wanted to spend some time thinking. He sat in his car, which was now baking in the full sun. Samuel's jibe was a touch harsh; Daniel had some aptitude as a detective, but in Kenya such a move depended on who you knew, not what you know.

Even if the body had just been a dead prostitute, the police would have made a show of investigating. When Daniel had radioed in, Sergeant Murungi had told him just to continue to stand guard, since this had to be left to the city police. A few minutes later he was back on the radio telling Daniel that a top forensic team plus support was coming from Nairobi, and that Samuel and Joseph were on their way.

But the men who had arrived were clearly not a top forensic team, or indeed any sort of forensic team. Daniel would have laid a small wager that they weren't even policemen. This was a clean-up operation, not an investigation. What was going on?

He picked up his radio to share his concerns with the Sergeant. But he thought better of it. Samuel and Joseph would be back soon enough, and would make a full report. This gave Daniel a short window to do some detecting. Maybe this was his opportunity to make a big impression. Having made a decision, he pulled back out into the traffic towards Salama.

Just on the outskirts of town he came to Isaac's Garage. This was just about the first building you'd reach coming from Nairobi. And Isaac slept in the garage. Daniel was pretty sure the damaged vehicle would have tried its luck here.

He pulled in to the garage entrance. The workshop was fairly quiet.

Isaac's operation was quite small, just him and his son, John. John lived in town, with his wife and numerous children. Isaac was a proud grandfather, many times over. As Daniel got out, Isaac came straight over. It was almost as if Daniel was expected.

"Afternoon Isaac. How's business?"

"Good enough." Isaac's wrinkled face was smeared with oil, which had also got in his few remaining hairs. Many people would have long since retired at his age, but Isaac needed the money, so retirement wasn't an option. "You got a problem with that old car?"

"Yes. It's a police car. They've all got problems. But that's not why I called."

"No? So just a social call is it? I've not got time to talk. I'm very busy."

This was patently untrue. There was one car up on the ramp, and another in the corner. Neither owner appeared to be waiting. "Where's John today?"

"I let him stay home. Probably making more babies." Isaac yawned, exposing his few remaining teeth.

"Been a long day has it?"

"Long enough."

Isaac was never the chattiest person, but his answers were briefer and less friendly than usual. Daniel thought he was on to something. "What time did you start today?"

"'Bout usual."

"So your usual would be what, about half seven?"

"Bout that."

"But it was much earlier today, wasn't it? About three o'clock." This was just a punt, but he saw the look that passed across the old man's eyes.

"Why would I start then?"

"Because you had a lorry in. The one with the damage from hitting a zebra. Must have been a bit of a mess."

Isaac looked at him for a long time. It wasn't a stare, or a look of surprise, but a long look while he weighed things up in his mind. "It wasn't a lorry."

Bingo. "What was it then?"

"They said there'd be big trouble if I talked to the police."

"There could be big trouble if you don't. They've got some big shot detectives from Nairobi on the case." Daniel was sure this wasn't exactly true, but it was good pressure. "It won't take them long to make the same guess I have. They come in here, you get carted off to the city. Be there days, and then where's your business? You tell me, I keep them away."

Isaac breathed out a big sigh. "It was a truck. Toyota."

"A truck? How did that manage to drive away?"

"They said they just caught the zebra, passenger side. It had pressed the cab on to the wheel. They'd managed to pull this back by hand enough for the wheel to turn when they ran straight, but any turn to the left caught the wheel. They must have taken all the left hand bends really wide. The bumper was missing, but they said they had it in the back. The door wouldn't close, so they must have held it all the way."

"So what did you do?"

"They didn't care what I did, so long as they got going quickly. So they got me to cut off a large piece of the cab, so there was a hole through the floor. Then I welded the door shut."

"Where's the bit you cut off?"

"They took it. Put it in the back."

"Did you see in the back?"

"No. They kept me at the front."

"How much did they pay?"

"$100. US."

"Good business. Did you get the number?"

"No. I don't want no trouble here."

"No." Daniel wasn't surprised. But, he wondered, how many witnesses would have noted a Toyota truck, with a mangled wing, no bumper and a door welded closed as it drove down the Mombasa Road? Probably none. They'd take much more notice of an undamaged truck! Whilst this was a lead, he didn't think it would go as far as he'd hoped.

"But it had writing on the side."

"Really?" Suddenly things were brighter. "What did it say?"

"Heavenly Flower Export."

Daniel had his notebook out now. "You said 'they' before. Just a driver and passenger?"

"Yes."

"Describe them."

"The driver was a big man. Maybe six feet. Must have been close to 100kg. Looked like a Luo."

"Luo, huh?"

"Yes. And although he was dressed casual, he had some big rings. Not cheap ones."

"What about the passenger?"

"Well, for a start he was white."

That was a surprise. Isaac saw this. "Yes. White guy. Shorter than the driver. Well built, muscular. Tattoos over both arms. He had a big cut on the side of his head, and a bruise around it. And on the other cheek he had a long scratch, looked deep. But he looked like someone who'd make nothing of that. And he didn't. Just went into my toilet and cleaned up a bit."

"Kenyan?"

"Couldn't tell from the way he spoke. But he was well sunburnt, so no local white. I reckon he was British."

Daniel made some more notes. "Was the driver hurt?"

"He limped a bit, so maybe had hurt his leg. Left leg."

"I bet they were in a bad mood."

"Maybe before they knocked me up. But they were pretty pleased when I agreed to get them going again. Having a bit of a laugh with me."

Given that these people had just dumped the woman's body, Daniel couldn't work out why Isaac was left alive. Were these people so cocky that they didn't need to get rid of this witness? At that time of the morning it was likely no-one else would have seen them. "Did anyone else come in while they were here?"

"Old Moses called in. He was off to market and needed some oil. He was surprised to see the light on, so pulled in. He had no cash on him, as always, so he's going to owe me."

"He saw your visitors?"

"Yes. He just walked in. Took the oil, and left."

"Did he speak to them?"

"No. They seemed a bit cross, presumably because it delayed me working."

"I reckon you ought to let Moses have that oil on the house. He probably saved your life."

Isaac looked surprised. "Why so?"

"Your friends killed a white woman. Dumped her body just off the road. They hit the zebra as they drove off. You're a witness, and you've given me a description. They'd never have let you live if no-one had seen them in here."

Surprise turned to shock. Then Isaac let out a long, low whistle. "I thought they were bad. But not that bad."

Daniel put away his notebook. "I'm going back to the station now to report. But I'll be back later to talk some more."

As he turned to go Isaac stopped him. "There's more," he said.

"More?"

"Yes. There were people in the back."

"People? How do you know? Were they talking?"

"No, but I heard them move."

"How do you know it was people, and not an animal?"

"It sounded like crying. But sort of muffled. Didn't sound like an animal."

"Muffled like what?"

"Well, I could hear sniffling. But maybe there was something over the mouth."

"Like they were gagged?"

"Could be. And one last thing."

"Yes?"

"It wasn't flowers in there."

"Why not?"

"It was sitting too low on the back axle. Flowers ain't that heavy."

"Which way did they go when they left?"

"Mombasa."

"Thanks Isaac. I'll keep this to myself for the moment. If those Nairobi detectives come, just answer their questions. Don't volunteer anything. And don't say I've been here – they hate us country boys interfering."

Isaac smiled. "Shit on them."

When Daniel arrived back at the hut that passed for a police station in Salama, the twins were on their own. Sergeant Murungi had left early. He apparently had a headache. The headache was called Mercy, and she lived in a shack a couple of hundred yards from the station. Mercy was a full fourteen stones of real woman, and the worst kept secret in Salama. The only person who didn't know that everyone else knew was Sergeant Murungi. It had got to the stage where Mercy and Mrs Murungi were, if not friends, then at least on nodding terms with each other.

"Have you been detecting then?" Samuel's tone was a lot less sarcastic this time. Both he and Joseph appreciated that Daniel was smart enough to have found something out.

"A bit, yes. But I'm going to keep that to myself for a bit."

"Why's that?" Samuel quickly reverted to a less friendly tone.

"You saw the way that one man headed towards the car when I opened the door." It wasn't a question.

"Yes."

"Well, I reckon these are really dangerous people. Not knowing stuff might be safer."

"You don't think they were policemen, do you?"

"Do you?"

"No."

Daniel could see there was an opportunity to make some more enquiries, without interference. "Since the Sergeant's not here to stop me, I'm just going to nip up to Franklin's Grocery. Is the electricity on at the moment?"

"Been on an hour or so. Reckon it won't last much longer."

"OK. I don't expect to be that long."

Franklin's Grocery was the biggest store in Salama. It was still only a shack really, but it was a big shack. Franklin had got a prime position on the main road, and expanded from groceries into a cheap and cheerful truck stop. The food was reasonable and inexpensive, and the buses also now stopped there. In relative terms, Franklin was pretty wealthy, enough to buy himself a real luxury, a computer. It would be many years before broadband arrived here, and the electricity supply was erratic even on a good day. But you could get access to the internet.

Franklin had time for Daniel, because Daniel never shook him down for a bribe. Unlike Sergeant Murungi, who needed the money to keep his two women. So he was happy to let Daniel have the occasional go on the computer. But he was curious.

"So, what you wanting to look up then?"

"I just want to look up a couple of things for a current investigation."

"So, this would be about the dead white woman then?"

News clearly travelled back quickly. "Yes. I've got a couple of leads. But I wouldn't go talking about this Franklin. The people who did this may come back."

Franklin sat with him to help; Daniel wasn't any good with computers.

They started with Heavenly Flower Export. This was easy. It had a web page, and Daniel noted in his book the holding company it operated under. Some of the major companies supplied were listed, and he noted these as well.

If the van had been carrying flowers for export though, it wouldn't have been driving to Mombasa. Mombasa has an airport, but it would have been illogical to drive there from Nairobi, which had a big enough airport of it's own. And Isaac had said it wasn't likely to be flowers, and something heavy would be cheaper shipped.

Franklin thought for a bit. "There are two ports in Mombasa. There's the old port, which has the fishing boats, plus a few dhows. That's on the east of the island. And there's a deep water port on the west, Kilindini Harbour. I've been to the old port, but never the big one.

I reckon the dhows take stuff up and down the east coast, probably a lot of traffic to Arabia. The deep water port will take heavy stuff, and containers."

"Well, I bet the dhows smuggle a lot."

"Sure they do. But there's lots of people there, so you'd have to be careful. If you were doing anything really bad, better to do it in the big harbour."

"You ought to join the police Franklin, thinking like that."

"What, for your pay? No thanks. Anyway, let's look up the harbour, see what we can find out."

The Kilindini Harbour page wasn't particularly user friendly. However it had something called a KIN, listing a number of ships. "What's a KIN?" Daniel asked.

"No idea. But there seems to be one for each day, so I'd take a guess that it's just a list of expected arrivals."

The current KIN listed all ship arrivals due in the next ten days. There were a lot. The spreadsheet listed eighteen container ships, fifteen conventional ships, nine tankers and one 'other'. However if the van was due to meet a ship it was presumably one that had already arrived. But the previous KINs were still up on the site, so they called up the one from eight days ago. This had even more, with fifty one arrivals listed. Franklin printed the list, just before the electricity went off.

Since the break in supply was rarely less than three hours, Daniel thanked Franklin and headed back towards the station. It was now deserted; Joseph and Samuel had clearly decided the Sergeant wasn't coming back, so they might as well have a short day themselves. This suited Daniel, who wanted to sit and think. He felt he had done well today, and gathered a lot of very useful information. But he needed time to work out how it all fitted together. And to work out who in the world he could tell about what he came up with.

*Chapter 7*

Barry was back at the hospital the next night, but Michelle was very tired, and said very little. Derek sat with her the whole time. After half an hour she was fast asleep, so Barry slipped away. He didn't go at all the night after, although he couldn't say why. But the following night he regretted that, and was at the hospital promptly at six.

She was wide awake this time, but on her own. As soon as he came in her eyes brightened." I thought you weren't going to come back."

"I'll come if you want me to."

"Even though I'm a cripple?"

It was so matter of fact that Barry was shocked. "Why should that matter?"

"It matters to Justin."

"I know. He told me. I can't believe he could be so callous."

"Well, he never loved me anyway. And I've only lost a leg. You're dying of cancer."

"Am I? What makes you think that?"

"You said you were. Before you hit Wayne. On the bus."

Barry was surprised. "You know him?"

"He works for Justin's dad. Same as my dad. And me. Do you have cancer?"

"No. I made that up."

"Why would you say something like that?"

"I just wanted to say something that made him think what he was threatening was pointless. But it didn't work."

"Dad's dying of cancer."

A wave of guilt hit Barry. "I'm very sorry to hear that."

"It's not your fault. He's got lung cancer. Used to smoke like a chimney. He's given up now. Locked the gate after the horse has bolted, as my mum would have said. The doctor said he had six months, and that was three months ago. I was going to look after him, but I won't be able to do that now. He's had a bad turn today. That's why he's not here tonight."

"Do you want me to look in on him?"

Michelle looked at Barry. "That's very kind of you to offer. But I think he'll be OK for the moment."

They sat in silence for a bit. Barry was happy with this. But Michelle clearly wasn't. "You're not very talkative, are you?"

Barry smiled. "Not hugely, no."

"But will you answer questions if I ask them?"

"I might. Depends on the questions."

"OK. Firstly, I'm assuming you're not married, because you've got no ring."

"I might have taken it off before coming."

"Maybe. But you'd also have had to take it off before getting on the bus every day. Don't look surprised. Since I'd realised you were looking at me, I thought I'd check! Have you got a girlfriend?"

"No."

"Why not? Good looking bloke like you. Even if you are a bit old."

"I'm only forty. I might not be interested in women."

"Don't think so. Not unless you thought I was a man."

"All right. Could be because I'm an accountant."

"You an accountant? Stop messing me about. I've never met an accountant as fit as you. They're all small and hunched, with moustaches. What do you do really?"

"I'm an accountant. I told you. Although these days I'm a manager in charge of accountants. And many of them are young and female. But I do like to keep myself fit."

"I didn't mean 'fit' in that sense. Why haven't you teamed up with one of the women in your office then? They must have been throwing themselves at you."

"Because they work for me, and that wouldn't be right. Or fair. Let's talk about you."

"More comfortable than talking about you? OK, but it won't take long. What do you want to know?"

"What do you do?"

"I work for Justin's dad. I just do things around the office, filing, post, that sort of thing. Dad's worked for Mr Young for years. When Justin and I got married, they gave me something to do."

"What had you done before?"

"I worked in Sainsbury's, up by Swindon Village." Barry looked blank. "It's on the road out to Junction 10. You don't pass it the way you come in. I was on the tills. I'm not a great intellectual, but I liked working there, and the people I worked with were great. But Justin wanted me somewhere he could see me."

"You said he never loved you. So why did you marry him?"

"Well, Dad's always worked for Mr Young. Mr Young thought it would be good. Keep Dad close to the business. Justin didn't seem to mind."

"You make it sound like some sort of arranged marriage."

"It was, sort of. Dad wanted it, and I didn't mind. I've not really wanted for anything, except children maybe. And Justin's never hit me, and I don't think he sees other women. He's not like that."

"It's hardly romance though, is it? And now he's dumped you."

"You don't understand. That's just the way it is."

"I don't understand how you can take it so well. What sort of business is Mr Young in?"

"Imports."

"What do they import?"

"All sorts. Machinery. Food. Chemicals."

"Why are they based in Cheltenham? It's not by an airport, or by the sea."

"Mr Young likes the racing. He's got a big place in the Cotswolds. He owns a couple of horses. Cheltenham's just the office. They've got warehouses down at Avonmouth somewhere. Not that I've ever been there."

"What does your dad do?"

"He did a lot of driving, but not so much now. When Justin started up in the business he was put working with Dad. But Dad's ill, so he's been replaced by Wayne. But Mr Young still keeps Dad on the payroll."

"Very nice of him."

Michelle yawned. She suddenly looked less bright. Barry realised that all the talking had taken a toll. "Look, he said." I'm going to head off now, so you can get some sleep."

"OK. I am tired. But come again tomorrow."

"I can't, I'm afraid."

"Why not?" For the first time she looked unhappy.

"I've got to go away. Just for a few days. We're pitching for an account with a Dutch company. They've got offices in Britain, but they want me to go out to Leiden to their head office."

"On your own?"

"No. I'm going with a colleague called Linda." He smiled. "But we'll be in separate rooms. I'll come and see you when I get back. You'll probably be out on the general ward then."

"I'll miss you."

Barry had been looking forward to the Leiden trip since it was arranged a month previously, but now he wished he wasn't going. However he was professional enough to be able to get on with business despite this. Their presentations went well, and the board of AKL Holdings seemed happy with what they were shown. But Barry and Linda were less impressed when they looked at the books. These were a total mess.

Over dinner on their fourth night, Linda suggested that they'd need to stay a bit longer than they intended. She had known Barry for a long time, and, truth to tell, before she had married, harboured some hope he might ask her out. But she didn't hold it against him that he hadn't, and then life turned out differently for both of them. However, despite how he held his thoughts and emotions to himself, she probably knew him better than anyone.

"Right then Baz. Spill it."

"Spill what?"

"Come on. There's a girl, isn't there?"

"Not in the way you think."

"No? What other way then?"

"Someone I know is in hospital. She's had her leg amputated following a car accident." Barry felt quite bad misleading Linda like this, but the ploy was entirely successful.

"That's very sad. How's she doing?"

"OK, I think. But I do want to get back and see how things are going. However, I'm not going to risk anything by leaving too early."

"To be honest Baz, I don't think we can lose this one. Conversely, I don't think they can afford to lose us!"

"No, that's pretty clear. It's certainly in the bag. And I think our price might have gone up a bit. But I'm sure we can sort it."

"We'll need to take on more staff to do it. It's going to be a full time job for someone."

"I'll see if I can persuade Rebecca to let us recruit someone."

It was a week before Barry was back at the hospital. This time he brought a big bunch of flowers. He had phoned to find if Michelle had been moved out of the High Dependency Unit. She had, and was now on Dixton Ward, on the third floor of the College Road Wing.

He stopped at the ward reception desk, to ask where Michelle was. She was in a side room, not in an open bay.

"She'll be glad to see you," said the nurse. "I'll sort out those flowers for you."

Barry went in to the room, with a big smile on his face. But one look at Michelle and it drained straight away. She was crying, and looked like she'd been crying for a long time. She looked at Barry, and the tears became a flood.

He quickly sat down next to her, and took her hand. She was clearly in no condition to speak, so he didn't ask any questions. He just waited till she was ready. It was a good ten minutes before she had calmed enough to speak. She looked at Barry and said simply, "Dad's dead."

"Oh Michelle, I'm so sorry. When did he die?"

"Yesterday morning. He was on his way here......" She had to break off again, and cried some more. Barry continued to wait. "Someone said he started to cough, and couldn't stop. They say he burst a blood vessel in his brain. He was still alive when he got to hospital, but he died before they could even tell me he was here."

"Michelle, I'm really sorry. I don't know what to say."

The nurse came in with the flowers, and put them on a small table by the bed. At the sight of them Michelle burst in to tears again. Barry held her hand tight. The nurse looked at them and said, "Visiting hours finish at eight. But you can stay longer if you need to."

"Thanks."

Still sobbing, Michelle's eyes rested on the flowers. She looked at them for a bit, and then with her free hand reached out and touched them. It was her left hand, and Barry suddenly noticed that the ring was no longer there. "They're beautiful flowers."

Barry didn't answer. In truth tears had formed in the corners of his eyes, and he didn't trust himself to speak. But he loved the feeling of her hand in his.

"Barry."

"Yes?"

"I've got no-one now. Mum died when I was young, and I've got no brothers or sisters."

"Will Justin completely desert you?"

"I think they'll give me some money. But that will be it. Now Dad's gone, they've no real use for me."

"What do you mean?"

"I didn't tell you the full truth before. You said it was like an arranged marriage. But it was a bit more than that."

"How?"

"Dad wasn't really Mr Young's driver. He was his partner. But there was some trouble, and Dad had tried to leave in some way. I don't know the details. But Mr Young found out, and believed Dad was double-crossing him. I think to stop him they threatened me, and the price Dad had to pay was me marrying Justin. So that way they had a hold over him. And he was no longer the partner, just one of the boys."

"Do you think they would have hurt you if he hadn't agreed to the marriage?"

"No. But they would have killed him." Like so much else she said, it was so matter of fact. "These are dangerous people Barry. Don't get mixed up with them."

"I won't. You said you've got no-one now. Would I be any good?"

Michelle looked at him for some time, searching his face. She didn't appear to have found any answers there. "Why would you take me on? You know nothing about me. I'm just a girl off the bus. Not a very bright girl. And I'm a girl who mostly knows very nasty people. And I'm a cripple."

"Stop saying you're a cripple. It doesn't change who you are. But you haven't said why would you let me. Remember I know a lot more about you now than you know about me."

"That's true. I suppose I ought to find out more about you before I give you an answer."

"Seems only fair."

"OK. First question. Where do you live? I know it's not Gloucester because you turn off up the M5."

"I had no idea you were watching me as much as I was watching you!"

"But I was watching you because you were watching me."

"I live in Worcester."

"Worcester? Why don't you come by train rather than driving and taking the Park & Ride?"

"The police asked me the same question. I just like to listen to music on the way in. But my office has no car park. Why do you use the Park & Ride?"

"I don't like driving in town traffic."

"That's reasonable. But as a matter of interest why was Wayne on the bus? I can't see that was good for his laddish ego."

"He's just lost his licence, and he didn't want the embarrassment of being seen in town being driven by a girl. The Park & Ride was a better option, but that was his first day. Where did an accountant learn a move like that? You weren't fazed at all by the knife, and what you did was pretty neat."

"There are elements of my past about which I'm not too proud."

"But you're going to tell me about them." It wasn't a question.

"Yes. But not tonight. And it's probably about time I left."

"No. You're not going to leave yet."

"No? Why not?"

"There's something you have to do first."

"What's that?"

"You're going to kiss me."

A strange expression spread across Barry's face. Michelle couldn't work out what it was. It was like fear, but it wasn't that. It was something deeper, more complicated. She thought it better to back away. "You don't have to if you don't want to."

Barry didn't answer. Instead he knelt on the ground, put his arm around the back of her head, and lifted her face towards his. Their lips met, gently. But Barry held there, and pressed harder against her. Then, quite suddenly, but not roughly, stopped, took his arm away and sat back on the seat. Michelle was very surprised to see tears running down his face.

"Go home now," she said, kindly. "But please come back tomorrow. It's Saturday, and visiting times start at three. We're going to need longer to talk."

*Chapter 8*

It was a remarkably pleasant day, quite out of keeping with the occasion. St Mary's Priory Church was in the centre of Monmouth. It was full to overflowing.

It had taken a long time for the body to get back to Britain. The Kenyan authorities had said they needed to carry out an autopsy. Despite the delay, this was hardly thorough. The report said that Sylvia Murungaru had died from a single gunshot wound to the head. It also concluded that she wasn't killed at the location at which she was found.

Despite the deterioration that had set in, a second autopsy was carried out back in Britain. This found evidence that Sylvia had suffered physical ill-treatment before she died. There was bruising to her head and body.

There was still no sign of her husband. Patrick Murungaru and their children had disappeared without trace. There was no official comment from the Kenyan authorities, but off the record the view was that they had also been killed, but their bodies better hidden.

An inquest was opened and adjourned, before Sylvia's body was released. Even after that there was lengthy debate as to whether to hold her funeral, or wait for news about the fate of her family. Eventually her parents took the decision to proceed. It was six weeks after Sylvia died that she could finally be laid to rest.

Steve and Deborah were there. The Priory Church had probably never been so full. It was standing room only at the back, and the doors were only closed with difficulty. Lots of Steve's college friends were there. Sylvia had always been a very popular girl, for several reasons. But she always managed to stay friends with people, and Steve even saw her former husband Harry among the mourners.

Sylvia was buried in the churchyard. It was an incredibly sad affair. At the end, Steve hung on, to catch up with a number of old friends. During one conversation he was surprised to see Sylvia's parents approaching. They weren't wandering across via other mourners, but seemed to be making a beeline for the small group he and Deborah were talking with.

"Steve Smith?" It was a question that wasn't a question.

"Yes, Mr Jones. This is my wife, Deborah."

"Pleased to meet you. When you were on television a few years ago, Sylvia said she knew you."

Despite the solemnity, Deborah had to bite inside her cheek to stop herself laughing.

"We were good friends, yes."

"Do you mind if we step to one side and talk in private?"

Steve had no idea what this was going to be about. "Do you mind if Debs stays with us? She doesn't know anyone else here."

"Of course not. She will have a view on what we're going to say."

This was getting more intriguing, and possibly a touch alarming. Steve was desperately hoping that it wasn't going to be embarrassing.

They moved back towards the churchyard wall. "Dr Smith," Mr Jones started; it was clear he was going to do the talking.

"Please, it's Steve."

"Thank you. Steve, I said Sylvia said she knew you when you came on the television. She told us that you were always good at working things out, and finding solutions to problems."

"I think she was flattering me."

"Well, we think not. So we'd like to ask you a favour."

Steve was at least relieved the conversation wasn't going the way he feared. But he also knew where it was now going, and this was much more alarming. "Please ask. I'll help if I can."

"Thank you. Given your friendship with Sylvia, I'm certain you will have followed the newspaper coverage in detail."

"I have indeed."

"And you will therefore be aware that the Kenyan authorities have not tried particularly hard to investigate the case."

"It's certainly been more Inspector Clouseau than Miss Marple."

"At least Clouseau was trying. I don't think they have been."

"You suspect some sort of cover-up?"

"Don't you?"

"Well, given that as well as the murder of a prominent person, the fact that a government minister is missing might have galvanised quite a bit of activity. But there seems to be no real evidence of that. To me it has all the hallmarks of a political crime."

"We think that as well. To be honest Steve, I was thinking of flying out to Kenya, to try and get some answers. But Marjory said what good would that do? I'd have no idea where to start. But we hoped you would come today, and we determined to ask you if you could make some enquiries for us. You have some experience in this sort of thing, and would have a much better idea of what to ask. And you've travelled so much as well. We've hardly been anywhere."

"I've not spent much time in Africa. But I assume the British police are involved?"

"Of course. They've interviewed us. And I know some have flown out to Kenya for an official visit. But as I said, this is political, and the British police will be handicapped by protocol, so very restricted as to what they can do. I know it's asking a lot, but we wondered if you would fly out and see if you can dig up anything at all. You've got to remember that Sylvia's dead, and there's nothing we can do for her now. But it's our grandchildren that are missing."

Deborah's hand caught Steve's, and gave it a slight squeeze. Steve turned, and caught her eye. "Do you mind if Debs and I have a brief chat alone about this?"

"No, you must do that. And we won't hold it against you if you say you can't help. But we had to ask. We'll go back and talk to some of the others."

Steve and Deborah stood in silence for a few seconds, just looking at each other. Steve broke it first. "Well?" was all he said.

"No, you say."

"I hadn't expected this. I fully agree with them that the truth won't come out from Kenya. But I've no idea what I could do. And yet I feel I owe it to Sylv to do something to help her parents, and her children."

"But it's not as simple as just flying out, is it? These people have killed at least one person, and possibly more. And prominent people at that, people who would have security. There is no just going and asking questions. Any probing would put you in immediate danger. And now you have other responsibilities, not just yourself. I don't want to live the rest of my life without you. And nor do our children."

"Put in those terms, there's no way I can do this."

"No, not if put in those terms. But I know if you don't help, you'd regret it. If not for the rest of your life, at least for a long time. I know you wouldn't do this if I asked you not to. So I'm not going to ask that. I'm just going to ask you to be very, very careful. Don't come back in a box."

"In many ways I'd prefer it if you would ask me not to. I'm not sure what I can achieve, apart from getting killed, or causing some sort of diplomatic incident. But I suppose one thing I do have is contacts. I'll do some digging here, hopefully without drawing attention to myself. I'll only go out if I think I can make progress. We'd better go and tell them what we've decided."

The drive back to Oxford allowed Steve and Deborah plenty of time to discuss what Steve could actually do to investigate Sylvia's death. But even if it had been much longer, they wouldn't have come up with many ideas. They agreed on one thing, that the murder was undoubtedly politically related.

Steve's best idea was to see which newspapers, if any, had correspondents based in Kenya; the harsh economic wind blowing through whatever had replaced Fleet Street had led to papers slashing overseas staff. But Steve had good contacts with most papers, from his Chairmanship of the Climate Change Commission.

Back home, Steve did a quick search on the internet. Of the quality newspapers, the Times, Guardian and Telegraph all had Africa correspondents based in South Africa. But the Independent's reporter was based in Nairobi. This was good. Steve had only recently been interviewed by the Independent's Environment reporter, and he felt sure he could ring him on an 'off the record' basis. Much better to ring than to e-mail.

"Tom Simons speaking."

"Hello Tom. It's Steve Smith here. Climate Change Commission."

"Hello Steve. What can I do for you? Have you got some breaking news? Like finding an interesting bit in Hans Meyer's report?"

"Come on Tom, that's hardly fair. It's a very interesting report. But I'll admit it could be more readable."

"Well, he could have put on page three that he'd been having cocktails with Lord Lucan, and no-one would notice. So I'm guessing this isn't about the Commission?"

"No. I want to ask a favour about something completely unrelated. Sylvia Murungaru was a friend of mine."

"Really? I didn't know that."

"We were at college together. Her parents spoke to me yesterday at her funeral. They don't believe the investigation is being taken seriously in Kenya, and they asked me if I could make a few enquiries."

"Why would they ask you that?" Then realisation dawned. "So, your past is coming back to haunt you?"

"To a degree, yes. But there's no relation between what happened then and this case."

"So what are you after?"

"I could do with an introduction to your Africa correspondent, Giles Anderson. I see he's based in Nairobi, whereas most of the others are in South Africa. And he wrote quite a lot of challenging articles at the time. Do you think he'd give me some help?"

"Well, I don't know. I've never met him."

"Really? Why not?"

"Because he's in Africa. We don't fly everyone home for the office Christmas party. Papers don't have that sort of money. Everything is stripped to the bone these days. I've not even spoken to him. But I can get you his contact details, and e-mail him to expect contact from you."

"Thanks. That would be very helpful."

"No problem. But while we've been talking I've been on our intranet site, and he's on leave at present. Due back on Monday apparently."

"Is he on leave in Britain?"

"No idea. But his biography saws he's from Zimbabwe, so he could be there. I'll e-mail you some contact details, and cut and paste a bit from his biography as well."

"That would be really useful. I don't suppose it's worth asking if you could keep this chat off the record?"

"It's always worth asking. But you're right. Nothing is ever off the record. Politicians always say that something is off the record when they most definitely want it on the record. But if you're going to do some stuff with Giles we'll have the story anyway, so there will be no advantage to us in spilling anything at present. Good luck."

Next, Steve checked back through newspaper websites to find out where the police were from who had been out to Kenya. This took some searching for, but when he finally tracked them down it was no surprise they were from the Gwent police. Steve did have a good contact in the police, but that was in Nottingham. However, you have to start somewhere.

One phone call led to another, and within an hour he was dialling what he hoped was the right number.

"Gwilym Evans speaking."

"Is that Inspector Evans?"

"That's right, yes. Who's asking?"

"You won't know me. My name's Steve Smith. I was a good friend of Sylvia Murungaru."

"Steve Smith, you say? It's a common enough name. But you're not the Steve Smith who was involved in the Jack Davis murder case?"

"I am. But I'm surprised you remember that."

"I was only Sergeant Evans then. But I was stationed at Aberystwyth. I went up to the house in Cwmystwyth. It was the most exciting case I've been involved with. But what can I do for you?"

"I was at Sylvia's funeral yesterday, and her parents asked me if I could look into how the case was progressing."

"So, you don't think we're doing it well enough, isn't it?" But Steve could tell this was said with a smile.

"I bet you've done all you can. But you'll know that someone not acting officially might be able to do a bit more. I was wondering if I could come over and chat to you, so that you could perhaps give me some contacts, and point me towards avenues you were unable to explore."

"It would be a pleasure. She was a good sort, Sylvia, and she deserves better than she's getting. Tuesday would be a good day."

"Shall I come to the station?"

"Goodness me, no. I'm on leave that day. Meet me at the Old Nags Head, on Granville Street. About twelve thirty. I'll look at an old paper so I recognise you. But, just in case, I'll be the chap with the big, red beard."

*Chapter 9*

"You said there were things in your past you weren't happy with."

"Yes."

"You're going to have to do better than one word answers today. You're going to be doing most of the talking. Have you been in prison?"

"No." Michelle didn't say anything. He was going to have to continue. "But when I was young I got mixed up with what my mother would have called a bad crowd."

"Tell me about it."

"That won't be easy. I've never told anyone about this stuff. It's so much in the past that it's like someone else's life now."

"But I'm in hospital, and need my only visitor to talk to me. And you did kiss me yesterday. But really, I would like to know."

"But I don't know if I can tell. It will be painful bringing it all up again." He took a deep breath. "OK. Be prepared for the worst. I'm assuming you can tell I'm from Birmingham? OK, daft question. Anyway, I was pretty good at school. Got a hatful of GCSEs, and went into the sixth form. I wanted to be a chemist."

"What, like at Boots?"

"No. A proper chemist. Developing new drugs. That sort of thing. But going in to the sixth form was a real change. We were treated as adults, me and my friend Chris, Chris Adams. Perhaps we needed more discipline. We started to stretch the boundaries. And in the evenings we started to spend quite a bit of time hanging about on the street. We got into a group that were a sort of gang; they called themselves the Stacks, after the local factory chimneys. At first we'd just hang out in the evening, but then we started skipping school.

The school started to get on our case. My parents were told I was truanting. They were perhaps not as surprised as they should have been, but they were really disappointed in me because I'd shown so much promise. But discipline wasn't their thing, and they had no idea what to do. So they didn't do anything. Instead the school gave Chris and me an ultimatum. No more truanting, or no more school. So we took the easy option, and left."

"What did you do?"

"I was fortunate because Chris's dad owned a small company. He gave us jobs in his warehouse. It was just manual work, but I rather enjoyed spending whole days in physical activity, not mental."

"But if you were so bright, didn't you find it boring?"

"To a degree yes. But I found being mentally lazy easier that being physically lazy. Anyway, Chris and I spent our evenings with the Stacks. I can barely remember what we did; just night after night of hanging around. A lot of drinking, and a bit of low-level vandalism. Just wasted time. Four years of my life, what should have been the best years. But I barely noticed my former friends all going off to college."

"I can see the work would have made you strong. Did you do boxing, or something like that?"

Barry laughed. But it was a hollow laugh. "No. I wish it had been something like that."

"So, what then?"

"There were other gangs. There was the Simpsons, they called themselves that after the television series. There was one called West Street, who mostly lived, not surprisingly, on West Street. And there was the Packers, but I've no idea where their name came from.

There was a lot of rivalry between the gangs, and a lot of name calling. That sort of thing. But at some point we moved from taunting each other to violence. I don't even know how that happened, but it seemed to be a very short step. It wasn't even the Stacks at first, but West Street and the Packers. They just started fighting. Then they had territories, which the others couldn't cross. This immediately dragged in the Simpsons and us; we'd have lost face if we didn't have our own territory.

So the area was carved up, and fights became frequent. They were mostly quick affairs, just testing the boundaries of our territories. Fists and feet, nothing more. No serious injuries. But people started to complain, and so police patrol cars started to appear at regular intervals.

So the fights almost became prearranged, at quiet spots, and lasted only until the police arrived. Then everyone dispersed. Occasionally someone would be picked up by the police for questioning, as a kind of warning. I was, on a couple of occasions, but I was never charged with anything."

"How did you feel about the fighting?"

"Well, hard though it is to say it now, I got a real buzz out of it. I hardly ever got hurt, but I happily knocked about the other side. I started going to the gym to build myself up more, although as you said my job had already greatly improved my strength. Chris was also involved in the fights, but he wasn't prepared to put in the same effort as me. It was great to be lads though."

"So, what happened to make you leave all that behind?"

"Tuesday the 21st of March."

"What do you mean?"

"Some dates just stick out in your mind. That one in particular. It changed my life."

"What was special about it?"

"Nothing really. It wasn't my birthday, or Chris's. But it was Craig's, and Craig was in the Stacks. And Craig was pretty stupid, even by his low standards, that on his birthday he went to an off-licence in Simpsons' territory. The Simpsons were pretty pissed off at the time, because they'd lost territory to West Street, but Craig was all they had to work on, so that's what they did.

They gave him a terrible beating. Even on the ground they kept kicking him. They broke several bones, and he lost consciousness. He was a blue light job on his way to hospital, and word quickly got back to us. No-one even thought of a hospital visit. Nothing would have suggested that Craig would have liked flowers anyway. Everyone knew that what he would want was revenge, and that was what he was going to get.

So we gathered up, and just walked into Simpsons' territory. I noticed that some of the crew, including Chris, had armed themselves with clubs, but I barely gave this a thought. Everyone knew this was an escalation, and all we cared was that some of the Simpsons would be joining Craig in hospital shortly.

The Simpsons were probably regretting their action, and certainly would not have wanted a full on encounter with us. But they had no choice, and soon they were at the far end of the street. They also had armed themselves. There was no shouting, no taunting. Just menacing quiet as the two sides moved towards each other. It was like some sort of mediaeval battle.

It was long, and it was really vicious. The numbers of us standing went down, as the injured started to pile up on the floor. You just wouldn't believe people could fight like that, for nothing."

Michelle had been listening, in increasing horror. "Were you hurt?"

"I was bleeding from the head, but I wasn't really hurt. To tell the truth I was just getting into it. Chris was proving to be quite expert with his club, and wasn't hurt at all.

He was advancing on one of the Simpsons' leaders, who was standing with his club, just beckoning him on. I was too busy myself to watch, but I caught something out of the corner of my eye that made me turn. The Simpson had dropped his club, and I saw something flash in the street light. I shouted "Knife!", but it was too late. He lunged at Chris, just the once, and backed away. Chris stopped, and was looking down at his chest. I could see the blood pouring through his fingers.

At that moment we heard sirens. Everyone ran off. I ran over to Chris, but as I reached him, he fell to the floor. A pool of blood was just spreading out around him. The sirens were really close. So I just took a last look at him. I knew there was nothing I could do, so I just ran off."

"What, you just left your best friend there? Was he all right? What did you do?"

"I just went home. I let myself in, and ran up to the bathroom, hoping no-one saw me. I had a shower, to wash off all the blood from my head. This was still bleeding, so I put a towel round it, put clean clothes on, and went to my room. I stayed there, just waiting to see what happened. I didn't know what would come first, but everything was bad. And I just couldn't get the picture of Chris in that pool of blood out of my mind.

And yet nothing happened. There were no phone calls, no knocks at the door. By maybe midnight I was mentally exhausted, and went to bed, but I couldn't sleep for a long time. I just lay there with things circulating in my mind.

But I must have dropped off eventually. My mum woke me up at eight o'clock She thought I'd slept through my alarm and would be late for work. So I got up, and had another shower to wash the dried blood out of my hair. I did have a large scab forming, which I had no chance hiding. But otherwise I looked OK. So I got dressed, and started to go down stairs.

As I was going down there was a really loud knocking at the door. My mum answered it. I could see it was someone in uniform, and he was asking for me."

"Did you give yourself up?"

"There was no point doing anything else. I just carried on down and said 'I'm Barry Clark.' Mum looked terrified. There were two of them. They actually asked me to 'accompany them to the station'. It was comedy police talk. But it wasn't funny.

They didn't say anything as they drove me to the police station, and I kept quiet. I was put in an interview room. There was a lot of activity, and I saw several of the people involved in the fight, from both sides."

"But what had happened to Chris?"

"I didn't know for definite at that point, although I was pretty sure. I'd had no word at home, and the police weren't saying. They put me in a seat at a table, and then sat opposite. They didn't say anything for maybe five minutes, just stared at me. I assume this was just to try and unsettle me, but I kept cool. Two key things hadn't escaped me. There was no tape recorder on the table, and I hadn't been cautioned.

When they finally spoke, they asked me about my head injury. I said I'd hit my head at work. Clearly they didn't believe me, but gave me the long silence again. Then they asked me where I'd been at nine o'clock the previous night. I said I'd been at home, with a sore head."

Despite the serious story, Michelle laughed. "That was pretty smart!"

Barry smiled. "I was quite pleased with it. But they said they'd got half a dozen people who said I was with them on Canal Street. I said they must have been mistaken, but the police said the people were pretty sure. Me, and Chris Adams. They looked for a reaction, but I tried not to give one. So they asked me if I knew Martin Barratt."

"Who was he?"

"I told them I'd met him a couple of times. Tall, thin, blond hair. They asked me when I last saw him. I knew the answer to that one. Last night. He was sticking a knife in Chris at the time. But instead I just said a couple of days ago."

"Why didn't you tell them he knifed Chris?"

"Because that would have told them I was there. And also it would be grassing, and I wouldn't grass."

"Even with what he'd done?"

"No. I know it's stupid now, but I didn't then. Then they asked me when I last saw Chris. I said we'd left work together yesterday. This wasn't untrue. It just wasn't the answer.

They asked me why I wasn't concerned about Chris. I said why should I be, had something happened to him? They said he was in hospital. When I asked how he was, rather than what had happened, I effectively gave it away. They said I knew what had happened, because I was there. I asked if I could see him. They said there wasn't a lot of point. They were really callous about it. They said he was in intensive care, and that he'd be leaving there in a coffin. His parents were there, deciding whether to turn off his life support."

"Oh Barry. How did you cope with that?"

"I started to sob a bit. So they came back at me again, and asked where I was at nine o'clock. I took a deep breath, and just repeated that I was at home in my room.

They just looked at each other, and without speaking got up and left the room. But if they thought making me sit alone would break me, they were mistaken. I was really glad for this time alone. I assumed that Chris had died at the scene, so the fact that he was effectively dead was something I had already thought through over the previous night. But what I found hardest to think about was Chris's mum and dad, sitting by his dead body, dead but for the blood still circulating, having to have the courage to agree to the switch being thrown.

What a waste of a life. And for my part, I'd been party to that waste. What had it all been for? Fun? Some sort of macho posturing? The rest of the gang – what were they to me? I didn't particularly like any of them, they were just people I hung around with. If it had been any one of the others, deep down would I have really cared? Anyway, I knew it was all over now.

The policemen came back in, after maybe half an hour. I'd steeled myself for more questions, wondering how long I could hold out. So I was really surprised when one of them said I could go. They said they'd got enough witnesses without bothering with me. But they said they were sure Chris's parents would be delighted with the support I'd given to the investigation. They just told me to piss off. And that was their words.

There was of course no lift home. It was pouring with rain, and I didn't have a coat. I was soaked through, but even so I walked home very slowly. But I wasn't thinking; quite the opposite. My mind was just numb. When I got home I brushed off Mum's questions. She clearly still had no idea what was going on, and was desperately concerned about me. But I was in no condition to talk, and just went straight to bed.

"What happened after that? Did they charge you with anything?"

"No. But Chris's dad sent word that he never wanted to see me again, and I was of course sacked."

"So, how did you get from there to here?"

"Listen Michelle, I've never talked this much about myself before. To anyone. I'm finding it very difficult."

"Is there worse to come?"

Barry's answer wasn't entirely truthful, but Michelle wasn't to know that. "I did manage to sort my life out. I sat at home for a few days, in my room, just thinking. It had become painfully clear that I was wasting my life, and I bitterly regretted my earlier decision to leave school. But I decided I wasn't going to brood. Instead I was going to do something about it.

I was twenty two years old. But because I'd been working for several years, and living at home, I'd managed to save quite a bit of money. So I decided I needed to go back to college, do my A levels and try and get to university.

I packed a rucksack with just enough clothes for a few days. Without really saying anything to my parents, I left home. I caught a train from New Street to Bristol Temple Meads. By eleven o'clock I was in Bristol city centre, somewhere I'd never been before."

"Why Bristol?"

"It was a case of why not? It was far enough from Birmingham, and I didn't want to go to London, or north. I picked up a local paper, and was immediately disappointed about how little property there was, and how expensive it was. But it was important to get a base. So I found the address of a relatively cheap guest house. It was in Newtown, on Clarence Road, and I bought an A-Z and walked the mile or so. It was called The Willows, and even this wasn't cheap, or cheerful. But I didn't intend staying there for long. I dumped my rucksack and headed straight back into town.

It was four weeks later, much longer than I'd hoped, but pretty quick in the circumstances, that I was sitting in my new flat. It was small, and, on the edge of St. Paul's, definitely not in the best part of town. And at nearly £700 a month, it was not cheap. But it was furnished, and I'd got it for six months.

At that price my money wouldn't last long. First and foremost I needed a job, and any other plans would need to be put on hold. But I had no qualifications, so there was not a lot I could do, and nothing was going to pay much. But I was really lucky, and got a job as a barman."

"But I thought you were going to go to college."

"I was prepared to take my time. I spent fifteen months working really long hours, just saving up. I'd almost so settled in to it, that I could have abandoned my plans, but Nick give me the push I needed."

"Who's Nick?"

"He owned the bar. He became my best friend. Still is really."

"I'd like to meet him."

"Maybe. Anyway, I signed up at Filton College. I intended working evenings and weekends, and going to college during the day. By that time it wasn't so much that I needed the money, but that I didn't want to let Nick down. Nick was pleased that I didn't just hand in my notice, but he wouldn't allow me to do those hours, So I did Friday night and the weekend.

I did three A levels in a year. I was really determined, but it was hard work. I think combining all that studying with work would have been a real strain to anyone with any sort of social life. Also I wasn't working enough to break even, despite a frugal lifestyle, so it was really one shot to get the results I needed.

But I was quite confident I could do it, and applied to university. I really wanted to stay in Bristol, so I was very pleased to get an interview. They offered me a place, but I had to get three As!"

"I bet you got them though."

"Yes."

"I left school at sixteen. I got three GCSEs. And I'm not going to tell you what grades."

"But you weren't a violent thug, who ran away while his best friend died."

"You're not that violent thug any more. You're not the same person when you grow up. I thought I might be clever when I was little. And you saved my life, when you could have been killed. Did you do chemistry at university?"

Barry was pleased she'd remembered. "Yes."

"What was university like?"

"It was the most wonderful three years of my life. I just loved the work, and the social life. But I also kept on working at the bar all through."

"But you were a lot older than the other students. Did you have a car as well?"

"Yes, I'd bought a cheap second hand car when I moved down."

"I bet you were really popular with the girls. Did you sleep with lots of them?"

"You certainly ask some pushy questions! Mostly I didn't think it was fair to abuse my advantages. Not too much, anyway. But I admit I wasn't a saint."

"Any long term relationships?"

"Not really, no. But, changing the subject, so I can finish quickly, I got a good degree. But my plans hit a setback. There was a recession, and the chemical companies weren't recruiting. Although I got a couple of interviews I didn't get the jobs. In part I think the fact I was late going in to education counted against me. I wonder if they suspected I had a past.

So I was now twenty seven. I knew I needed to do more than bar work. I really needed to get a more professional job, while still applying for chemistry jobs that might come up. So I applied for a whole range of jobs where having a degree was the important thing, not what degree it was.

But I have to say it was with some despondency that I took the job I was offered at Perkins. They're a medium-sized accountancy firm, mostly based in the south-west. Accountancy is what careers officers pushed any scientist towards, because they always think any real science jobs are so few and far between. And they're probably right.

And yet, within a few days of starting, I realised I rather took to it. Perkins seemed to think so too, because they immediately signed me up for an accountancy course, back at Filton College!

Although I passed this with good marks, and even though I realised I was rather good at this accountancy lark, I still hankered after a job in chemistry. So I put in the occasional job application, and tried to keep up to date by subscribing to various magazines. But it was no use, and I was now an accountant. And still am."

"So, is that the end of the story?"

"I think so."

"I don't."

"What do you mean?"

"When you kissed me yesterday, you were kissing someone else, weren't you?"

*Chapter 10*

It was six o'clock when Barry stepped into the Victoria Bar. He'd come straight from the hospital, and he was missing the evening visiting hours.

Nick was behind the bar tonight. "What, twice in two months? So, you becoming a regular now?"

"Last time I was here you asked if I wanted to talk."

"Do you want to now?"

"Possibly. I'd like the option anyway."

"Jude should be here soon. She had a slight babysitting hiccup. Can you nurse a pint for a few minutes?"

"I didn't realise she had children. I thought she was a student."

"She is. But a student who got a bit too drunk one night."

"It happens. Yes, I'll be fine. I'll take myself over to the corner. But you'll be busy soon."

"It's a bit slower since your time. Doesn't really get active till after eight, even on Saturday. I'll be with you soon."

It was ten minutes later that Nick sat down with Barry. He just looked at Barry, waiting for his friend to start. Eventually Barry said, "There's a girl."

"I always thought that when you said that, I'd be saying 'whoopee-do'. But I reckon this isn't a whoopee-do moment."

"No."

There was a pause. "Was that the whole talk?"

"Maybe. But I've just spent two hours telling someone things I've never told anyone before. Stuff I've never told you."

"She must be pretty special."

"Must she? I think it's a lot more complicated than that."

"When you say you told her stuff you've never told anyone before, does that mean you've not told her your more recent past?"

"Yes."

"But I can understand that. You'd consider it a betrayal."

"Probably. In a way I wouldn't be sure of my motives. But even that's not it."

"You never used to talk in riddles, but I know you don't give much away. But would I be right in saying that you're not in love with this girl?"

"That would be true. But only half the story."

"I would ask if we will get to meet her. But I've got a better idea. Chris and I are having our twentieth anniversary party four weeks today. Bring her along."

"Thanks Nick. I will if I can."

"If you can? Let me guess, the complication is that she's married."

"She is married, yes. But, funnily enough, that isn't the complication." Barry looked at his watch, and seemed to reach a decision. "Look Nick, I've got to go. Thanks for talking. But I've got somewhere I need to be." He got up and started towards the door, and then turned back to say, "Her name's Michelle."

Visiting time was almost up when Barry stepped back into the Dixton Ward. Michelle had clearly been crying, but her face brightened immediately she saw him.

"I'm sorry," was all she said.

"Don't be. But I do need to tell you more."

"Not now. Give it more time. But I need to talk to you."

"What about?"

"They say they would like to send me home in a few days. But I haven't really got a home to go to. Dad's gone, and Justin won't have me."

"Will you come with me?"

"I'd like that. But you'll have to go to work."

"I'll take some leave. I've got lots unused. Have they said anything about getting you mobile again?"

"You mean, when are they going to stick on my peg leg? They say that the stump has shrunk nicely, and that I can have a temporary leg fitted. They'll give me a day on Monday with the physio, to get used to walking on it with crutches. But if I've got somewhere to go, then I can go on Tuesday."

"That'll give me a couple of days to get the place tidy."

"I bet it's tidy anyway."

"True. I am an annoyingly tidy person. To get it ready then."

"What are you going to get ready?"

"Well, I'll have to make up the bed in the spare room for a start."

"Why? Are you expecting visitors?"

Barry stared at her. "Well, you are a pretty forward little minx, for a married woman."

"You deserve something for what you told me today."

Barry spent the evening thinking about sorting things out. But in the end he touched nothing. He needed Michelle to see the way things were. After that, maybe some things could be moved.

He arrived promptly at three o'clock for the Sunday afternoon visiting hours. But looking through the glass window he was surprised to see Michelle already had a visitor. Barry could only see his back. He was tall, well-built, greying hair. Barry guessed he would be about sixty. He opened the door noiselessly, and stepped in. Michelle was looking very serious, perhaps even a bit fearful. But as Barry entered, she looked towards him, and half smiled.

Seeing the look, and the smile, the man turned. Barry saw that his guess was about right. He also was pretty sure he knew who his visitor was. Michelle confirmed it. "This is Mr Young. Justin's dad."

Barry could easily see the family resemblance. In many ways Mr Young looked like an older version of Justin. Just a normal sixty year old, if there is such a thing. But the look in his eyes set him apart. They were cold, and even at rest slightly hostile. But his greeting to Barry was cordial enough. "You must be the chap who saved our Michelle's life. I'd like to thank you. Edward Young." He extended his hand.

There was nothing to be gained from any other course of action, so Barry took it. "Barry Clark," was all he said.

"Barry, is it? Do you mind if I call you that?"

Barry could see he was going to be called that, whether he minded or not. "No, that's fine. Is it Edward, or Mr Young?"

This seemed to take the other visitor aback somewhat. It was clearly an unexpectedly forward question; 'Mr Young' would be what most people would say, instinctively. But he surprised himself when he said,

"My friends call me Ted."

Barry knew that it was only a very minor point, but that he had won round one. But he also knew that in this relationship, in the long term defeat was much more likely than victory.

"So Barry, what do you do?"

"I'm an accountant."

Mr Young looked surprised. "I find that rather unlikely."

"So do a lot of people, apparently. But I can assure you that it's true."

"Are you any good at it?"

"I seem to be doing all right so far. Sorry to be a bit forward, but I am surprised to see you here, given what Justin's attitude has been."

A shadow crossed Mr Young's face. "I don't agree with what Justin's done. However it's done now, and Derek was an old friend. I'm not going to besmirch his memory by neglecting his daughter. But what I don't see is why you, apparently a total stranger, are taking it on yourself to take her on."

"Let's not have a 'does she take sugar' conversation here. Michelle can make her own decisions. I made an offer, and she accepted. Admittedly, she may not have had a lot of options."

"Is it all right with you, Mr Young?" Michelle seemed quite nervous that it wouldn't be. But it was Barry that answered first, cutting off options to the older man.

"I'm sure Ted will be happy if you're happy."

Barry knew he'd been shot a look, but Mr Young concurred, "Course that's fine, Shell. I'll fill Barry here in on what else we've agreed."

Barry was sure that Mr Young only needed to agree with himself. Michelle's views were unlikely to have figured.

"I'm sorting out Derek's funeral. It's the least I can do for my old friend. I'll also get the boys to sort out the house, and pack up his things. Don't think he's got a lot. It's a company house, so there's no sale needed. Also we'll pack up Shell's things, and get them delivered to your place. Tomorrow evening convenient?"

There was no point arguing. "That will be fine."

"We'll need the address."

There was no-one Barry was less keen to give his address to, but there was no way round this. But anyway, it would take them no time to find it anyway. They could just follow him home. So he wrote it down on a piece of paper, and passed it over. Mr Young glanced at it. "Worcester?"

"That's right."

"OK. Be in around seven. I'll leave you alone now. Bye Shell." And he was off.

There was a few moments silence between them, and then Michelle spoke. "You took a risk there, Barry. He doesn't like anyone to get the upper hand."

"I don't scare easily. I've got no-one to be scared for."

"You have now. But haven't you got any family?"

"I've got a sister. She's in Australia. She's a few years older than me. But we've not spoken, or communicated at all, for ten years."

"Why ever not?"

"We fell out."

"You don't seem the falling out sort. At least not with decent people. Was this something to do with your past?"

"No. But her attitude to me was probably established then. Like so often in families it was to do with money."

"Did you lend her a tenner and she never returned it?"

"Not exactly. But I see I'm going to have to tell you."

"I'm afraid so. Get used to it."

"She's called Molly. I think my parent's had a thing about five letter names ending in 'y'. She got married to a chap called Richard just before Chris died. Richard was some sort of small businessman. I never really knew what line of business, but he was a smarmy, slimy individual. I didn't trust him an inch. He was a few years older than Molly, and she was infatuated with him. And my parents really took to him as well. There were comparisons made between how I was wasting my life, and how well Richard was doing.

But a couple of years after I started at Perkins my parents died."

"Barry, I am sorry. What happened?"

"They were driving back from a night out in Birmingham. They were hit head on by a speeding car, which was being chased by the police. They both died at the scene. I don't think they'd have known a thing about it, fortunately.

I was given time off work to arrange the funeral and, since I was now an accountant, I got to sort out their affairs. Losing my parents was a tremendous shock, but I hadn't expected what came afterwards. When the will was read, I found out that my parents didn't have a penny to their name. Their main asset was the house, but they'd re-mortgaged that a few years earlier. It took some questioning before I found out what had happened. Richard's business had allegedly been in difficulty, and Molly had persuaded them to do this. The money had of course all gone, along, soon after, with Richard.

I was furious, not surprisingly. It was the first I'd heard of it, and I realised Mum and Dad had just been conned. It wasn't because of the money in itself, but in the way this had happened. I was just thinking of the pressure they must have been put under to do this. And Molly herself wasn't in the slightest bit apologetic. Instead she just abused me, and suggested that with my history I didn't deserve anything anyway.

So I left a lawyer to sort out the final details, and never spoke to her again. Indirectly I heard that she had married someone else, and moved to Australia. One of my cousins did pass me her e-mail address, but I've never written, and neither has she. And to be honest Michelle, I have no regrets about that."

"So we're both on our own now. What about your friend Nick? Is he like family to you then."

"In a way, yes. Nick and his partner, Chris."

"Does she work in the bar as well?"

"She's actually a he."

Michelle's eyes widened. "You mean Nick's a homosexual?"

"You'd better not have a problem with that. We wouldn't stay friends for long."

"No, it's not a problem. I've just never met a homosexual before. I don't think Mr Young would be very tolerant."

"I suggest the word 'gay' is a touch preferable to 'homosexual' these days. And I bet you've met plenty of gay people. You just don't know they are gay. Anyway, Chris doesn't work in the bar. He's an architect. And you could meet them soon. They've asked us to a party."

"When?"

"Four weeks yesterday. It's their twentieth anniversary. I've told them I'm bringing someone."

"Did you tell them it was a cripple?"

"No. I didn't think that was necessary."

## Chapter 11

The Old Nags Head was a quaint old pub, with a labyrinth of corridors and tucked away niches. Tuesday lunchtime was clearly a quiet time, and there was hardly anyone in. But even if the place had been packed Steve would have had no difficulty picking out Inspector Gwilym Evans. He was a big man, and his beard seemed even bigger. He would have been difficult to push past at the bar, and it would have been a brave person who tried. Steve wondered what they'd made of him in Kenya.

"What will you be having?"

Steve looked at the beer on offer. "That's very kind. Pint of London Pride please. What sort of food do they do here?"

"The curry's pretty good. It's what I'm having."

"Good enough for me."

Orders made, they retreated to a corner, just in case more people came in. "It's good of you to see me at short notice, Inspector."

"Since it's Tuesday lunchtime, and I'm off duty, you can call me Gwil. Can I call you Steve?"

"Of course."

"Well Steve. Before you start asking me questions, can I ask you one?"

"Fire away."

"With that Jack Davis business, why didn't you just come down to the police station?"

"Because I didn't think you'd believe me. At least not immediately. When you found the two chaps tied up, you'd have been more interested in me than what was on a data stick. And Lynda Cooper was still free, and she would have convinced you to pass that over to her before you'd looked at it."

Gwil thought about that for a minute. "I bet that's only part of the reason."

"How do you mean?"

"I reckon you have an inherent mistrust of authority. I reckon you really only trust yourself."

"That's probably true. But you'll agree I've been given good reason to have that view."

"Maybe. But self reliance can become a problem. Sometimes you need to call in the cavalry."

Steve laughed. "I'll bear that in mind. But anyway, all that was a long time ago."

"I bet you thought that was the end of your adventures."

"If only. But life has been quiet since we came back from Peru."

"Too quiet?"

Steve smiled. "I had thought not. And I did think long and hard about whether to take this on. But, you know what, I've got a little feeling in my stomach, just like I did before. It's that sort of mixture between excitement and apprehension. And I've missed it."

"Be careful that feeling doesn't take you over."

"I appreciate the warning. I've got responsibilities now, so I'll be very careful. Is it OK if we get down to business?"

"Sure thing. What sort of information are you after?"

"I'm not entirely sure. I suspect I'll have seen everything you found out, so I'm much more interested in suspicions and informed speculation. Details of key people you talked to would be helpful. I'm pretty sure because you agreed to see me that what has been in the press so far is a long way from the truth."

"I can certainly give you some pointers. But before I start I do need to say something. When we got back, the press asked us lots of questions, and probed the things you want to know. But of course we didn't provide them with anything useful, just gave them the plain facts."

"I'd have expected the press to be questioning. It was big news at the time."

"So, since you are a complete stranger to me, aren't you surprised I'm prepared to talk to you? Why would I trust you to keep anything I say off the record?"

"I hadn't thought of that. But since we're meeting here, I'm hopeful that you will give me information that you didn't give them. So yes, I am curious why."

"Well firstly, I'm prepared to trust you, because your history makes clear you are to be trusted. And I checked back to your contact in Nottingham, who vouched for you. So, given that, I'm prepared to talk to you because I want the truth to come out, and it hasn't yet. But I don't know what the truth is.

Monmouth's a small town. When I moved over here from Aber, I got married. My wife Liz was in the same class at school as Sylvia, and they were good friends. Liz was at the funeral. I couldn't be, because I was working. She wants justice for her friend, and so do I."

"When you say you want the truth to come out, the truth compared to what? Nothing's come out yet. The last report I found in the *Daily Nation* said that police still had no clear motive. There didn't even appear to be any theories. But there was no suggestion this was political."

"There was no suggestion it was anything at all when we were there." Gwil broke off as the curries arrived. Steve couldn't help but notice that the policeman's curry was twice the size of his.

"What's that? Protection money?"

Gwil laughed. "If only. Marion here is Liz's aunt."

The barmaid laughed. "Look at the size of him. Do you think he could last on a standard portion?"

By mutual agreement they left off talking till they'd eaten. When they'd finished, and Gwil, despite the huge portion, finished first, Steve asked, "How many of you went?"

"Just two of us. I went with Simon Roberts. He's also an Inspector."

"Are you Detective Inspectors?"

"No. We're both uniform. They always send uniform, to be a bit more showy. But God, it was too hot for uniform."

"Is there a formal report of your investigation?"

"Yes. Of course."

"And is it available to the public?"

"It's never been made available. But a Freedom of Information request would quickly turn it up."

"I'll make one as soon as I get home."

"I'd do that. But read this while you're waiting for it to arrive." Gwil dropped a report on the table.

"Thanks Gwil. That'll save some time. But of course I'll put the request in anyway, just for form's sake. Does it say anything worth reading?"

"Not really. The names of the people we met may be of interest. But I don't think you'll get access to them. We briefly met the Minister of State for Provincial Administration and Internal Security. He's in charge of the police. Then we got rather longer with the Commissioner of Police, a chap called Mutula Oparanya. He assured us that every possible line of enquiry was being followed."

"Of course he did."

"I know he would say that. But he was very earnest. And to be honest I felt he was a thoroughly decent chap."

"What about the Minister?"

"He was a bit stranger. If anything I'd say the principal impression I got from him was embarrassment."

"What do you mean?"

"Well, I couldn't quite put my finger on it, and it's even harder to put it in to words. It was something like Kenya should really be famous as a tourist destination, not for this sort of thing."

"So, not like he was part of some conspiracy then."

"Yes. But not exactly. I'm trying to think of some sort of analogy. It was kind of, like, when you're in the supermarket with your kids, and they're having a bit of a tiff, and one knocks over a pile of tins. You try and pretend they're not with you."

"Ah." Steve thought for a bit. "So, what you are saying is that he may have been aware of something rumbling along below the surface, but he had been surprised when it all ended in tears before bedtime."

"That sort of thing, yes. But between us we're making a lot out of a little."

"Better to make a lot out of something, than something out of nothing. Did you spend all your time talking to senior people, or did you get nearer to the action?"

"We got a day out with a Chief Inspector, with his driver. He took us to where Sylvia's body had been found. Not surprisingly there was nothing at all to be seen there. For all we knew, they could have taken us anywhere."

"Where was the place?"

"It was outside Nairobi, on the main road to Mombasa. But it said that in the papers. It wasn't far from a dump called Salama."

"I'd seen that name in the paper. Did you speak to any witnesses?"

"No. We did talk to a couple of the detectives who said they'd been to the crime scene. But to be honest, I don't think they had been."

"What makes you say that?"

"They were sketchy on key details. Who'd found the body? Had it been hidden? Did they find any tyre tracks? That sort of thing."

"Like any evidence at all, in fact?"

"Just about, yes. But we did get to speak to the pathologist who'd carried out the autopsy. Not without a bit of difficulty, though."

"What sort of difficulty?"

"Well, it took a couple of days before he was produced. They said he'd been on holiday. Must have been an adventure holiday."

"Why?"

"He'd got a black eye."

"And presumably he was not over forthcoming."

"Indeed. Not much to say for himself at all. Died from a single gunshot wound to the head. Was killed elsewhere, and the body dumped at the scene."

"Did you ask him how he'd missed the other marks on her body?"

"Unfortunately this was before the body had been returned. We weren't able to see it, which, since Sylvia was a friend, I was quite relieved by. But I wish now that we'd pushed for that."

"No, it was better that you didn't. Because if you'd seen the marks, they would have been added to the report, and we wouldn't have seen what seems like a cover-up. How much of what you've said is in the report?"

"All of it, apart from the speculation. And the black eye."

Steve went and got Gwil another pint. Gwil asked Steve about how well he'd known Sylvia at college. Steve answered carefully, but there was a smile in Gwil's eyes. "She was a looker, wasn't she?"

"She was indeed."

The smile moved from Gwil's eyes to his mouth. "You lucky bastard. Anyway, what do you propose to do now?"

"I'm going to talk to the Africa reporter for *The Independent*. He's based in Nairobi. I intend flying out there, and I'm hoping he'll give me a hand. But I really don't know much beyond that at the moment. I might take a trip out to the place you mentioned, you know, the dump."

"Salama."

"Yes. See if there were any witnesses. And I'd quite like to pursue the thing you said about the policemen you spoke to, the ones who you didn't think had been at the scene. Why wouldn't they let you talk to the ones that had been?"

"They may have seen something that we weren't meant to find out. But I have my own theory."

"Which is?"

"There weren't any real policemen at the scene."

"Now we are into real conspiracy territory! Thanks for your help Gwil. I'll keep you informed about anything I find out."

"Good luck. You'll need it. Don't forget, people who kill once have no reason not to kill again."

"I've promised Deborah I'll be careful."

*Chapter 12*

Michelle sat in the chair at the side of her bed as Barry packed the few things she'd had into a small bag. She was wearing long black trousers, so all Barry could see was the bottom of her prosthesis. He moved the wheelchair right up to the chair.

"Move it back a bit," she said. "I want to show you what I can do."

He did as instructed. Michelle picked up her crutches, and with some difficulty pushed herself up. She had one big wobble, then steadied herself. Slowly she walked over to the wheelchair. It wasn't really walking. Her real leg took a step, then she pulled the artificial leg after it. Arriving at the wheelchair, she slowly turned herself round so she could sit down. Barry could see the effort etched in her face, plus, he noted with concern, some pain. But he knew it was important for her to do this herself, so he just held the chair. With relief Michelle dropped in, and passed the crutches to Barry. "Home, James," she commanded.

"Certainly, madam." Barry put her bag on her lap, and added the larger one full of hospital supplies.

They said little on the drive to Worcester. Michelle didn't really know what to expect at Barry's house. Barry knew what she would find, and was sure it wasn't what she was expecting.

They turned into Tavern Orchard. "That's an unusual name for a road," Michelle remarked.

"They often name roads after what they knocked down to build the houses. I bet there was an old orchard here, next to a pub."

"That's actually quite sad."

"I nearly bought a house on Duck Meadow, round the corner."

"I hope they didn't build that on the ducks."

Barry reversed on to his drive, so that Michelle had the shortest possible walk to the front door. He firstly opened the door, and turned lights on in the house. Then he opened the passenger door, and helped Michelle out. She steadied herself, and then struggled to the door. Barry held her arm while she negotiated the step, and then she was in. He took her in to the lounge, and sat her down in one of the armchairs. "Would you like some tea?"

"Yes please. White, no sugar."

Barry could see her eyes were moving around the room. He left quickly, and only returned with the tea on a tray. He put this on a small table, handed Michelle her cup, and sat in the other armchair.

She said, "You're going to have to talk to me."

"I know."

They both sat for a few minutes, looking at the opposite wall. Michelle broke the silence. "Who is she?"

There was a large photograph looking back at them. It was a picture of a couple on their wedding day. The bride was radiant, not just because she was a bride, but because she was an exceptionally beautiful woman. The groom was Barry.

"Laura."

Michelle turned to look at Barry. His voice sounded odd. There were tears on his cheeks. "You said you weren't married. Are you divorced?"

"No."

"But she's left you…….. Oh." Understanding suddenly set in. "Barry, I'm so sorry. When did she die?"

"Two years ago."

This time the silence was very long. Then Michelle said, "I should go."

"No, please don't. And where would you go? Besides, I've got a pile of boxes next door, delivered last night."

"Is the rest of the house a shrine to her?"

"No."

"But everything has been left as it was before she died? All her clothes still in her drawers?"

"Pretty much, yes."

"Can you tell me about her?"

"I couldn't start to do that. But I'll tell you what happened."

"Only if you feel up to it."

"No, I need to do it. But I'll need something stronger. Would you like some whisky?"

"I don't know if I'm allowed it. But I'll take a risk."

With some alcohol inside him, Barry felt more able to start. "Laura was my boss's PA. We got on well from straight off really. She was bright, and very beautiful. But much more than that, she was just such a warm and loving person. I couldn't believe she could fall for someone like me. Especially with my past."

"But you told her about it."

"To a degree. But she wasn't interested. All she said was 'That's not who you are now'."

"That's true enough."

"Maybe. Anyway, we got married ten years ago. It was wonderful. We thought about starting a family straight away, but we decided we'd concentrate on our careers for a bit. I was five years older than her, so that wasn't a problem."

"Did you never get round to it?"

"No. We started to try. But we didn't get anywhere. After about two years we wondered if there was something wrong. So we went to see a doctor. I assumed it would be something to do with me."

"Why?"

"Because it's usually the man. But they quickly established it wasn't me. So Laura started having some tests. She had a pelvic examination, and the doctor was a bit concerned and sent her off to a specialist.

There was a lump. They said all sorts of reassuring things, but took a biopsy. The results came back in a few days, and it was ovarian cancer.

From then they were completely honest with us. They said the cancer was quite advanced, and that the prognosis wasn't good. But she had surgery and chemotherapy. She lost all her beautiful hair. But all this did was give us a brief delay. It was a really aggressive cancer, and she was dead within a year."

Michelle said nothing. Barry could see that she was just looking at the photograph. Eventually she said, "Well at least I know why you were looking at me on the bus."

"It was a shock when I first saw you."

"Did you think I was a ghost?"

Barry half laughed. "No. But I did start to wonder if she had a sister

I didn't know about."

"You said at the hospital that you'd wanted to talk to me. I guess I was wrong about why."

"I wanted to see if you sounded like her as well. To see if you were like her."

"Was it painful being reminded of her in that way every day?"

"No. Quite the opposite. I found it strangely comforting. After all, it would have been easy enough for me to avoid seeing you if I'd wanted to. Just get a later bus."

"That's true. But you'll know now that I'm not like her. She's Laura, and I'm Michelle. Did you bring me back here to keep being reminded of her?"

"No. I brought you here because I didn't think you had anywhere else to go."

"If that's the case, it was very kind of you. But I bet you've made up the spare bed."

"Yes, I have."

"What if I say I won't sleep in it?"

"Are you likely to say that?"

"Yes. Look Barry, I'm not her. But she's not here, and I am. I know you don't love me, after all, why would you after a couple of weeks? But you seem to like me, and I like you. That'll probably do to be going on with.

I don't intend to be more difficult for you than I have to be. I want to do as much for myself as possible. So in a minute I'll be going to the toilet, on my own. But I'm also going to want a bath, and that I can't do on my own. So, like it or not, we're going to be up close and personal.

But it's more than that. I've been sleeping on my own in the hospital, and I don't like it. I'm getting a lot of pain from where my leg was. I want someone there to put his arm round me when it hurts too much. And there's something else, but I'll tell you about that later. Can I have a look round?"

They had dinner on the kitchen table, because the dining room was full of boxes. Afterwards Michelle sat on a dining chair and instructed Barry to open each box in turn to identify its contents. Then, having pinned down her essentials, Barry carried these upstairs, to the main bedroom. The rest he would carry up to the spare bedroom tomorrow.

Michelle was getting tired. "Bath time," she said; She tried to make it light and flippant, but this was a big moment.

Barry carried a dining chair up to the bathroom, and started the bath running. He then offered to help Michelle up the stairs, but she just passed him a crutch and pulled herself up along the handrail. But the heavy way she dropped to the chair showed just what an effort it was.

When she had caught her breath she said, "This is a big moment for both of us. You're going to see just what a cripple looks like, and it may revolt you. And I'm going to see how you react, because this is what I am."

"You need to have a bit more faith in me than that. You're right though, in that I don't know how I'll react to seeing you with only one leg. More importantly, you don't know how I'm going to react when I see you naked!"

"If that is what you're thinking, then we're probably OK. I'm hoping you can undress me sitting down. Shall we take my top off first, with a view to distracting you, or work from the bottom up?"

"Trousers first." Barry carefully pulled her trousers down, and Michelle raised herself slightly to help. He left her knickers in place. Past the end of her stump, and over the prosthesis. He was pleased at how little the sight disturbed him.

Barry smiled at her reassuringly. "That went quite well. Now, as far as I can see, you can take your top off yourself. After all, I can still see two arms."

She smiled back. "True. But I'm very tired. So could you do it for me please?"

"If I must." He pulled her top gently over her head, and stepped back. She noted the pause, but said nothing. He put his hands behind her back, and was surprised to find removing a bra was just like riding a bike; when you'd mastered it you never forgot how to do it.

This time when he stepped back he gave an involuntary gasp, much more reaction that the prosthesis had got.

"Are you happy with those?"

"I'm not sure. I may just have to stand here for another half hour to make up my mind. Right, I'm going to take your leg off before your knickers, just in case they get caught."

"That would be sensible. But it will make it hard to get in the bath."

"We'll manage."

The temporary prosthesis was just a standard pylon, with the stump fitting in a plastic socket. Before Barry started on this, Michelle cautioned him. "The end is very, very sensitive. Just a slight knock can be really painful."

"I'll be gentle," Barry promised. And he was. He laid the artificial leg down, and looked at the bandages. "I presume you can't get that wet?"

"I can't soak it in the bath. But I must wash the end. And it must be dried really carefully. Then I've got some powder in the bag. And I've got some elasticated bandages to put on overnight."

"Well I must congratulate you on your planning."

"What do you mean?"

"If you're going to have to keep the stump out of the water, you at least had the sense to lose the right leg. Otherwise you'd have been sitting against the taps. So I need to take the bandages off."

"Yes. Carefully please."

And now the stump was fully exposed. The stitches were still in place, and the end was red and inflamed. It looked incredibly painful. But Barry didn't even mention it. He worked Michelle's knickers over her bottom, and carefully past the stump.

"Are you ready?" he asked.

"Yes," she said, and gave a little laugh.

"What's so funny?"

"Nothing. How are you going to get me in?"

"I'll lift you."

"Well, you'd better take some clothes off as well. Otherwise you'll get very wet.

Barry took his shirt off, much to Michelle's approval. He came to her stump side, and picked her up as though she weighed nothing at all. "Wow," she said. "You are strong."

He gently laid her in the water, with her stump resting on the side of the bath. Seeing that this might be uncomfortable, he folded a towel and put it underneath.

"Thanks," she said. "But we'd better make this a quick wash, because I'm not desperately comfortable. Can you wash the stump? Just clean warm water, with a clean flannel. I'll do the rest."

When she was finished, Barry draped a towel over the chair, so he could sit her in it and wrap her up so she didn't get cold.

"You're quite good at thinking ahead," she said.

"Thanks."

"But you've forgotten one thing."

"What's that?"

"I'm all wet. When you get me out, your trousers will get soaked."

Barry suddenly looked reluctant.

"Oh for goodness sake, Barry. Take them off. I've seen an erect penis before, you know!"

With a sigh he took his trousers off, and, without prompting, his boxer shorts. If he'd needed to hang up a towel, he certainly had a convenient place.

"Cor. That's almost as long as my leg. OK, can you get me out?"

Again Barry had no difficulty lifting her. He put her on the chair, and wrapped the towel round her. Then he dried himself off.

"Please don't get dressed again. Now I feel we're equals."

Barry dried her carefully. He brought some tissue paper to make sure the stump was completely dry. "Shall I put some clean bandages on?"

"Not just yet. Can you carry me in to the bedroom, please."

He laid her gently on the bed. "Now," she instructed, "just stand there and look at me." This he didn't find difficult.

"Well, what do you think?"

"You are very attractive."

"And how much does the leg put you off?"

Barry didn't answer. He knelt down, and kissed the end of her stump. She gently put her hand on his head. "Thank you," she said. "Now, come up here and kiss me."

Barry lay down next to her. "Look, Michelle. I've not planned for this. I've not got any condoms."

"So?"

"But what if you get pregnant?"

"What if I do? Look Barry, I said that you deserved something for all you'd done for me. But in fact I need this more than you do."

"Why?"

" I'll tell you after." And she pulled his head towards hers.

But afterwards she was too tired to talk. Barry put new bandages on, and covered her over with the duvet. Then he snuggled up next to her, and they went to sleep.

It was still dark when he woke up. He realised Michelle was sobbing. He put the bedside light on and stroked her face. "What's wrong?" he asked.

"It hurts. It hurts so much."

He was very concerned. "Have I made the bandages too tight?"

"No, it's below that."

Below that? What did she mean? Was she not properly awake, and rambling?

"It's where the leg was. I know it's gone, but it still hurts. They told me it would, but I can't see how it can hurt if it's not there."

"I suppose all the nerves are still there, and they haven't worked out it's gone yet."

"That's what they said. They called it 'phantom pain'. But it's not phantom at all, it's very real."

"What does it feel like?"

"Well, before now it was like what you said, that the bandages were too tight. But bandages below where they cut it off. But this is different. It's like it's there, but twisted round behind me. But if I breathe carefully, I can get it under control."

She lay and breathed deeply in and out, concentrating on her breathing. After about five minutes she had it under control. "That's better," she said.

"It's good that you can control it."

"Well, I've controlled it up till now. Since we're both awake, is there something we could do?"

"Yes. You can talk to me."

"That's not what I was thinking of."

"I know. But you've still got something to tell me. After that you might get lucky."

"What have I got to tell you?"

"What you didn't tell me before."

"Oh. That. Well, you might find this hard to believe, but when we made love earlier, it was my first time for months."

"Really? But I thought Justin didn't have another woman."

"He hasn't. I'm certain of that."

A rather unexpected idea was starting to form in Barry's mind. "Had he had many girlfriends before you?"

"Not that I'm aware of."

"So was it his idea to marry you, or his dad's?"

"I'm not really sure."

"I bet you're not. Despite what you say, it looks like you do know another gay person."

"Are you suggesting Justin is a homosexual?"

"Gay. Gay, gay, gay. It's so much friendlier a word. Yes, quite possibly. And I reckon any suggestion of this would be very embarrassing for his father. So you were very definitely a marriage of convenience! It would also explain why he took the first opportunity to get rid of you. I bet you didn't make love very often in all the time you were married."

"It was OK to start with, but very quickly became less frequent. I reckon it won't take you long to catch up and overtake."

"That sounds like a challenge. And since it's unlikely you'll let me get back to sleep until I oblige, let's get on with it."

*Chapter 13*

If Barry had thought that he was taking in an invalid, who would need careful looking after, he couldn't have been more mistaken. Michelle had every intention of establishing herself. Her first question was the most difficult one.

"Barry, you're going to need to make a decision. Will you let me move some of Laura's clothes to the spare room? I'll pack them away neatly. But I'll need a place to put my things."

Barry knew this was going to come. But he felt that he had to acquiesce. Actually he found this easier than he thought. Last night had helped him move on, much more than he ever would have expected. Not the making love, surprisingly, but the caring. Laura wasn't suddenly going to move out of his life, but she was moving over, and letting someone else in.

Michelle opened the big wardrobe. "Wow. She had some beautiful things."

"She did love to dress well. And could she shop!"

"Well, you'll know that I wasn't good at clothes. I bet you thought I only owned a single pair of black trousers."

"I did see you in a brown dress one day?"

"Really? The trousers must have still been wet." She was touching Laura's clothes as she spoke, just feeling the quality. "It wasn't that we couldn't afford expensive clothes. Far from it. Justin's got lots of money. Sports car, four-wheel, I think he's got a boat somewhere. I could have had whatever I wanted. But I grew up not having a lot, and I didn't really see the need."

"Would you like to try on some of these? You must be quite a similar size."

She looked at Barry. "Are you saying that because then you can even more imagine me as Laura?"

"I know you could see it like that. But it's the opposite. It's quite hard to think of someone else wearing her clothes, but they are really nice, and it would be a terrible waste to throw them away. And I think you'd look good in them, but as Michelle, not Laura."

"I don't see many pairs of trousers here, but there are some lovely tops I could try."

"Why not try some dresses? I can see you might not want to go out in them, but you could wear them in the house."

"But you'd be seeing my leg the whole time."

"I'm hoping I showed last night that I'd be seeing everything but the leg."

"I'll put some trousers on for now. Remember, you've got to get me down to the hospital to get me booked in for physio. But when we get back, I'll put on a dress. I've just thought of something else to do with one of those dining room chairs."

The first significant obstacle they had to overcome came on Friday. Derek's funeral was going to be emotionally draining for Michelle. For Barry, it was the unwelcome opportunity to meet members of the Young family again. He had no idea how many would be there, but there was no-one he was keen to see. Whilst not in any way afraid of them, he knew that prolonged contact would give Ted Young the upper hand.

But it was only a small affair, at the Coney Hill crematorium outside Gloucester. The Youngs were there, senior and junior. Otherwise there was no-one Barry recognised. He was pleased that Wayne, the youth whose face he'd rearranged, wasn't present; it might have put a different complexion on matters if the Youngs had made that connection.

Michelle had decided it would be best for her to be in the wheelchair. There was likely to be too much walking for her level of ability with the crutches. As they entered, Barry saw everyone turn round to look at them. He was surprised when Justin came over to them.

"Hello Shell," he said, in a reasonably friendly voice.

"Hi Justin. How are you doing?"

"I'm fine."

"Have you had an accident?"

"Just walked into a door. Is he looking after you?" There was a nod towards Barry.

"He's been brilliant."

"I'm sure he has." You could read into that what you liked, but Barry was pretty sure what he was meant to read into it. But he didn't bother to respond.

The ceremony was fairly brief. There were no refreshments afterwards. Ted Young clearly hadn't pushed the boat out. But he did come and talk to them.

"You doing all right, Shell?"

"I'm fine, Mr Young. I'm looking forward to coming back to work."

"Really? That would be difficult. We've got no wheelchair facilities."

"I won't need those. I've got an artificial leg. I'm walking again already. In a few weeks I'll be fine to come back."

"Fair enough. If you're going to be able to do that, let me make you two an invitation."

Barry had no desire to accept an invitation from this character, of all people, but he waited to see what it was.

"I've got a horse running in the Cheltenham festival, four weeks today."

"What, in the Gold Cup?" Barry was prepared to be very impressed.

"Sadly, no. That's out of my league at the moment. No, in the Vincent O'Brien County Hurdle. But it should be a good day. Especially if I win."

"Is that likely?"

"You've got to always hope. Otherwise why bother taking part?"

Barry looked at Michelle. She nodded. "That's very kind, Ted. We'll look forward to it."

"I'll send a car to pick you up."

"No need for that, Ted."

"I insist."

"OK." Barry thought it best to capitulate, before the offer became a threat.

Michelle's recovery moved on much quicker than Barry had expected. She was rigorous with her attendance at physio. She quickly relieved Barry of taxi duties, getting herself to the bus stop. Initially the effort made her very tired, but as Barry was finding out, she was a very determined woman. With this determination she rapidly got stronger.

Barry went back to work, with a new enthusiasm. Linda immediately saw the change in him. "Right Baz. There is definitely a girl. Now you are really going to have to tell me."

"OK Linda, I surrender. Yes, there is a girl."

"You can't stop there. You're going to need to tell me everything. Especially after that trick you pulled in Leiden."

"That wasn't a trick. I did get back to visit someone in hospital. And she had lost her leg in a car accident."

"If you say so, I'll believe that bit. But who's the girl?"

"She is. The one who has lost her leg."

Linda stared at Barry. He couldn't interpret the look on her face. When she spoke there was a note of genuine concern in her voice. "What's this all about Baz?"

"No need to be concerned Linda. It's only that the woman I've moved in with me has just lost her leg in an accident. And incidentally she's already married. To a gangster."

"Now I know you're taking the piss."

"Funnily enough, I'm not. Look, would you and Brian like to come round to dinner on Saturday? Then you can meet her."

Given what Barry had said, it was no surprise that Linda accepted with alacrity.

"But one more thing," Barry warned her. "Be prepared for a surprise."

"Something more surprising than her being a one-legged gangster's moll?"

"Yes."

He wasn't at all surprised that Linda and Brian arrived spot on seven o'clock. She would normally be pretty punctual, but Barry guessed, correctly, that they'd been sitting outside for a few minutes to make sure they weren't a second late.

He took their coats, relieved Brian of a bottle of wine, and led them in to the lounge. Laura was holding a large bunch of flowers. "Linda, Brian. This is Michelle."

Barry was watching Linda's face. But he knew immediately that he should have told her first. The colour had drained completely away. "Fuck me!" was a most un-Linda like expletive. The flowers dropped to the floor.

Michelle was standing on her crutches. She was wearing one of Laura's tops, with trousers to hide her leg. She realised that Linda had not known what to expect, and so she took charge. She stepped forward, and held out her hand. "Hello," she said. "I'm not a ghost. Barry should have told you how much I look like Laura. Come and sit down."

"Thanks," said Linda. "I need to. Close to I can see the differences. But you do look so like her." She picked up the flowers, and handed them to Michelle.

"That's very kind of you, Linda." Michelle laughed. "I know how much I look like her. It's why Barry always caught the same bus, so he could look at me. But I don't think that's why he rescued me from the burning car – I think he would have helped anyone."

"Rescued you from a burning car? What burning car?"

"Didn't he tell you about that?"

"No." Linda looked at Barry. He just looked embarrassed.

"Well, he'll hate me saying it. So I'll send him out to put these in some water, and to look after the dinner, while I tell you the story."

Back in the office the following Monday, Linda sat with Barry. She thought it was time for a serious talk. Barry was ready for this, but he let her have her say.

"Right Baz. You're going to need to listen to your Aunty Linda."

"I know. So hit me with it."

"Well firstly, she's very nice. And I mean that."

"That's a good start."

"And you clearly get on quite well."

"Yes."

"And I bet she's not sleeping in the spare room."

"No."

"But she's not right for you, is she?"

Linda may have expected a strong denial from Barry, but there wasn't one. "No, probably not."

"So this could all end in tears, and, given her disability, that could be a real problem for her."

Barry could sense this was an accusation, and that Linda thought he was acting badly. He realised that Linda thought he was taking advantage of Michelle.

"I know exactly what you're saying, Linda. But I'm not taking advantage of her. Or, rather, we're taking advantage of each other."

"How do you mean?"

"We both agree that this relationship may well not go anywhere in the long term. I asked her to stay because she had nowhere to go. But it was her that insisted that we slept together. We both have our reasons. You know mine, and I know hers. We may not fall in love. But we do like each other, and we may continue to like each other enough to stay together. The key thing is that we're in this with our eyes open."

"Fair enough. Now, was the gangster thing a joke?"

"No. Far from it. Her husband is the son of a significant local hood."

"Aren't you taking a terrible risk there?"

"Surprisingly, not in the slightest. Fact is, he's probably gay, and happy to have her off his hands."

"A gay gangster? Brilliant! Mind you, he'd have to be gay not to want to stay with her, however many legs she's got."

"Yes. And if you're suggesting that things might have been different if she wasn't gorgeous, you're probably right."

"But do you see her, or Laura?"

"Funnily enough, from the moment I talked to her in the hospital, it was her and not Laura. But I am worried about the connections. We may joke about gangsters, but her former contacts appear to be entirely unpleasant. And they are still in the picture."

"So, is she a crook as well?"

"I don't think so. But her dad definitely was."

"Well, be really careful. Apart from anything else, if you get tainted with that sort of contact it would be very bad for business."

"I am aware of that. Thanks for your concern Linda. I do appreciate it. But I'm going into this with my eyes fully open."

Michelle was really happy living with Barry, in a way she had never been with Justin. What she liked most was that while she was determined to try and keep house for him, he insisted on sharing all the jobs. Justin had not lifted a finger for housework. Michelle wondered if this was the result of Barry's two years on his own, but she was pretty sure that this was just the way he was.

But there was one thing she was not looking forward to. Nick's party. It wasn't that she didn't want to go to a party. She loved parties. Although she had no idea what to expect of a party organised by a gay couple. All sorts of peculiar ideas raced around her head.

No. What was worrying her was meeting Nick. She knew he was Barry's closest friend, although she was aware that Barry was not currently in regular contact with him. She also knew now that he had been best man at Barry and Laura's wedding. Michelle feared Nick's reaction would be like Linda's, but much worse. She begged Barry to warn Nick, but he wouldn't.

"It's not fair on me, and it's not fair on him."

"I know that. But if I prepare him, he'll put on his best appearance for my sake. I want him to accept you as you. So I'll need him to be surprised."

"Have you at least told him about the leg."

"No."

"What have you told him then?"

"That you're called Michelle. And that you are married."

"Great. That will really endear me to him."

"Why? What's wrong with 'Michelle'?"

"Ha ha Barry. Let's just hope it doesn't ruin his party. After all, it's his day, not mine."

Michelle contemplated getting her hair cut short, so as to look less like Laura. But she decided against this. Although Barry insisted her resemblance to Laura wasn't the reason he had offered to bring her home, she didn't believe him. He might be convincing himself this was the case, but she was pretty sure subconsciously this was still the true reason. If she cut her hair, she reckoned there was a real chance he would react adversely. He wouldn't throw her out, no question of that, but he may well cool towards her. And since he didn't love her, she decided this wasn't a risk worth taking.

Instead she concentrated on her fitness and walking. Her physiotherapist warned her that pushing the limits could result in months of setback. So she didn't overdo any one spell of exercise on her prosthesis. However, she didn't miss a single programmed session, either at the hospital or at home.

Also she realised that arm strength was as important as leg strength. So she enrolled in a gym, and took on a programme of upper body exercises. This, she reasoned, would help her with her crutches. She was so successful that by the time of Nick's party she felt confident enough to leave her crutches in the car and go in with just a stick.

The Victoria Bar was a blaze of lights. It was nine o'clock, and the party was well under way. Even with the windows closed they could hear the music. Barry slipped his car into the car park at the back. Although Barry knew the back entrance, they walked round to the front. As Barry pushed the door open, a wall of noise hit them. At one end of the bar, on a small stage, a four-piece band was belting out a raunchy version of '*I will survive*'. Under disco lights, couples of various persuasions were dancing a variety of dances. No-one turned to look at them.

Most people were dancing, so Barry led Michelle to one of a small number of seats at the furthest point from the stage.

"Why are we coming over here?" she asked, or, rather, shouted.

"Don't you want to sit down?" he yelled back.

"No. I want to dance."

"Is that a good idea?"

"It is if you hold me."

"Happy to give it a go. But don't push it."

"I won't."

Having grossly abused Gloria Gaynor, it was now the turn of Abba and *Waterloo*. Holding Barry resolutely by the shoulders, Michelle was moving in a surprisingly free way. Barry was pretty convinced that the amount of rubbing he was receiving in his groin wasn't entirely down to her disability.

Over Michelle's shoulder he suddenly caught Nick's eye. Nick was dancing with a woman, but to Barry this wasn't a surprise; Chris wasn't a great fan of dancing, and Nick would take whoever was willing, whichever gender.

"Glad to see you here Barry," he yelled.

At this moment Michelle looked up and straight at Nick. Barry saw the look of surprise leap into Nick's eyes, but was pleased to see it passed away in a second. "And you must be Michelle."

"Hi. Are you Nick?"

"Yes."

The music suddenly stopped. "Half hour break," Nick informed them, still shouting a bit while his ears recovered. "There's some food if you want it. But come and have a quick chat first."

They walked back to the seats Barry had initially headed for. Although it had only been a couple of dances, Michelle was clearly already in need of a rest. Barry could see Nick looking at her, the limp really pronounced even though Barry was supporting her round the waist.

"I'm really glad you could come. And it's good to meet you Michelle. Barry's told me all about you."

"No he hasn't."

"Quite right. He's told me nothing at all. In fact, he's gone out of his way to keep you a mystery."

"Well, you've already seen two reasons for that."

"I've seen that you look remarkably like Laura."

"Yes. And you were watching me limp."

"I did notice."

Michelle hitched up her trouser leg, exposing the bottom of her prosthesis. Nick barely flickered. "So, you're a bit Heather Mills. That doesn't seem to constrain you at all."

"So how was it you realised so quickly I wasn't Laura? Barry's friend Linda took a real time."

"Well, your hair is very like Laura's, and there are some striking similarities facially. But the way you move is so different, and I don't mean the way you walk. Laura certainly wouldn't have been grinding Barry like that!"

Michelle laughed. "I do get a bit carried away. Anyway, Barry says this is your anniversary. So, congratulations."

"Thank you. Yes, we've been together for twenty years, and it's five years since our Civil Partnership. Did Barry tell you he was our Best Man at that?"

"No. I didn't know gay couples had a Best Man."

It was Nick's turn to laugh. "You don't know many gay people, do you?"

Michelle blushed deeply. Nick felt bad about this and continued, "It's just that you said gay like someone who isn't used to using the word in this context."

"It's true. I've been working really hard to make sure I said gay. Barry says it's a better word than homosexual."

Just as Michelle said this, Chris joined them. There was a look on his face that Barry wasn't too keen on. But he stood up and greeted him. "Chris. Good to see you. And happy anniversary."

"Thanks Barry."

Michelle had struggled to her feet. "Hello Chris. I'm Michelle. Happy anniversary."

"Thanks." This was curter. He turned to Nick. "I've got to get some drinks for the band. They'll be starting up again in a few minutes." He turned to go, but Barry saw that as he did, he passed a comment to Nick before walking off. An expression like thunder flashed across Nick's face, but it was gone in an instant. Michelle had been sitting back down, and had missed that. Barry caught Nick's eye, and an expression passed between them, but nothing was spoken.

"I'm going to grab some food," Nick said, and he headed over to a table that was already starting to look greatly depleted.

Barry turned to Michelle. "Will you let me get you something, so you can keep your strength for some more dancing?"

"Good idea. But I won't want much."

Barry went over to grab a couple of plates. He'd noticed that despite what Nick had said, he'd actually gone nowhere near the food table. He'd followed Chris back towards the band, and, after Chris had put down the tray of drinks, was in animated conversation with him. The two of them then disappeared through a door behind the stage. Barry was very concerned by what he was seeing, but took the food back to Michelle and didn't mention anything.

The music started up, and Michelle dragged Barry back to the dance floor. But three more dances, and she was very tired. So Barry helped her back to their seats, and they sat and watched the others. But dancing to Michelle wasn't really a spectator sport, and Barry realised this. "Shall we head off home?"

"I am tired. Will you mind? We've not been here very long."

"No, it will be good to get home. But I'm glad Nick has met you."

"He's nice. I don't think Chris likes me though."

Barry looked at her, but said nothing. He then looked round the room for Nick, so they could say their goodbyes, but he wasn't anywhere to be seen. Barry had a bad feeling about this. But he couldn't go looking for him through the private rooms, so he helped Michelle to her feet and they headed towards the door. But just as they got there, Nick joined them.

"Off already?" he asked. He smiled as he said this, but Barry could see it was a forced smile. There was strain on his face. Barry didn't mention this.

"Yes. Michelle gets tired very quickly."

"I'm sorry," said Michelle. "But it was fun to get out. I love dancing to that seventies music."

"That really is a gay thing," said Nick, with a bit more of a smile. "The closest we come to a stereotype."

They both saw Michelle suppress a yawn. "Thanks very much Nick," said Barry. "I'll give you a ring next week."

"That would be good," said Nick, and Barry knew his suspicions were correct.

## Chapter 14

Franklin Orengo's relative wealth meant that as well as the store, and his truck stop café, and his computer, he also had a relatively decent vehicle. It was a Toyota pickup. Initially he would use this to go to Nairobi for supplies, but fairly quickly he reached agreement with some of his trucker customers to drop stuff off, for a small fee. This fee was for the drivers of course, not for the transport companies. And recently he'd picked up a reasonably smart Toyota Corolla as well. Owning two vehicles in Salama marked you out as someone really special.

The other commodity his wealth gave him was free time. He had staff to run the store, although he was there himself most days. He trusted his staff not to cheat him too much, and would occasionally spend a day on some other pursuit, most often female.

But after Officer Kipruto's visit, his curiosity was roused, to the point where he could not keep still. How he waited five days was a miracle as much as a mystery. Franklin knew not to go to the police station. Apart from anything else, this would remind Sergeant Murungi that he hadn't shaken Franklin down recently.

So Franklin pitched up at Daniel's shack in the early evening. Daniel hadn't arrived home yet, but his wife Esther was expecting him at any moment. She asked Franklin in.

Franklin knew Esther well, although not as well as he had tried to know her. She was already married to Daniel at the time, and Franklin was drunk. It had taken a sharp slap across the face to persuade him her refusal was absolute. This might have been a cause for some friction, but Daniel was well aware of the fact, and he and Esther still laughed about it.

Franklin had barely sat down when Daniel arrived. He looked at the visitor quizzically, taking baby Noah from Esther. "Hello, little man," he said to his son. "I wonder what Uncle Franklin is after. Although I think I can guess."

"You can't leave me hanging, man. What's the story?"

"There is no story."

"Come on. You've got all those leads. What did the Sergeant say?"

"He told me to leave it."

"What? I can't believe that, man." Franklin's eyes narrowed. "How much did you tell him?"

"Fortunately, not too much. All I told him was about how the so-called detectives had behaved. And I told him about the zebra, and how the vehicle wouldn't be drivable. But I didn't tell him I spoke to Moses."

"What did he do?"

"Well, to his credit he got on the phone to Nairobi. I was outside, but couldn't get all he was saying. He made two calls, and after the second he called me in. He said they'd told him that the investigation was going well, but they didn't want it compromised by interference from the local police. He said they'd told him any local officer getting in the way would be instantly dismissed."

"Wow. A proper cover-up."

"So it seems."

"So what are you going to do?"

"Well, I was thinking about doing nothing. I don't fancy losing my job."

Franklin didn't like the sound of that. "So you're just going to quit?"

"You've got a better idea?"

"Yes. Do you fancy a holiday?"

"Where would you be thinking?"

"I bet you've never been to Mombasa."

"You're right. I've heard it's nice."

"OK then. Here's my suggestion. Take a couple of days off, to make a long weekend. We'll go on a trip to the coast." He turned to Esther. "That's you as well. We'll stay in a cheap hotel – my treat. Have a look at the ocean."

"And the port?"

"I'm sure it's an interesting place. But of course you won't be a policeman if you're on holiday, so won't be investigating anything."

Daniel looked towards Esther, expecting strong opposition. "What do you think?" he asked.

She took him by surprise. "I bet Noah would love to go in the ocean."

Daniel went back with Franklin to the store for a bit of research on Franklin's computer. They called up a map of Mombasa. A quick look showed the location of Kilindini Harbour on the west side of Mombasa Island. "How well do you know Mombasa?" Daniel asked.

"Quite well. It's maybe a six hour drive from here, on a good day. My brother Wycliffe lived there for several years. A couple of roads cross over to the island at the top. But most workers live off the island. There's a number of cheaper suburbs, and some real slums. Wycliffe lived in a place called Likoni. It's very rough in places, but there's a free pedestrian ferry across to the island.

There's a beach right near, called Shelly Beach. But much better you can get a cheap bus down to a place called Ukunda, maybe thirty kilometres south. It's by Diani Beach, which is absolutely beautiful. Esther and Noah would love it."

"So, they would get a bus to the beach, and we'd do some exploration at the harbour?"

"That would be the plan."

"It's not much of a plan Franklin. There's a lot of ships. We have no idea which one, if any, they would be meeting. And we have no idea how often the van goes that way. It may have been a one-off journey."

"That may be true Daniel. But I don't think you really believe it."

"No."

"So. Tell me what you think is going on."

"Well, it would be pure guesswork. But, I'm thinking something like this. I reckon the dumping of the body was largely incidental to some other trip. They were taking something heavy, so definitely not flowers. I bet this is a regular journey, and almost certainly criminal. Regular, but who knows how frequent. If it's just one specific ship, it could be months between shipments."

"Maybe I could help out there."

Daniel looked questioningly at Franklin. "How would you do that?"

"You know I have a lot of contacts. And a bit of money to spare. I've looked up your Heavenly Flower Export. It operates from a small unit just outside the main Nairobi Industrial Area. It's only a short step to the Mombasa road. I've had my cousin Patrick swing by and have a look at it."

"Franklin, he needs to be careful. These are really dangerous people."

"Don't you worry Daniel. I've told him that. He's no fool. He's just driven past to check it's there. But I can get it staked out, find out how many people work there, how often vehicles go in and out, just some general info. And if a truck heads off down the Mombasa Road, we'd hear about it."

"So, are you saying we'll cancel our trip to Mombasa, and wait to follow the next truck when it comes through?"

"Yes. Easy."

"But it could be months before the next truck. I think we ought to stick to the first plan."

"Why? You've got no real idea where the truck would be going. They may not go direct to the port. Or they may unload outside the port into another container. They might not go to the main port at all; they could make some sort of illegal loading to a boat outside the main harbour."

"Well firstly, you promised Esther and Noah a trip to the ocean, and I'm not letting you renege on that. And secondly I do know where they are going, or at least we're pretty sure. I agree they may not take the Heavenly truck in to the harbour, and I even think it's more likely that they don't. The dockers would notice it wasn't flowers being loaded, and it would be too many people to keep quiet. But I doubt they'll ship illegally. I don't think they'll break any law they don't have to. But I still think it would be useful for us to have a look round the harbour."

Franklin looked uncertain. "It's an international port. Deep water. It's bound to be very secure. To anyone without money for bribing. I hope you're not suggesting I do that?"

"What, are you suddenly moral?"

"No. But I don't want to throw money away."

"Well, you won't need to. You forget, I'm a police officer. I'll ask some questions, and get in for a look around."

"Surely that would just give the game away. And put the bad people on to us."

"It would, if those were the questions I asked."

Again Franklin looked baffled. Then slowly his face cleared, and a smile started to spread across it. "So, you'll invent a totally spurious crime that you are investigating, and use that as a pretext to get yourself in."

"To get us in."

"But I'm not a police officer."

"No, and I won't pretend you are. But I have a good idea what you could be. We'll both need to dress smart. I'm going to be plain clothes."

"You don't want to dress smart if you cross over from Likoni. You wouldn't stay smart for long. I think we'll have to go down in my Corolla. I'll have it cleaned up nicely to make it look more official. OK, tell me the rest of the plan. And I'll get Wycliffe to give us a cheap hotel in Likoni. This weekend too early?"

## Chapter 15

Barry didn't ring Nick. Instead he took Monday morning off, and headed back down to Bristol. As he expected, Chris was at work. Nick was finishing off clearing up from Sunday night's opening. They sat in the same corner Barry had used on his return to the Victoria Bar, just before Michelle's accident.

"Is it bad then, Nick?"

"It's beyond bad. It's all over."

"Are you sure? Could I help? I'm happy to talk to Chris if you need an intermediary." Barry paused, and then said something that had troubled him all Sunday. "This isn't a row about Michelle?"

"You're right. We did have a row about that. But it's been falling apart for years. I actually think our Civil Partnership was just a way to paper over cracks. I don't think there's anything you can say Barry. It really is all over. Chris actually moved his stuff out yesterday. I don't know where he went. But I have a feeling he didn't stay on his own."

"Oh, Nick. I'm really sorry to hear that. Look, if you want to have a break, close up for a few days and come up and stay with us."

"That's very kind of you. But I'd rather bury myself in the bar. I've got lots of friends here, and I can wallow in their sympathy. And maybe I'll pick up a good-looking younger model as well."

"Is that what Chris said about Michelle."

"Not exactly."

"Well, spill it then."

"He called her a cheap slapper."

"Did he half hear something, and guess she was homophobic?"

"Well, isn't she?"

"No. Not at all. It's just that she's no experience of outwardly gay people. But I'll bet you a pound to a penny her husband is also gay."

"Really. He must be available. Is he young and good-looking?"

"He's about thirty, tattooed, and a gangster."

"A gangster eh?"

"Well a crook at least. And, although I've no direct evidence, I bet a violent one."

"Charming. Michelle seems OK though. We need to talk about her."

"Hold hard. We were talking about you."

"Yes. And I don't like that. So now we're talking about you. After all you appear to be shagging a one-legged Laura look-alike, who's married to a gay gangster and must be fifteen years your junior."

"Eighteen."

"Nice work if you can get it. She's surprisingly articulate for a gangster's moll, but I don't see you as soulmates. Not like you and Laura. Is it just the likeness?"

"I don't think so. She is fun company, in a way I don't think I'd tire of quickly. We do get on well. From my point of view I could see it lasting. Maybe like would grow into love with time."

"Like an arranged marriage?"

"Sort of. We were brought together by fate, not by lust. Although I will say lust comes into it now."

"At your age you'd better be careful you don't do yourself a mischief. Mind you she is very attractive, for a woman. But I'd say her features were not as fine as Laura's. She's maybe a bit more earthy."

"You think she's got coarse features?"

"No, not that. Far from it. But she's a bit more earth-mother than Laura."

"I'd certainly agree with that. Laura would take an age, making sure her make-up was perfect. I don't think Michelle has much in the way of make up. But she doesn't really need it. But my real problem is with the crooks."

"So they are unhappy about you taking her away?"

"No. They gave her to me." Barry told Nick about Michelle's accident, and what Justin had said.

"So if they are happy with being shot of her, where's your problem?"

"Her father-in-law has taken a shine to me."

"He's also a crook?"

"He is the crook. The rest are his minions."

"Now that could be a problem. Especially given your line of work." Nick mused for a bit, then added, "I bet that's it. He's not taken a shine to you. It's to what you do. How neat would it be for him to hook in a tame accountant. Could help him clean up his ill-gotten gains."

"That's what I'm fearing. Although I'm sure he'd already have an accountant."

"Maybe his current one is getting a bit shop-soiled in the eyes of the authorities, so he needs a clean one. And I assume he's the sort of person who wouldn't take no for an answer?"

"I suspect people who say it to him live to regret it. If they live."

"Isn't that a bit melodramatic?"

"I hope so."

"Well, the best thing to do is to keep your distance, and hope he loses interest."

"That would be nice. But we're off to the Gold Cup meeting with him on Friday. He's got a horse in one of the support races."

"I didn't know you liked racing."

"Don't be silly. I can't abide it. As a friend once said – all that raw dog food."

"Well, I'm not sympathetic. I'd love to go. But I suggest you put an each way bet on his horse. For form's sake."

Gold Cup day dawned bright and clear. Barry had hoped that the recent rain would have continued, on the very unlikely hope that the day would be cancelled, but it was a glorious day for mid March. He wondered what sort of car would be sent for them, and he vaguely imagined a Rolls Royce, with a uniformed chauffeur. So it was with a touch of disappointment when he saw it was just an Audi, even if a fairly up-market one, driven by Justin Young.

"Morning, mate. You ready?" Yet again the greeting was fairly friendly.

Barry was determined to make the best of today, so made sure he was equally friendly, although there was a touch of chiding in his reply. "She's just re-bandaging her stump, to make sure she'll be comfortable all day. She won't be long."

"Do you want to get her chair in the boot, or will she need it to get to the car?"

"She won't need a chair. Just her stick."

"Really?" Justin seemed genuinely surprised.

"Yes. She's walking pretty well already. Last weekend she was dancing."

"Now you're taking the piss."

"No, I'm not. She only managed a few, and she did get very tired. But there's no holding her back."

A smile half crossed Justin's face. "That's my girl."

Barry wanted to say that she wasn't Justin's girl any more, she was his. But that might have been a bit too confrontational. And anyway, he had a sneaking feeling that more to the point he was her boy.

Michelle appeared at the door. "Got everything?" she asked.

"I'm not sure what else I might need."

"Good. Let's go then. Hi there Justin."

"Hi Shell. It looks like you're doing great."

"Getting there."

Barry had for obvious reasons never been to Cheltenham Racecourse, and he had only a vague notion of where it was. There was a series of enormous car parks, and the main car parking for the *hoi polloi* was several hundred metres away down the hill. But Justin pulled in to a disabled parking space, right next to the main entrance. "Dad knows the Managing Director."

Michelle didn't object. "Thanks Justin," was all she said.

Barry had been expecting to be out on one of the terraces, maybe having lunch in one of the restaurants. But Justin took them through the entrance, up in the lift to the fourth floor, and led the way to private box number 4050. There was no-one there when they entered. "Dad's probably down with the trainer. And he'll be showing the others his horse."

"How many of us are there today?"

"Just six. Dad's got a couple of potential new business partners. If you wait here I'll go and see how they're doing. Do you want me to put any money on for you?"

Definitely time for a political gesture. Although he had the sort of feeling he might as well have been putting a match to the note, he passed over a twenty. He remembered Nick's advice. "Put a tenner each way on Ted's horse. What's it called?"

Justin smiled. "Not been studying the form then? It's called *Young Folly*. Might be his little joke, but probably sums up the chances. Still, he'll be pleased. See you in a bit. We'll be eating here at twelve thirty."

Barry looked at his watch. Quarter past twelve. "OK Justin. We should be OK entertaining ourselves."

Glass doors led to a terrace. Michelle was just stepping out, so Barry joined her. Michelle leant on the railing. "Great position, isn't it?"

They were just before the finishing post. And just behind the racetrack were the Cotswolds. It was a remarkably fine view. "Have you been here a lot?"

"Quite a few times, yes. I think Mr Young liked Justin to bring me when he was entertaining. I think he thought of me as a bit of an ornament. You know, distraction for the clients."

"What sort of clients?"

"Just business partners. Exports."

The terrace to the left was empty, but to the right Barry noticed a couple of younger teenage girls, quite possibly twins, also looking at the view. "Hello there," he greeted.

"Hello." Before they managed any other conversation they were joined by a man, who Barry presumed was their father.

"Hello, Michelle," he said. "Is Ted here today?" Barry was surprised by the first name terms.

"Hi Mr Gordon. Hi Liz, hi Beth. Yes, he's downstairs, with Justin. He's got a runner today."

"Really?" Mr Gordon sounded genuinely interested. "Does it have any chance?"

"Mr Young says you've always got a chance. *Young Folly*. It's in the second race. Barry here's just put on a tenner each way"

"I'll nip down with the girls and put something on it as well."

Barry sat down next to Michelle, surveying the scene before him. "It's a great view from here," he said. "But wouldn't it be more fun out there with the crowd?"

"We'll only stop up here while we eat. Then Mr Young will want us to go down to the terrace. That concrete one down there, at the end of the grandstand. It's for the owners and trainers."

Barry heard the door to the box open, and he stood up to greet Mr Young. But it was the food arriving, so he sat down again. "All this must set him back a tidy sum."

"He's loaded. You should see his place in the Cotswolds."

"I hope I never do."

Barry heard the door to the box open again. This time he turned to the see the Youngs enter, with their guests. These were two smartly dressed black men. Barry got up and went back inside to meet them, leaving Michelle outside.

"Hello Barry. Glad you could join us. Can I introduce the Ndesandjo brothers. Haji and Darweshi. From Tanzania."

One of the guests held out his hand. "To save Mr Young embarrassment, I'm Haji."

Barry took the hand, and that of Darweshi. "Barry Clark. I'm a friend of Michelle's. She's Ted's daughter-in-law."

"Mr Young tells me you're an accountant."

Barry worked hard to keep control of his features. "Yes." Should he say more? Something like 'but not his'? But he delayed too long, so missed the chance. So it was better to change the subject. "Have you seen his horse?"

"Not yet. Mr Young was showing us around the racecourse. It's a fine place."

Ted took over. "You should come out here and look at the view. And come and meet Michelle. Then we must eat."

The cold buffet lunch was excellent, and accompanied by what Barry was sure was a very fine wine. But wine wasn't his strong point. Afterwards they sat outside on the terrace, ready for the first race. Ted chatted to the Gordon family, like old friends, and also to the elderly couple on the terrace to the left.

The first race was the JCB Triumph Hurdle. Ted explained to the Ndesandjo brothers about the type of horses. Barry wasn't really listening, but he caught something about novices. Whether horses or jockeys he wasn't sure. "Right," Ted instructed, "just as soon as this is over, we're off. Justin, you take Michelle to the stand. We're going to the saddling box. Here, put these on. You'll need them for access." He passed Barry and the brothers a badge each.

"Here Barry, have a look at this." Justin passed Barry the racecard. He saw that the Vincent O'Brien was run over the same length as the Triumph Hurdle, and the novices in the first race were the horses. From the card he could see that Ted's horse must be five years or older. And his jockey would be wearing some fairly garish pink and black stripes, with a pink cap. It wouldn't be the thing to wear in some of the rougher parts of Cheltenham, after dark.

"It doesn't say the odds in here."

"Of course not," said Ted. "They change all the time. What are they now?"

"20-1," said Justin.

"Is that good?" asked Barry.

"If you win, yes."

The runners were off. The start was in the far distance, but they raced up and turned round the circuit. Away they went into the distance, and then back and up the straight. Excitement was mounting as a close finish seemed in prospect, but in the last few strides a grey forged a couple of lengths lead. An audible groan reached their ears.

"Outsider," said Ted. "Beat the favourite. Come on then, we're off."

"See you in a few minutes," Barry called back to Michelle.

Down in the lift and outside, they crossed the road, passed the parade ring, to the saddling boxes. *Young Folly* was in the third box. Ted greeted the jockey. "Good luck Bill. How's he feeling?"

"He feels pretty fine Mr Young, sure he does." Barry half smiled at his stereotype of a jockey actually being the reality. Then Bill was mounted, various adjustments made, and he was off round the parade ring.

"OK," said Ted. "Let's take our places." The Owners and Trainers stand was pretty full. They picked out Michelle and Justin part way up, and made their way through to join them. At the same time the horses emerged through the underpass, and set off down the course.

Ted had his binoculars out and was looking down the track. He seemed pretty satisfied with what he saw. "He's looking good. Moving nicely."

Barry checked the racecard. Twenty eight horses were listed. A quick count only came to twenty four. "Where are the rest?"

"There are four non-starters."

All Barry could see now was brown dots, heading away, each with another dot, this time multi-coloured, sitting on its back. In the far distance there was some milling about, a longish delay, and then Ted shouted "They're off!" This was followed almost immediately with "They're over the first!"

The dots got closer and bigger. Almost immediately in front of them the horses took the second. They were mostly in a tight bunch, and going so fast Barry couldn't make out what position *Young Folly* was in, but he seemed well placed.

"He's lying fifth!" Ted was starting to get excited. The runners were disappearing round the circuit. They took the third, fourth and fifth with no problems, but a faller at the sixth caused another horse to refuse. There was no alarm from Ted, so Barry assumed *Young Folly* was unaffected. As far as Barry could tell, the seventh was negotiated well, and the horses were now getting spread out. The excitement was starting to get even to Barry.

"Where's he now, Ted?"

"I think he's still fifth, but he's close up on the next two."

The leader and second were now several lengths clear of the rest, and the race for first was going to be close. But no-one in Ted's party was in the slightest bit interested in that. *Young Folly* was now fourth, well clear of the fifth, and close on the back of the third. They raced towards the final hurdle. First and second cleared it and streaked past, to end up in a photo finish. Well behind them *Young Folly* came to take the last just half a length behind *Sixty Stars*.

Ted was now shouting at the top of his voice. "Come on Bill, take him. Take him." The whole party was shouting, and even Barry couldn't stop himself joining in. *Sixty Stars'* jockey had a quick look round, which was a mistake, because the horse just clipped the hurdle. It wasn't enough to make him fall, but it just briefly disrupted his stride. *Young Folly* eased past a length. They raced for the line, and *Sixty Stars* was coming back strongly. But the finishing line came just in time, as far as those in the Young party could tell.

"Yeeeeeeeeeesssssssss." If he'd made it any longer, Ted would have suffocated. "Let's go!"

Most of the party started to charge down the stairs. Barry had almost forgotten Michelle in his excitement. Remembering himself, he stopped and turned back. She had a broad grin on her face. "Go on," she said. "I'll see you back in the box."

The horses were making their way back. Ted met *Young Folly* part way. Bill leaned over and took the upreaching hand. Ted took the reins, and walked back with the broadest smile on his face. Barry, Justin and the Ndesandjo brothers waited for him. There were handshakes all round. Ted, although not exactly lost for words, was lost for vocabulary. He just kept repeating "Third" with the occasional "Third, at Cheltenham."

As a group they went back through the underpass, into the parade ring, and through the gate to the Winners' Enclosure. *Young Folly* took his place at number three, with the unlucky *Sixty Stars* next to them at four.

Bill went with the others to be weighed in. After a minute or two's standing around, Barry had returned to his normal calm state. "So Ted, how much do you win for coming third?"

"Eight thousand."

"Wow." Barry was surprised. "That's more than I expected."

Justin laughed. "It'll cover his expenses for a couple of weeks, tops."

Barry, ever the accountant, did some quick mental arithmetic. So, he thought, he's probably spending two hundred thousand a year, just on this. But he just said "I'd better go back and keep Michelle company."

"OK. Take the brothers with you. Be with you shortly."

As they made their way back, Barry took the opportunity to probe. "So, Darweshi, what line of business are you in?"

"You're better at names than most British people, Mr Clark."

Barry suspected this wasn't a compliment, but evasion. "My clients wouldn't hang around long if I didn't get their names right." He tried a different approach. "I'm assuming you're exporters, since Ted runs an import business. And I work for a firm mostly working with importing companies."

This was a very risky strategy. Barry assumed that, since he was Ted's guest, if the brothers were crooked they would assume he was too. But if it did encourage them to let something slip, it would also suggest he was at least prepared to be crooked as well.

"We look to supply to expatriate Tanzanian communities. Things they miss from the home country."

Well, that didn't sound particularly criminal. And Barry didn't get the impression it wasn't the truth.

Haji added, "We're interested in storage at Avonmouth."

They were back at the box. Michelle was back sitting on the terrace, chatting to the Gordons. Mr Gordon was very pleased with himself. "Barry isn't it? Thanks for the tip. The girls put an each way on *Young Folly*, and I put ten on the favourite."

"Did that win? I must admit we didn't really notice!"

"I bet you didn't."

Ted and Justin were back much quicker than Barry expected. Ted had champagne. "Got to celebrate properly."

"Isn't Bill joining us?"

"Goodness, no. The jockeys don't mix with owners. And anyway, he's got a ride in this next race."

Justin reached in his pocket, and handed Barry a wad of cash. "Sixty quid," he said.

Barry was surprised. "Sixty? I hadn't expected that much."

"You won fifty for the place, with your stake back."

Ted was surprised. "You put money on him?"

"A tenner each way. It seemed only polite."

Ted's smile appeared completely genuine. "Well, your courtesy has been well rewarded. Let's toast. To *Young Folly*. And to new business relationships."

Barry sincerely hoped he was talking about the Ndesandjos, but deep down he thought differently.

## Chapter 16

If Kenya had a Trade Descriptions Act, the Paradise Guest House would have fallen foul of it. As Franklin would have said himself, you don't stay rich by wasting money. But Esther thought it was fine, and Noah was too young to care.

They had arrived the previous evening, after dark. Straight after breakfast they had caught the bus down to Diani Beach, and spent a couple of hours there. Esther was happy with this reconnaissance, and she was sure she could get down on her own the next day.

Back in Likoni they had a quick lunch. Noah was tired, so Esther was happy to be left alone while Daniel and Franklin did some exploring. Dressed in casual clothes, they strolled down to the ferry, and crossed to the Island.

Getting off at the far side, they took a good look at the map. The Kilindini Harbour was about three kilometres away. They set off at a holiday pace, strolling up Mbakari Road and Archbishop Makarios Road. They turned left on Moi Avenue, but very quickly after the roundabout saw the security at the main port entrance. The side road they passed was also closed off.

Rather than approach closely enough to be observed they tracked back, and turned up Zanzibar Road. They continued north along Shimanzi Road, with the sprawling Shimanzi Industrial Area to their right. To the left, all entrances to the port were either closed, or had security. From here it was not possible to say how much further the port went, but it could be a long way.

It was clear that there was no easy way to sneak in here for a look round. Another approach would be necessary. So they turned east along

Makande Road, and down the main Jomo Kenyata Avenue right back in to the old town, past Fort Jesus to Mombasa Old Port.

Mombasa Old Port was nothing like its more modern replacement. This was just a heritage port. There were a dozen or so dhows along the waterfront, most of which appeared to be offering harbour tours. This was clearly not the sort of place you'd choose to smuggle from.

They were now both tired from traipsing round. Franklin was clearly starting to get a bit bored. "What now, Mr Policeman?"

"Well, I fancy a beer. And a bit of different company. Follow me."

Daniel walked up to the board for one of the harbour tour boats, the *Emerald Princess*. He looked at his watch. "They've finished for the day. Let's go on board."

They walked up the gangway. No-one was obviously about. But after a couple of minutes a fairly elderly man appeared from the cabin.

"Sorry. Next trip not till tomorrow."

"Thanks Captain. I've seen that outside. But I'm not after a tour. I'm from *Coast Weekly*. I'm doing a bit about trade from Mombasa. I was hoping I could persuade you to take a few drinks with us, and answer a few questions."

"I'm the Mate, not the Captain. I'll have a word with him and see if I can come with you."

He was back pretty quickly. "He says no more than two drinks."

They walked back towards the old town, and stopped at the first bar they passed. It was a rough looking area, but the Mate seemed pretty happy. Franklin got three beers, but, thirsty though they were, they'd barely started theirs when the Mate drained his in one. With just a quick bit of eye contact with Daniel, Franklin ordered up another. This nearly went as quickly. A third was brought, but this one was just cradled in the Mate's hands. "What you want to know?"

"Does any cargo go from the Old Harbour these days?"

"Hardly any. A few dhows go round to Arabia. Pirates mostly kill the trade. Not worth the dhows paying protection money. Almost everything goes from Kilindini."

"Did you used to work on the dhows?"

"Sure. Went all over. Zanzibar, Mogadishu, Aden. Five years did nothing but Dubai. Good money in those days."

"What sort of stuff?"

"Anything. Pick up and drop off along the coast. Carpets, electricals, second hand pickups, tusks, whatever."

"All legal?"

The Mate smiled. "Of course not."

"But now everything goes from Kilindini?"

"Yep. In and out. They load grain. Bring in oil. And there's a big container port up at Port Reitz."

"Port Reitz? Where's that?"

The Mate looked surprised. "You don't know Reitz?"

Daniel quickly amended his cover. "I'm new. Only started on the *Weekly* last month. That's why I'm talking to locals, to get a real idea of what's going on."

"Good plan." The mate looked at his now empty glass. Without a word, it was refilled. "Kilindini is a huge harbour. Goes right round off the island. Port Reitz is the far end. Right by the Oil Tank Farm. You going to talk to them?"

"Yes."

"Not sure the security will let in a reporter."

"I'll ask nicely." Daniel got the map out, and the Mate pointed out the entrance at the top of the Nairobi Road.

"OK," said Daniel. "Thanks for all your help."

They left him at the table, with enough money for number five. Daniel was pretty pleased with the result. Night was just starting to fall, so they moved quickly back towards the ferry.

That evening, after dinner and Noah had gone to sleep, they discussed the plan for the next day. Esther would take Noah down to Diani Beach, and the men would don their smart clothes, and drive round to Port Reitz.

They started early the following morning, and crossed again on the Likoni ferry, this time in the car. Traffic was light, not surprising for a Sunday. Getting through the town, they crossed over the Makupa Causeway, and turned left at the roundabout. Encouragingly they were following a couple of container lorries. Just before the port entrance they pulled into a layby, where several lorries were also parked up.

"OK Franklin. You ready?"

"Sure?"

"You got your story straight?"

"Trust me."

"Right. Let's go."

They got out of the car, and walked smartly up to the security post. A uniformed security guard stepped out, and held up his hand. Daniel pulled his ID out of his pocket.

"Morning. I'm Detective Constable Daniel Kipruto of the Salama police. This is Franklin Orengo of the Co-operative Insurance Company. We're investigating the theft of agricultural machinery from the Salama District. We have reason to believe it may have been brought here, and we would like to have a look round."

The security guard did not look particularly impressed. "No-one told me you were coming."

"I'm the police. We don't tend to tell people we're coming."

The guard clearly wasn't especially bright. He scratched his head for a few seconds. "OK," he said, finally. "I'd better let you go through."

Daniel decided gratitude wasn't appropriate. "Yes. You'd better. Otherwise I might start thinking you're involved." With rather more urgency the guard waved them through. He then moved to speak to the driver of a container lorry that had just pulled up.

They followed the road through, heading towards the water. Quickly they realised that even this container section of the port was pretty large. To be a touch systematic, and to get an idea of the layout, they walked towards the eastern end. There were many railway tracks at this end, and some accumulations of containers. Three large cargo vessels were moored here, two partly loaded and the other empty. Some container lorries were passing by, and small cranes were picking the containers off and loading them.

They headed back west. This was where the bulk of the containers sat, in front of the giant oil tanks. Four large cranes were actively loading two ships. This was a much bigger operation. In all the port was probably a mile long.

After three hours of nosing around, they were making no real progress. It was time to start asking questions. Daniel approached a small group of men taking a break around a small van, mugs of tea in their hands. He pulled out his ID again, and gave his spiel about missing agricultural equipment. Everyone shook their heads, not surprising since there was no missing machinery. Then Daniel took a risk. "Anyone seen a truck from Heavenly Flower Export? One of those was also reported stolen."

One of the men looked up. "When was that?"

"Bout three weeks ago."

"They were here around then. But it wasn't a stolen van, just normal."

"Normal?"

"Come about every month. But they'd smashed it up a bit. Probably reported it stolen, to claim the insurance."

"They'll be in trouble if they have. Mr Olengo here is from the insurance company."

The men laughed. But the first one said, "You'd still better pay them. Don't want to argue with them!"

"Where do they unload?" asked Daniel.

"They move stuff into a container up by number 1."

"Show me."

With some reluctance the man got a buggy, and Daniel and Franklin squeezed in. The container was deep within a block of others. It was red, and unmarked. Daniel tried the door, which was unsurprisingly locked. He listened. There was a low humming coming from inside.

"Refrigerated?"

"Could be. Never seen inside. Maybe part refrigerated. Would have to be battery, so don't think it could be the whole thing."

"What ship do they load in?"

"*Sea Empress*. Out of Rotterdam."

"Well, agricultural machinery doesn't need refrigerating, so it doesn't look like these are our men. But my friend here may see them about the insurance on their truck. Thanks for your help. We'll have a bit more of a look round."

After the buggy had departed, Daniel and Franklin sat on the ground, backs to the container. "What do you reckon, Daniel?"

"I reckon we've seen enough. Let's get back. Esther will be back soon. And I'm worried we've asked too many questions."

Next day they drove back to Salama, starting early. They had a reasonably clear run, and were back by three o'clock. Franklin dropped them off, and headed back to the store. Daniel still had the rest of the day off, and he wanted to spend time playing with Noah.

Just before dark there was an urgent knocking, at the back of the hut. Daniel looked at Esther, and went to see who it was. He opened the door, to see Samuel, in his police uniform, looking really distressed. "Hi Samuel. What's…"

"No time. You've got to get out. There are men at the station, asking for you. They've beaten the Sargeant really bad, and Joseph too. Didn't see me, outside. They gonna kill you I reckon. Get out now!"

"I must warn Franklin."

"Too late for Franklin. Go now. Take nothing."

"Where shall we go?"

"Try Uncle Amos. But go now." And Samuel was gone. Panic gripping him, Daniel grabbed Noah, and with Esther ran out into the gloom.

## Chapter 17

It was almost spot on six thirty that the Kenya Airways flight from Heathrow touched down in Nairobi. The sun was just coming up, and the temperature was near perfect.

Steve cleared customs, retrieved his luggage reasonably efficiently, and headed out of the exit. He scanned the cards and quickly picked out his name. He stepped across. Before he spoke the man said, "Dr Smith?"

"That's me."

"Hello there. I'm Kiboi Muthui. Giles asked me if I could pick you up. He's got a bit of a problem this morning."

It was pretty clear that Kiboi Muthui was making sure straight off that Steve didn't assume he was just Giles Anderson's driver. "You work with Giles?"

"I'm a freelance journalist. But I mostly work with Giles."

"Pleased to meet you. I'm Steve." They shook hands. "What's Giles's problem this morning? Nothing serious I hope?"

"Far from it. One of the kids isn't well, so is off school. He's just had to wait till the maid comes back from shopping. He's going to meet us at the Pasara Café. We'll have breakfast there. Giles said you were a touch cagey about what you wanted to do, but that it was about the Murungaru affair."

"I'll wait till we're all together before giving the details, if that's OK. Saves repeating it all."

"No problems. Let's go then. He'll probably be there before we are."

There was a real laid back feel to the Pasara. The clientele was about half and half black and white. Many of the whites were tourists, and the blacks appeared well heeled.

Giles was already there. He waved them over, and rose to greet Steve. Steve recognised him from a picture on the internet. He was well over six feet tall, and broad; he would be an imposing figure in any gathering. "The famous Steve Smith. Very pleased to meet you."

"I like to think of myself as previously famous. Thanks very much for helping out."

"That's no problem. The Murungaru case has gone incredibly quiet, and, with a bit of luck, you'll stir something up. That should give me a good storyline for a week or two. Unfortunately local political unrest doesn't score well in London."

"No. A bit like climate change. Well, there's no point in not telling you exactly what I plan."

"That would be great. And, since you've had the decency not to suggest otherwise, I can assure you that you can implicitly trust Kiboi here as well."

Steve looked at Kiboi. "I didn't for a moment think otherwise. Otherwise why would you have asked him to fetch me? But you make a good point. I've no idea who can or can't be trusted, so I was going to work on a plan of trusting no-one."

"I'd endorse that," said Kiboi earnestly. "The case is undoubtedly political, and the police are also heavily implicated."

"So, what's your plan then Steve?" asked Giles. "I'm assuming you have a detailed idea of what you want to do."

"I do. But clearly I'll have to be flexible, to respond to events. Today, can you spare me the time to go through everything you've gleaned?"

"Of course. Unfortunately that won't take too long."

"I appreciate that. Well, after we've spoken, I'm going to go to the Jomo Kenyatte University of Agriculture and Technology."

Giles and Kiboi both had surprised looks on their faces. "Why?" asked Giles. "Do you think they are involved in this?"

"Goodness, I hope not. No, I'm visiting Professor Daniel Abukutsa."

"Is he a friend?"

"Well, I've met him a couple of times. He's doing some excellent work on genetic engineering of crops, for drought resistance. To maintain yields of African crops under hotter, drier conditions. They've got thirty million euros from the Belgians for research."

Kiboi's faced broke to a smile. "It's a cover."

"Of course. Professor Abukutsa is assiduous in putting his results on the internet. And I could easily speak to him on Skype. But I'm meeting him at the university, and he's taking me out to his experimental station. I'm having dinner with him and his family tonight. After that, as far as he is aware, I'm going on a short safari to the Masai Mara. I'll tell him nothing about my real purpose."

"So, what's your plan for tomorrow? Kiboi and I have kept the next two days clear, to help out if we can. Unless a big story breaks, of course."

"That's very kind. Well tomorrow it would be good to talk to a reasonably senior police officer."

Giles seemed a bit miffed. "What do you think you'll find out that we haven't?"

"Nothing at all. My line will be that I'm an old friend of Sylvia's family, and that they'd asked me, since I was coming to Kenya, to see how the investigation was going."

"But isn't there a danger that you'll stir them up?"

"I certainly hope so. Because if I stir them up they might make a mistake. Give something away."

"Well, you clearly like to live dangerously." Giles smiled. "But I like your approach. What next?"

"The day after I'd like to have a quick look where the body was found. And then go on into this dump, Salama."

"It won't take long to see the sights there."

"I don't want to see the sights. I want to go to the police station. If there is one."

"That I didn't expect. Tell us why."

"I've spent a lot of time thinking about this, and I've come up with a bit of a theory. Sylvia was dumped just off the main road. And then some alleged Nairobi police…"

"Alleged police?" Kiboi seemed surprised.

"I spoke to one of the British policemen who'd come out after the body was found. He had a theory that no genuine police had been at the scene. Just his hunch, but a policeman's hunch. Anyway, these Nairobi 'police' investigated the crime scene, and took the body back to Nairobi.

So, now we're going to assume there's a conspiracy. We might as well, because if it's just a bungling investigation no-one will get too upset. My view is that Sylvia's murder wasn't planned, but happened as a result of some cock-up in whatever the crime was. Her body was unceremoniously dumped, and someone was then contacted, and told to clean up the mess. I bet a number of hours elapsed between the body being dumped, and the cleanup team arriving. And I suspect that Nairobi to Mombasa road is pretty busy."

"Very."

"So it's quite possible that someone reported it to the police. And Salama is the nearest place. So I think it's worth asking at the police station there whether they know anything."

Kiboi looked doubtful. "Even if they do, they'd almost certainly have been told not to speak to anyone about it. Especially not to a couple of whites."

"I'm sure you're right. But I was hoping you'd indulge me in a little bit of play acting."

"Play acting?"

"Yes. And please don't take offence at this. What I suggest is that Giles and I say we are friends of Sylvia's, and again want to ask if there's any information we can take back to the family. Kiboi, would you be prepared to pretend you were our driver." Steve paused for a second. "Or, better still, a late replacement for our driver."

"I can live with that. Why a late replacement?"

"I'm assuming that English is commonly spoken among educated people, but what's the language on the street?"

"There's dozens of languages in Kenya, and most of them are spoken in Nairobi. But the general language is Swahili. Giles here is pretty fluent."

"The usual driver for a couple of white people would be expected to speak English. But if they have to make a late replacement, he might not speak much English. Maybe also not look so smart. You might be able to chat to the locals in and around the police station, moan about being dragged out at short notice, and see if you can pick up a few odds and ends."

Kiboi was smiling. "I like the way your mind works. Happy to play along."

"And Giles would have to pretend he doesn't speak Swahili."

Steve had an excellent afternoon and evening with Professor Abukutsa and his family. Whilst he was doing that, Giles arranged for him to meet the following day with Assistant Commissioner of Police Vivian Kibet,

Kenya's highest ranking woman police officer.

The meeting with the Assistant Commissioner was perfectly friendly, and as useless as Steve predicted. Yes, the investigation was continuing. Progress was slow. There were few leads. And so on. Steve had no doubt that she was being completely honest. He thanked her for her time, and said he would take back to Sylvia's family the knowledge that solving this crime was still high priority.

They set off early the following morning. Kiboi had taken his role to heart. He was fairly scruffily dressed, and from the off pretended he didn't speak much English, just to get into character. Steve took the opportunity of the two hour drive to Salama to look around him. He was surprised to start seeing game animals soon after leaving Nairobi. There were topi, gazelles, zebra and even a couple of distant giraffes.

As they approached Salama, they decided there was nothing to be gained trying to find out where the body was found. There would be no evidence after this time. Instead they just headed into the town.

The first thing they passed was a large burnt-out shed. A drunkenly leaning sign said it had been 'Isaac's Garage'. They continued into town, and, towards the middle, passed another burnt-out building, that looked as though it may have been a large store.

"Is this something to do with the political violence?"

"Probably. But to be honest there's so much outside Nairobi this just wouldn't register. Driver."

"*Bwana?*"

"Pull up and ask the way to the police station."

The police station was only a concrete shack, but this in itself made it a class above the town's other accommodation. Kiboi parked outside. Steve and Giles went in the door, and Kiboi just leant on the car. Steve noticed immediately that a couple of people wandered across to speak to him.

Inside the station there was one bigger, but not big room, with a couple of desks. They could see a second, smaller room at the back. Two uniformed policemen were sitting at the desks. They looked up as the white men entered, and both got up to greet them.

"Hello," said Steve. "My name is Steve Smith. I hope you don't mind us calling in."

The two officers looked fairly blank, and Steve was starting to think they were just a bit dopey when Giles tried a few words in deliberately broken Swahili. There was a reply, and the policemen and Giles all smiled.

"You'll have gathered that they don't speak any English. Let's whistle Kiboi in." Giles walked to the door, and did indeed whistle for Kiboi. There followed a conversation between them in broken English and even more broken Swahili, before Kiboi spoke to the policemen in Swahili. Immediately, Steve noted, the smiles disappeared off the policemen's faces. One walked across knocked on the door to the smaller room, put his head round the door, and then beckoned Steve and Giles across.

Inside, and making the room cramped, was another desk. There was another policeman here, a sergeant. He didn't get up when they came in. Instead, he beckoned them to sit down, difficult, since there was only one chair. A second chair was squeezed in, and they both sat.

The sergeant stared at them for a few moments. It was long enough for Steve to see that he had some fairly recent looking scars on his face. Also the little finger on his left hand appeared dislocated. He was a sour looking man, and clearly not pleased to see them.

"You ask about Sylvia Murungaru?"

"Yes."

"Why you ask about her?"

"My name's Steve Smith. I am a friend of the family. They would like to know how she died."

"She was shot."

"We know that. But by whom?"

"Nairobi police investigate."

"Yes. But not very well." Steve took a punt. "Which of your officers saw the body?"

Again the sergeant stared. Much too long a pause. "No-one saw the body. Nairobi police saw it."

"But if no-one saw the body, how did the Nairobi police find it?"

"Someone must tell them. No Salama police see anything."

"Doesn't that upset you, those Nairobi police not letting you get involved?"

"You must talk to Nairobi police. Now, I have much to do."

Steve glanced at Giles. "OK. We'll go now. Thank you for your time."

The sergeant didn't get up. He just looked down and started writing. They left the room. Only one of the policemen was outside, but the other came back in as they opened the door. He passed them without a word.

They got back in the car, and Kiboi said, "Where to, *bwana*?"

"I think we can leave that now."

"Yes, *bwana*," said Kiboi with a smile. "Did you find out anything useful?"

"It's quite clear they know something, but they are too scared to talk. Did you get anything?"

"Well, a bit. About two months ago that garage we saw, Isaac's Garage, burnt down one evening. Isaac wasn't in it apparently, and he now appears to be in hiding somewhere. And the store owner was murdered in a botched robbery, and his store burnt down, in the same evening."

"Unlucky evening."

"Exceptionally so. Because the house of a local police officer called Daniel Kipruto also burnt down."

"I don't suppose he was one of the policemen we saw?"

"No. And he and his family are also missing."

"Excellent work, Kiboi. That would explain why the sergeant wasn't keen to see us there. I bet this missing policeman holds the key. I reckon he saw the body. At least." But a frown crossed Steve's face. "But if he was going to be easy to find, they'd have found him. So how will we find him?"

"Funny that. I was just wondering that myself, as I stood by the car. Then one of those policemen walked up, and took a good look at the car. He said I'd got a bald tyre at the back, and bent down to point that out. Well, the tyre is fine, but I noticed he dropped a piece of paper as he bent down. As he went back inside I picked it up. Would you like me to stop and see what it says?"

"Why not?"

Kiboi pulled in, and smoothed out the crewed up paper. He read, "Ngulia Tsavo."

"Is that all?"

"Yep."

Steve said, "Tsavo's a National Park, isn't it?"

"Yes. About two hours from here, further along the Mombasa Road."

"It's huge," added Giles. "About the size of Wales. It's in two separate parts, Tsavo East and Tsavo West."

Kiboi thought for a bit. "I think Ngulia is one of the game lodges in Tsavo West."

"Anyone any ideas what it means?" asked Giles.

"Nope," said Steve. "But I think I'm going to pay this Ngulia place a visit."

"That'll set you back a bit. The game lodges are expensive, as are the National Park entrance fees. And you'll need a four wheel drive. Look, let's get back. Come round to my place for dinner, and we'll discuss how to take this further. Can you come as well Koboi?"

"Thanks for the offer Giles. But I promised my father I'd call and see him. He's not been so good lately. But I'll catch up tomorrow." Koboi suddenly smiled.

"What is it? Giles asked.

"Daniel Kipruto. It's the name, Kipruto. It would translate for you as something like 'born on safari'. Maybe that's significant."

Back in his hotel room, Steve considered the day's events. They had made staggeringly good progress, just asking some basic questions, questions anyone would have asked. Nothing of what they had found out had been at all difficult, yet none of it was reported to Inspector Gwil Evans, or indeed came up in the conversation with Assistant Chief Commissioner Kibet. Why would that be?

The answer was pretty obvious. They didn't ask, because they knew the answer. The conspiracy theory was well on track.

The phone rang. Steve assumed it would be Giles, arranging to pick him up for dinner. "Hello," he said, breezily.

"Dr Smith?" asked someone who was definitely not Giles.

"Yes. Who's speaking?"

"My name is not important."

A wave of apprehension swept over Steve. "That's unusual," he said. "Most people's names are very important. Otherwise their friends won't know what to call them."

The voice just continued in the same measured tone. "Your humour is wasted on me, Dr Smith. You have been asking questions which have upset a number of people."

"Presumably their names are not important either?"

"You need to stop asking questions."

"I get the impression some sort of threat is on its way."

"Dr Smith. You will stop asking questions. One way or another, if you get my drift. I suggest you leave Kenya immediately. Catch the London flight tomorrow."

"My flight is in four days time."

"I think you will find your flight is tomorrow. We took it upon ourselves to rebook for you. Be on it. And I suggest you stay in your hotel tonight, and till you leave for the airport tomorrow evening."

Steve paused, and then acquiesced. "OK. I'll do what you say. I'll be on the flight."

"A good decision Dr Smith. And we will be ensuring that you are."

"I'm sure you will."

The phone went dead. Steve sat down. He was much less shaken than he might have been. As he had demonstrated in his past, he was calm under pressure. He thought for some time, and then reached for the telephone and dialled Giles's number. He was aware that this conversation would almost certainly be intercepted.

"Giles. It's Steve."

"Hi Steve. I was just going to ring. I'm just setting off now."

"OK Giles, but there's been a change of plan. I'm afraid I can't come tonight, and I've got to fly home tomorrow. Something's come up."

"Nothing too serious, I hope?" Giles's voice was a mixture of surprise and concern.

"Pretty serious."

"OK. Presumably you'll need a lift to the airport?"

"That would be very kind. I'll eat in here tonight, but it would be good if you could join me, so we can make the arrangements. And I'll need to cancel my mini safari to the Masai Mara."

"But...." There was a pause, then Giles gathered himself. "Of course. I'll help with that. See you in about an hour."

Steve was sitting at a table for two in a quiet corner of the hotel restaurant when Giles arrived. From here they would not be overheard. "Hey Steve," Giles greeted him. "Presumably we talk in hushed tones."

"Yes. And it's all got pretty dangerous. To be honest, I really shouldn't have got you to come, because we are both probably under threat."

"Look, I'm a journalist. There's always some risk around a story. And after your phone call I have already taken a couple of precautions that I won't need to bother you with. I must be getting a bit rusty though. Masai Mara indeed. Good hint, but I nearly gave it away! Now, what's the story?"

Steve recounted his telephone conversation with the nameless man. Giles considered it for a bit. "You're definitely doing the right thing going home. And you can take back all the information we've got already, which could stir things up."

"Go home? I'll be buggered if I'm doing that."

Giles looked at him, wide-eyed. "You're either very brave, or just reckless."

"I suspect I'm a bit of both, but not so much."

"So, since this seems to be a bit of a forte for you, I'm assuming you've got a plan?"

"Of course. But when I carry it out, anyone who knows about it will certainly be in danger."

"You mean someone might beat it out of me?"

"Yes. Or Koboi. Who at least knows I'd be planning to go to Tsavo."

"Tell me the plan then, and I'll tell you how we might minimise the risk"

"It's quite simple. I pack up, and you take me to the airport in the early evening. I check in, load my bag, and then slip out of another entrance if there is one, and get into a four wheel that we've hired, through an intermediary. I then drive to Tsavo West, and stay a couple of nights to see what might turn up."

"And you're the master of plans? That one's pretty rubbish."

"So, can you help me smarten it up?"

"Possibly. But let's identify the weaknesses. Firstly, you're proposing to drive to Tsavo as if you were popping up the M1. It's a five hour drive, in daylight. You're driving in the dark, and the lodge will probably be many miles inside the Park. There are no roads there, just tracks. And anyway the Park is closed between dusk and dawn, and guarded.

Secondly, we have to cover the potential risks to others. Koboi has no family apart from his father, and I don't think he'd be at risk. But I've got my family to think of.

Thirdly, at some stage you'll have to leave the country. And they'll be looking for you."

"I'll do a deal with you. If you cover one and two, I'll tell you my plan for three."

"OK. But let's eat, since you're treating me. And that will give us some thinking time."

After a pretty reasonable dinner, Giles had some suggestions. "If you're going to do this, I see no solution but for all three of us to go. Admittedly that's going to up the costs, but it can't be helped. And Koboi and I will have to take our chances to a degree afterwards. I can get my family to stay for a few days with friends at the embassy, where I'm sure they'll be safe.

We'll have to drive in the night and park up for a kip before entering the Park first thing in the morning. I could book for the next two nights, in a false name. But you'll have to use your proper name at Ngulia, because you used it at the Salama police station; and it will be you anyone will be looking for. And we'll probably have to show our papers at the Park entrance, so we'll just have to hope no-one catches up with us for a couple of days."

"All that sounds good. And there's no need to worry about the costs. Sylvia's parents insisted they covered everything, and made it a condition that I let them know the full costs. The amount we're going to rack up shouldn't be too much of a problem."

"So what about the third part then?"

"There's an airport at Mombasa, just continuing down the road. I'm going to book a flight back to London in four nights time."

"Now that really is rubbish. They will obviously cover the two international airports. And they won't even have to cover Mombasa really, because you'd change planes in Nairobi!"

"Even better."

"How so?"

"I said I was going to book a flight, but I didn't say I was going to take it. I had a look at the map of Kenya, and I believe there is a land crossing south of Mombasa, at Lunga Lunga. I thought I'd cross over there in three days time, if you'd drop me off. If they think I'm getting that plane, I'll be out of the country before they realise they've missed me. I'm rather hoping you'd have a contact in Tanzania who could meet me on the other side."

"I could arrange that. An alternative though would be the Taveta crossing"

"Where's that?"

"Through Tsavo West. It's much nearer than Lunga Lunga, so a shorter drive in Kenya. You'd have a much longer drive in Tanzania, through to Dar-es-Salaam, but that shouldn't be dangerous. And the

Taveta crossing is a bit more of a backwater. But whichever crossing you use, you'd have to hope they weren't tipped off to look for you."

"That may be a long shot, but I'll be hoping that they think I'm stupid enough to actually be planning to be on the plane. And, since you did, I'm quite encouraged!"

## Chapter 18

Steve had a very boring time, sitting in the hotel all day. It had not taken long to book a flight from Mombasa. He'd done this from his room, since he wasn't really concerned about the line being bugged. In fact, he hoped it was, since it was important that they (whoever they were) believed he was taking that flight.

After that he packed his bags. His hand luggage bag was unfortunately small, so he couldn't get much in it. But he crammed in a few changes of clothes, his washing kit, and his valuables. There were some bulkier clothes he would be sad to lose, but that was the way it was.

It did not take him long to read the available newspapers, and he worked his way through the various leaflets. He even found himself wishing that he'd brought Hans Meyer's report with him – even if he'd not managed to wade through it, it would have helped him kip. No-one made any attempt to contact him, and the hotel staff gave a good impression of not noticing him hanging around.

Giles appeared at six. Steve loaded his bags in the car, and they headed off to the airport.

"So, what's the plan?" Steve had no idea whether Giles had managed to arrange anything or not.

"I don't have one. I met Kiboi, and explained the position in detail. He said he'd see what he could do. But I've heard nothing since. To be honest, I'm quite worried. I would have thought he'd have let me know if he'd got anything arranged. He would have been able to alert me to anything, without giving anything away to any eavesdroppers."

"Well, in the absence of even a Plan A, what I propose to do is check in immediately. Then I'll hang around for as long as possible, but if nothing happens, I'll just clear security and fly home. After all, we've made really significant progress with what we've got."

"Reluctantly I'll have to agree with you. I can't take the risk of just heading off with you. Kiboi was our best bet, and if he can't come up with something, we'll have to take the safe option."

Giles helped Steve into the terminal. After checking the flight details Giles said, "Look Steve, I'll leave you here. It will look suspicious if I sit a long time with you. I'm going to start working up what we've got into a story. But I'll delay it for a couple of days so you can report back first."

"Thanks Giles. You've been incredibly helpful. Maybe when all this is resolved I'll bring the family back on safari. If we can afford an ethical one."

"I look forward to that. Good luck Steve."

The queue to check in was already quite lengthy, and it took Steve three quarters of an hour to get to the front. He passed over his passport, and ticket. "I believe I've been rebooked on today's flight."

The man smiled and took his papers. After a short bash at the computer, he picked up the phone and said a few words. Still smiling, he passed back Steve's passport, and his boarding card. "Enjoy your flight, Dr Smith"

"Thanks." Steve turned, and was faced with an austere looking middle-aged woman, dressed very smartly. She wasn't in uniform, as such, but gave a very official impression.

"Dr Smith, please come with me."

"Who are you?"

This appeared to be a question no-one answered. "I have been asked to ensure that you get the flight tonight. Please come with me immediately to security. Steve was taken to the front of the security check. His minder watched him through, and followed him. No-one took any notice when she set off the metal detector.

"Come this way." Steve followed her through Departures, and through a small door she opened that led off into a corridor. This they followed for some time, before they stopped before another door. This one was locked, but the woman produced the key, unlocked it, and stood back to let Steve in.

"Wait here."

'Here' was a small room, bare except for a few chairs along one wall.

Before Steve could ask any questions, that almost certainly wouldn't have been answered anyway, he heard the door close behind him, and the key turn in the lock.

There was another door opposite. This was also locked. Steve gave into the inevitable, and sat down. The chair was not comfortable. He looked at his watch. It was two hours to the flight. This was turning into one of his most boring days, ever. And he hoped he wouldn't need the toilet.

Despite the discomfort, Steve did doze for a time. He was jerked from half sleep into full wakefulness by a noise outside the far door. He looked at his watch. Flight in fifteen minutes. This is pretty efficient, he thought. Get me on the plane, and then take straight off.

A key was turned in the lock, and the door opened. Any vague notion Steve had held that this would be Kiboi was immediately dashed. It was another middle aged woman, not the same one, but fairly similarly attired. "Come," was all she said.

Steve picked up his bag, and followed her out of the room. Another long corridor. Then through another door, and they were outside. A plane was just taking off. Steve could see in the distance what he assumed was his plane, with some bags being loaded. A Toyota four by four was waiting.

"Get in."

Steve walked to the passenger side. "No, in the back." Steve obeyed. The woman got in the driver's seat, and set off. Steve had apparently been wrong about which plane, because she headed off the other way. They appeared to be driving along the side of the building. The next instruction was rather more of a surprise. "Get down on the floor."

"What?"

"Get down on the floor. Now."

It wasn't a voice you disobeyed. Steve threw himself down. The car pulled up, and a brief conversation in Swahili took place. Then they set off again. After a few minutes the voice, much friendlier now, said, "OK, you can get up now."

Steve sat up. He was pretty sure that this was a beneficial turn of events, but he needed reassurance. "Who arranged this?"

"No talking. Just enjoy the ride." This appeared to have been said with a smile. So, Steve just sat back and waited to see what unfolded. They drove for about half an hour. Fairly early on they turned on to what

Steve was pretty sure was the Mombasa road, but it looked different in the dark. At a particularly dark spot, they pulled in, and the woman turned off the lights.

As they sat there Steve's eyes adjusted to the dark. He could just about make out the silhouette of a car, parked maybe thirty yards away. There were no lights in that either. They sat in silence for maybe fifteen minutes. In that time a couple of cars passed on the road, but didn't slow down or stop. Finally the woman said, "OK, we get out. Be careful."

Steve eased himself out of the car, and at the same time the other vehicle's doors opened. Two figures approached. Even when they were right on top of him, Steve couldn't see their faces, but he knew who they were. "Brilliant, Kiboi!" he whispered.

"Thanks." The silhouette turned towards the woman, and hugged her. "And many thanks to you Auntie. Here's the key. Get back now. I'll be in touch when we're back."

"OK Kiboi. Be careful. I'll keep an eye on your dad." There was a pause, then she added, "They're going to be pissed." And with that she was gone. The other car started up, and edged back on to the road before turning on its lights, and heading back towards Nairobi.

"Let's go," said Giles. "Kiboi, I'll drive first. You could do with a rest."

"Fine."

"Don't be too sure you'll get any rest," said Steve. "I'm going to want to ask lots of questions!"

"Don't," said Kiboi firmly. "Best not to know. We don't know just how pissed they are going to be, and what you don't know you can't tell them."

"Fair enough. But Giles, did you know about this earlier this evening?"

"Pretty much. But we needed you to look like you had no idea what was going on, which is easiest when you actually do have no idea what is going on!"

They drove for several hours. Steve was asleep when they passed through Salama. When he awoke, Kiboi was driving. Giles was asleep in the passenger seat. "How far now?" Steve whispered.

"I'll stop in about an hour. We'll go into the Park through the Mtito Andei gate in the morning. I don't want to stop in the town, so I'll pull in well off the road outside, and we'll have a sleep."

At seven thirty next morning they filled up the Toyota in Mtito Andei. Before they entered the park Giles gave Steve a small notebook and pen. "If we do strike lucky you're going to want to make full notes."

"Thanks Giles. I'd make a terrible journalist!"

At the park entrance Steve paid for the whole party, for three days. Neither the ticket officer, nor the bored looking female soldier, showed any obvious interest in them. Sylvia's parents were starting to rack up a large bill, but Steve was sure they'd be pleased by what he'd found out already. That was if he could get back to tell them.

Giles said, "There's no point going straight to Ngulia. It would look odd if we just sat around there all day."

"What do you suggest?"

"Let's see some game. One place in here I've always wanted to see is the Mzima Springs. A great place for hippos and crocs apparently. Since someone else is paying, we may as well go. Let's have a look at the map."

It was four o'clock when they arrived at the lodge. Whilst he had never taken his mind off his mission, Steve had really enjoyed seeing big game up close in the wild for the first time. Now, though, they had to wait in the hope that someone came to them. They checked in, and were introduced to the restaurant and bar manager, whose name badge announced him as Charles. Very quickly they were sitting at the bar in front of him.

"What can I get you gentlemen?"

They took their beers to the patio, and looked out over the wall. An eagle passed overhead, and a stork nonchalantly walked through the pond. In the distance they could see impala, which were spooked by two hyenas loping past. Charles approached them again. "Can I get you another drink?"

"Yes please, Charles. Three more beers. And have one yourself."

"Thanks very much, sir."

"And what's that structure over there?" Steve pointed at a rough wooden frame.

"You'll see, sir," said Charles, with a smile.

As dusk fell, a man walked out, looking very nervous. He was carrying a joint of meat. This he proceeded to tie to the frame. Then, rather quickly, he headed back."

"I suppose that's less cruel than tying up a goat," said Giles. "I wonder what they are expecting?"

Night fell, as quickly as always. A crowd started to gather on the patio. Then a loud whisper spread through. Something was moving. Very deliberately, and with no concern, or interest, in the onlookers, a leopard emerged from the scrub, and climbed up the structure. Camera flashes went off all round, but the leopard took no notice. For the next ten minutes it ate, giving the crowd a great spectacle. And then, as silently as it had appeared, it was gone.

And then dinner was served. It was accompanied by hyraxes running around the roof, a bushbaby coming to fruit, and porcupines wandering in the light outside. Steve was in heaven.

After dinner they sat on the patio till late. Conversation was desultory. They were now just waiting. But no-one approached them, and so eventually they wandered off to bed.

The following morning, after breakfast, they decided, as the previous day, to be tourists. So they headed off into the rhino sanctuary, a huge fenced off area to help the rhino population recover from poaching. The highlight of the day was coming across two cheetahs with a freshly killed impala. Not the highlight of the impala's day, though.

They were back about an hour before dark. Kiboi decided to have a nap before dinner, and Giles went to have a shower. Steve sat at the bar, and ordered a beer. Charles looked at him.

"On your own, sir?"

"For a bit, yes."

"OK Dr Smith. Quickly, come with me." And without another word, Charles disappeared through a door. There was no time to think, so Steve followed.

The door led outside. A very old, battered Land Rover was standing there, with two men by it. "Put this on."

This was not a request. Steve was blindfolded. Should he be worried about this turn of events? He felt not, there was no sense of threat, just precaution. So he just went with it. "Let the others know I'm OK."

"Sure."

He was helped into the front seat of the Land Rover, and carefully strapped in. They drove off. Steve lost all track of time as he bounced around, was it one hour, or two. The blindfold was good, he could not tell even if it was still light. Briefly an irrational fear passed him that he might just be dumped out in the bush, which wouldn't be healthy. He also had a feeling that he might not actually be being driven that far, just going in a roundabout way. But at last they stopped.

Still blindfolded he was helped out, and guided across fairly level ground. He bumped against what appeared to be a doorway, and he heard what he assumed was a door shut behind him. He was helped into a chair, and then the blindfold was removed.

He appeared to be in a small room, in a rough shack. There was only a small light, so he was not dazzled. He was in the only chair. The man who removed the blindfold joined the other on the floor, to the side. In front of him was a small family group, a man, a woman and small child asleep on her lap. The man was looking at him, with a slightly suspicious expression.

Steve took a punt. "Officer Kipruto?"

A frown crossed the man's face, but was quickly replaced by a slight smile. He nodded, but said, "No English."

This was going to be difficult, Steve looked at his two minders. They also shook their heads. But the woman spoke. "You Dr Smith?"

"Yes."

"You want speak my husband?"

"Yes, if he is happy to speak to me."

"Amos think you OK."

Who was Amos? She saw the expression on his face. "Charles not real name. He Amos. Amos Amakobe."

"The woman who was killed was Sylvia Murungaru. She was my friend."

"My husband find her. My husband investigate, with Franklin."

"Who is Franklin?"

"He is store owner in Salama. We think maybe they kill him."

"When we went to Salama, a big store had been burnt down. They said the owner was killed."

A tear appeared in Esther's eye when she heard this confirmation. She relayed the news to her husband, who looked forlorn. "They kill him. Kill us if they find us. Kill you if they catch you."

"A garage on the edge of town was also burnt."

"Garage Isaac's. He mended the truck. He dead as well?"

"No. He's missing. Probably hiding. Like you." Steve got out the notebook. "I hope you don't mind me taking notes. I don't want to forget any details."

"That OK."

"Thank you. Steve noted down the details about Franklin and Isaac, confirming them with Esther. Then he asked. "Do you know why they killed Sylvia?"

"My husband not know. But he tell what he do know. Then you go tell England police. Maybe then they make Kenya police catch people who kill, and we go home again."

"I'll do my best, Mrs Kipruto."

So, through Esther, Daniel told how he had found Sylvia, and how the Nairobi 'police' had taken her away, about the Heavenly Flower Export, its drivers, what Isaac had said about the load, and the refrigerated container that would go on the *Sea Empress*. When they had finished, and Steve had checked all details, some food was brought in.

After eating, Steve pulled out his wallet. "Officer Kipruto, what you have done has put you in great danger. But the information you have given me should help to bring the killers to justice. You must be in difficult circumstances. Please accept this money, not as a payment for the information, but from the parents of Sylvia Murungaru, to help you until you can get back home."

Steve passed across $300, his entire stock of dollars. Esther briefly hesitated before taking the money. "My husband thank you. And I thank you."

"If we can get through this difficulty, I would like to come back to Kenya with my family, and meet you back in your home."

"We pray for that day. But you must sleep here. No driving in Park in dark. Dawn they take you back. But will cover eyes again."

It was nearly breakfast time when Steve arrived back at the Lodge. He went straight to the room, where Kiboi and Giles were up, dressed and in earnest conversation. They broke off immediately when Steve walked in. "Thank goodness!" said Giles. "We found a note to say that you were OK, and expected back today, but we didn't know whether to believe it. What did you find out?"

"I'll tell you over breakfast. But I need a shower first. And then I think we need to get going straight away."

Rather than go back to the main road, they travelled on through the Park. This was probably slower, but undoubtedly safer. And it gave the maximum time for Steve to pass on everything the Kiprutos had told him. But it meant it was nearly three o'clock when they passed through the Old Mbuyuni Gate, and almost four when they reached Taveta, just before their fuel would have run out.

They dropped Steve just before the border post. Giles gave him some last minute instructions. "If you get through OK, it's about four kilometres to the Tanzanian post. But you can get a *boda-boda* to there."

"What's one of those?"

"A bicycle taxi. When you come out the Tanzanian side, someone will be meeting you. Not sure who, but they'll recognise you, so don't worry. You'll probably have to overnight in Moshi, before heading down to Dar es Salaam tomorrow."

"Thanks Giles. And thanks to you Kiboi. If the two of you let me know any further incidental expenses, I'll settle up later."

"Do you want me to hold off filing my story?"

"Shit. I'd completely forgotten you're a journalist. Of course you're going to file this. Can you hold off for just a few days? I want to tell Sylvia's parents first, rather than them hearing from the press."

"Given there may still be a substantial risk, I think it would be best if I filed straight away, but I'll request they don't go to press for a few days. After all, it's not a current story, but it's going to be after we publish! I'll get them to hold off till they've checked a few details with you, if you get through now."

"Sounds fair enough. But one more thing. Would it be possible to leave my name out of it?"

"Why would you want me to do that?"

"I'd like to do a bit more investigating back in Britain, and it would be easier out of the glare of publicity. If I can turn any more up, it could give you more of a story."

"I'll see what I can do. Anyway, you'd better get off."

"Thanks Giles. Watch and see what happens to me. If I get stopped, get away quickly and add that to your report. I won't mind then if you mention my name!"

With that, Steve shook both their hands, and walked off towards the border post.

*Chapter 19*

Just after lunch on Monday, Barry pulled into the car park of Perkins head office in Bristol. He took the lift to the fifth floor, and signed in at reception. The girl at the desk greeted him cheerfully, even slightly flirtatiously. "Hello Mr Clark. You're here to see Mrs Ellis?"

"Thanks Sarah. Yes. Is she ready for me?"

"She said to send you straight in."

Barry politely knocked at the door, and a cheery voice called, "Just come in Barry."

His boss was sitting behind a very large, and very clear desk. She got up to greet him, with a kiss. "Hi Barry. What's up?"

"Thanks for seeing me at such short notice Rebecca."

"To you it's Becky."

"OK Becky."

"So, is this about the figures? It's the second month in a row Taunton's pipped you. Are you worried your performance is slipping?"

"Well, Maureen is very competitive."

"And you're not?"

Barry smiled. "Maybe. But no, I'm not worried. Our figures are still going up, and I'm sure you're happy about the pressure we and Taunton are putting on the rest, and each other. No, as I said it's a personal matter, but it has potential consequences."

"You sound pretty serious. Potential consequences for you, or for the business?"

"Both."

"Well, I know you know you can trust me, so give me the details."

"Well, mainly I'm in a new relationship."

"Congratulations Barry." This was said with a smile, but there seemed to be a tinge of disappointment with it. "I bet a lot of the female staff will be disappointed about that. Presumably it's someone from the office, and we need to make some changes to management arrangements?"

"No, she doesn't work for Perkins."

"A client then?"

"No, it's nothing like that. The problem is, whilst I think she is completely innocent, she has very close connections with some very bad people."

"Ah! And would those connections have an interest in you professionally?"

"Yes."

"And are you tempted by their interest?"

"Good God, no! Not at all. But they are not the sort of people to take no for an answer."

"I assume you don't want to end the relationship?"

"No. And that's not just pigheadedness. But I will admit that I don't intend to be pushed around."

"Barry, do you think the woman has been used to snare you? It must be a possibility."

"No. My meeting with her was complete chance. However bad these people are, this was something that wasn't engineered." But Barry wasn't going to explain the circumstances. "Since you haven't asked, her name's Michelle."

"Nice name. Well, let's get some tea in. We're going to have a long think about this." She rang through to Sarah. "Can we have some tea please Sarah? And tell Jack that I'll have to delay our meeting till three.

So Barry, do you think this is a resigning matter?"

"Not yet, if you're prepared to stick with me. But it could easily come to that. Or at least I may have to take long leave at short notice. At the moment I think the chief baddy is just sussing me out. It's hardly a full time occupation for him at the moment. I think he's just preparing the ground for a later approach. But later may be soon, if you see what I mean."

Barry broke off as Sarah brought the tea in. After she left he continued. "The fact is Becky, I don't think there will be a resolution to this unless we can somehow put this character out of business."

"What do you mean?"

"Well as he's moving to try and snare me, I'll be moving the other way to catch him. If he wants me professionally, at some stage he'll reveal himself. I've got the clear impression that he's well known to the police, and that they would love to close him down. If I can get something on him, they will be straight in. It's the only way I can see that Michelle can have some sort of future."

"You mean Michelle and you?"

"Perhaps."

"Barry, what you are suggesting is incredibly risky. For you, and possibly for us. What sort of business do you think he's in?"

"He could have any number of lines, but I think it's mainly smuggling. He claims he's in imports, and apparently has property in Avonmouth. I want to get in there and see if I can find anything interesting."

"If he's criminal, he's hardly likely to let you poke around his store of loot."

"No, hardly. And I don't have any idea yet how to get in there. So I think I'll have to let him feel he's reeling me in a little, and wait to see what opportunities come of it. I think he's incredibly sharp, and would pick up immediately if I was even the slightest bit pushy. He'll have to genuinely think he's slowly corrupting me, and I reckon it's the sort of challenge that would amuse him."

"The way you are talking this might be some sort of game for you."

"No, it's definitely no game. But in some ways it may be a way for me to finally draw a line under the past." Barry didn't elucidate which bit of his past he meant, but it was a different bit than Rebecca was thinking.

There was a silence, while Rebecca was thinking. Barry didn't break it. Eventually she took a deep breath. "OK Barry. As you know, the first thing I should do is report this up the line. But I'm going to take a real chance here. From Perkins' point of view I'll work on the principle that you've just alerted me to a minor concern, and we'll agree to talk regularly to ensure there is nothing seriously wrong. And we'll meet regularly, but so as not to arouse suspicion we'll make sure that those meetings appear incidental. I don't want anyone, inside or out, to think we have concerns about you."

"If we keep bumping in to each other, people will think we're having an affair."

Rebecca just stopped herself from saying "If only!" Instead she just laughed, slightly forced. But then said, very seriously, "Just be very careful Barry. A lot of people would be very sad if anything happened to you."

"Thanks Becky. I will be careful. Very careful."

When Barry got home that evening, Michelle was sitting at the dining room table. "Hello," was all she said as he walked in.

"Hi Michelle." He bent to kiss her. "Is something wrong?"

"That depends."

"Very mysterious. Depends on what?"

"On you, mainly."

"OK. I'd better sit down as well."

Barry sat at the table next to her. "Right. If I pass out in shock, less far to fall."

Michelle took a long look into his face. He waited.

"I'm pregnant."

A broad smile crossed Barry's face. "I was expecting bad news!"

"You don't think this is bad news?" Michelle was looking very concerned.

"Why would I? Do you?"

"Not if you don't." She was also smiling broadly now.

"It's not the most surprising outcome, given what we've been up to."

"But I'm worried it's going to change everything."

"In time, it will certainly change everything. But not yet. I suggest we go out and celebrate. And then come back, and celebrate some more."

"That's my sort of plan."

But Barry was concerned. He'd just hidden it well. His concern wasn't about their relationship. If there had been no extenuating circumstances, he might even have considered suggesting they got married. But now it was a complication in his strategy in dealing with Ted Young, and gave him an extra area of vulnerability.

He had hoped that Ted was more needy than Barry had suggested in his conversation with Rebecca, and would move quickly. However, this turned out not to be the case. A month passed, with no contact. Barry did not believe that Ted had lost interest in him. He could only assume that something else was occupying his mind just at the moment.

It was tempting for Barry to just leave the matter. Maybe he had been mistaken in Ted's intentions. Or maybe Ted had found an alternative accountant. But Barry knew that Ted Young was the sort of associate you would never be free from, and that it was only a matter of time before he reappeared. And now Barry couldn't wait for that to happen in Ted's time; that could be months, or years. But how to force the issue, without arousing suspicions?

And then an opportunity arose, when Michelle announced she was ready to go back to work. Despite her pregnancy, Barry didn't try to persuade her otherwise. So Michelle phoned Justin, to see if her job was still available. When she came off the phone she looked a bit upset.

"What's wrong? Won't they let you go back?"

"That's not it. They're quite happy to have me back. But they just said they'd sack the girl they got in to replace me. I feel really bad for her."

"That is rather tough. But it's your job, and they shouldn't have employed anyone other than a temp unless they were sure you weren't coming back. When are you going to start?"

"A week on Monday."

"That soon?"

"Is that a problem?"

"No. Not at all. I'll drive you in, then take the car back out to the Park & Ride."

"No need to do that. They said you can park in one of their spaces. You can walk to your office from there."

"That sounds good. I've never actually asked, but where is Ted's office?"

"Eagle Tower."

"Eagle Tower? What, the 'Demolish it Now' building? That horrible tower block in the middle of beautiful Cheltenham?"

"Is that what they call it? It is hideous, I know. But the view is great from it."

So it was just over a week later that Barry pulled into the Eagle Tower car park. He got out and opened the door for Michelle. "I'll come up with you," Barry suggested, eager to push things forward.

"No need. I want to be independent."

Barry looked at her, side on. She was just starting to show, but easily overlooked if you didn't know she was pregnant. Michelle saw where he was looking.

"Are you going to go off me, now I'm getting fat?"

"You're not getting fat. You've got pregnant. And I bet you'll look really beautiful, the bigger you get."

"Huh. You're just saying that. What you mean is, however big I get, you're going to want to keep on making love."

"Only partly untrue. Can we keep on making love?"

"You try stopping."

Barry watched her walk across to the entrance. It was two weeks since she'd abandoned the crutches in favour of one walking stick, and her new prosthesis was working well. She fairly shot across the car park. Once she was through the door, Barry locked the car and headed in towards his office.

Michelle was really happy to be back at work. To her it was a further sign of her recovery, and her independence. For the whole week Barry dropped her off and picked her up. In the evenings he tried to glean any information from her, especially whether Ted Young had asked after him.

"He's hardly been in. Justin's been in a couple of times, but that's all."

"So what are you doing?"

"Normal stuff. Answering the phone, filing papers, sorting invoices. The other girl wasn't very good. Left things in a bit of a mess. I think that's why they were glad to get me back."

By the Saturday Barry was really frustrated that he had heard nothing. He needed some advice. So over lunch he asked Michelle, "Do you mind if I nip down and see Nick this evening?"

"What, a boys' night out?"

"Is that OK? You won't mind not coming?"

"No, that's fine. I am tired after working all week, so I'll just have an early night."

Barry arrived at the Victoria Bar an hour before opening time. "Hi Barry. For old times sake you can help me get ready."

"Jude got childcare problems again?"

"It's not Jude. It's Samantha. Jude's mostly stopped coming, to concentrate on her exams. And Samantha's proving a touch unreliable. I'm afraid I'm going to have to let her go. How's Michelle doing?"

"Brilliantly. She's gone back to work."

"What? With the gangsters?"

"Yes. And there's more."

Nick looked at Barry through narrowed eyes. "Is it what I'm thinking?"

"That her leg's regrown?"

"Stop pissing around Barry. She's pregnant, isn't she?"

"She is indeed."

"Is that a good thing?" It wasn't quite an accusation, but it was edging that way.

"I think so, yes. To be honest Nick, I'm really very pleased. And she wants you to be the godfather."

"I don't do God. You know that."

"Nor do I, and I don't think Michelle does either. But it's just a bit of tradition, if you can put up with it."

"If you want me to, I can certainly put up with it. Will all the gangsters be there?"

"Well, that's what I've come to talk to you about. I need some advice."

"Emigrate."

"That's one option. But I'd like to do something different. I'd like to get them locked up. But to do that I need to somehow get close enough to find out what they are up to."

"So what do you think I can offer in the way of advice?"

"I don't know. But I've really not got anyone else I can ask."

"Well, tell your Uncle Nick what you know, and we'll see what we come up with."

"The head chap is called Ted Young. He's got an office in Cheltenham, and runs a company called Gloucester Imports."

"What do they import?"

"Michelle said a variety of stuff. Machinery, chemicals and food were things she mentioned. She said there was a warehouse at Avonmouth somewhere, but she didn't know where; she'd never been there."

"And you suspect they are smuggling something?"

"I would expect the vast majority of stuff they import to be completely above board. But I reckon there's some dodgy stuff in amongst it. On Gold Cup day Ted......"

"Ted? Are you on first name terms?"

"Apparently. Anyway, he had a couple of guests, brothers from Tanzania who were in exports."

"He's an importer. I presume it's not unexpected that he knows some exporters. Rather crucial to the business. Wasn't it George Bush who said 'Most of our imports come from abroad'?"

"Demonstrating a deep insight into the trading economy, yes. The brothers said they were interested in supplying the expatriate community with things they miss from home. Not sure what that would include."

"Do all Tanzanian homes have elephant tusks hanging on the walls? That would be illegal."

"It might be ivory. Or drugs of some sort I suppose. The fact is, I've got no real clue. But right back at the beginning, when I'd gone to the hospital on the night of Michelle's accident, a policeman turned up to question me. A Detective Inspector, not just a uniformed PC. And this chap was convinced Mr Young and his son....."

"Michelle's ex-husband?"

"Not ex yet. But yes, Justin. He was convinced they were badder than bad, and dangerous to know. I bet he had his reasons. So I'd put money on some sort of smuggling operation."

"Do you have an address for this warehouse? We could go and have a look round."

"No. I'm sure Michelle could find out, but I want to keep her out of it. What I want to do is get invited there."

"Why would they invite you?"

"Because I'll get them to think I'm going to work for them."

Nick stared at Barry. "You mean you are prepared to ruin your reputation to do this?"

"Yes."

"Why the fuck, if excuse my language, would you do that for a woman you don't love, even if you have banged her up?"

"You're assuming I don't, or won't, love her. I'm starting to think that might be possible. I won't love her like I loved Laura. But why would I expect to? It's unlikely I'd ever love anyone like that again. And you're assuming I'm doing it for her."

"Well, who else would you be doing it for?"

"For me."

"For you? How does that work?"

"Because I have a past, something I'm sure you suspected when we first met. And in some odd, back-handed way, I want to repay a debt."

"Well, I'm sure society will be very grateful for your sacrifice."

"Society won't give a shit. And the people I'm repaying it for will never know. But I will. But there is one other thing. My boss knows I'm doing this. But she will completely disown me if it goes wrong."

Nick was very surprised. "Why would she let you do this?"

"She trusts me. But also, she's got a bit of a thing about me. Doesn't know I know, of course. More than a bit of a thing, if the office wags are anything to go by."

"Well, aren't you the popular one. How has she taken to Michelle?"

"She's not met her, but she knows about her. That won't be an issue."

"All right then. So in your new role as Caped Crusader, what advice do you want?"

"I need to appear corruptible. Not suddenly, but slowly. Slowly and steadily. Drawn into a web."

Nick thought for a minute. "This may not be much of a plan, but it's a start. Why don't you ask 'Ted' about his accountant? Purely a professional interest, obviously. You may get a feel for whether he is genuinely looking for a replacement. If that doesn't work, you could let slip you do freelance work."

"I don't."

"Yes you do. Probably slipped your memory. See where you can go from there. Do you do accounts for similar types of business?"

"Yes. And we've just contracted with a Dutch import company."

"Have you been asked to do anything dodgy over the years?"

"Of course. But before you ask, I never have done. A gentle word has always made them desist."

"But you are familiar with sharp practice? Familiar enough to recognise it, understand it, and advise on it?"

"I would have thought so."

"Well, if you get to the position where a question of that nature is asked, don't use the gentle word. Anyway, I need to get on with some work now. Can I get you a drink?"

"Only if I pay for it."

At that moment the door opened, and a young woman rushed in. Nick greeted her with forced friendliness. "Evening Samantha. Glad you could join us."

"I'm sorry I'm late Nick. Bus was cancelled. But I see you've got everything ready anyway."

Barry looked at Nick. "I think I'll pass on the drink, and leave you to it. Thanks for talking it through with me."

"Just because I did, don't for one minute think I approve. But keep me informed of progress."

"I will."

## Chapter 20

On Monday, Barry parked as what was now usual in the Eagle Tower car park. But this time he made a suggestion. "I've not seen where you work. Can I come up and have a look?"

Michelle was really pleased he was showing interest. "Of course you can. Have you got time?"

"I'll need to be fairly quick. But yes."

They went up in the lift to the fourth floor. Out of the lift they turned right, and came to a door with a sign saying 'Gloucester Imports'. It was a small, undistinguished sign, the sign of a place that didn't want to advertise itself. It was the sort of sign of a place that only needed to point out to people who were actually going there that they had arrived.

Michelle tried the door. It wasn't locked. "Mr Young must be in."

This was a good start, thought Barry. Michelle led him through the door, into the reception. There was a desk, with Michelle's chair behind. Behind her there was a section of filing. "This is my bit," she said brightly.

"Are you on your own here?"

"Mostly, yes. I answer the phone, file stuff, and do Mr Young's appointments. Through here," she pushed open a door to the right, "there's a kitchen." On the left there was a smallish kitchen area, with a sink unit, kettle and microwave. Opposite was a small office.

"Whose is that office?" asked Barry.

"Various people use it. The lawyer, if she comes in. And the accountant when he's here."

"I wonder if I know the accountant. Small world, accountancy. What's his name?"

"He's Paul Johnston. Must be mid sixties. Pretty bald. Do you know him?"

"Doesn't ring any bells. And I presume that's Ted's office through there?"

A door was facing them. It was pulled to, but not properly closed. Barry had noted this, and said the last bit slightly louder.

"Yes." But before Michelle could add to this, the door opened, and Ted was standing there. He smiled. "Hello Barry. Thought I recognised the voice. What are you doing here?"

"Michelle's showing me where she works."

"Nice of you to be interested. Did I hear you mention Paul's name?"

"Yes. When Michelle mentioned your accountant, I wondered if I knew him."

"And?"

"No, not come across him."

Ted looked at Barry for a second, clearly thinking whether to say something else. He very quickly made a decision. "Have you got time for a chat?"

"No, not really. I'm going to have to shift not to be late. Got to set a good example." Barry paused, as if pretending to reconsider, then added, "But what time are you off tonight?"

"I'm out from about ten, but will be back by four. Probably here till about six."

"I couldn't keep Michelle here that long. But I could probably call in about quarter to five, if that's any good to you?"

"That would be great. See you then." With that Ted disappeared back into his room, pushing the door to again.

Barry turned to see Michelle looking at him with some surprise. He put his finger to his lips. Then out loud he said, "I'll need to get on. But I could do with a pee first. Where's the loo?"

"The other side of reception."

"OK, thanks." They went back into the reception area, and Barry firmly closed the door, so that Ted couldn't hear what was said.

"What are you up to Barry? You don't want to get involved with Mr Young."

"I know that. I'll tell you this evening what it's about. To a degree it's about us. Anyway I must run. Literally."

He was back at exactly quarter to five. Michelle smiled at him. "He's expecting you. Just go straight in."

Barry hesitated outside the door, and instead of pushing it open, knocked. The voice inside called, "Come in, Barry."

He entered. It wasn't a particularly big office. Ted sat behind a largish, but not extravagant desk. There were a couple of armchairs, and a small drinks cabinet. And that was about it. "Drink?" Ted asked.

"No thanks Ted. Driving." Barry noted that Ted didn't take one for himself either.

"Where do you do your accountancy then, Barry?"

"I work for Perkins. I run the Cheltenham office."

"Big office?"

"Twenty three."

"So, are you more a manager than an accountant these days?"

"I keep my hand in."

"Suppose you'd have to. What sort of companies does Perkins have as clients?"

"Well, the companies themselves would be confidential. But all sorts really. Mostly medium sized."

"All UK?"

"Until a couple of years ago. We're doing some European now, when they have a significant UK operation. Some in your line, import and export."

"Do you do any of your own business?"

"What, on the side you mean?"

"Yes."

"Well, clearly I couldn't compete with Perkins for business. But they don't do small companies. So they don't actually forbid it. But it would be frowned upon."

Ted's question hadn't been answered. He wasn't sure if Barry was avoiding it, or evading it, so he asked again. "But do you do any?"

"I have. But not for a long time."

"Would you be interested in doing some now?"

"How would Mr Johnston feel about that?"

"It wouldn't hurt him to have some competition. Have a think about it."

"Will do, but I better get Michelle home now. She's doing well, but she gets very tired."

There was a noise outside. Ted said, "That'll be Justin back. I'll need a word with him. Can you see yourself out?"

"No problem."

Barry pulled the door to behind him. He could see Justin talking to Michelle at reception. "Hi Justin. How are you?"

"Fine mate. Shell's looking good too. You're doing her good."

"Hope so. You ready, Michelle?"

"Coming." Michelle picked up her bag, and came out from behind the desk. She passed Barry, who held the door open for her. At that moment the toilet flushed, and the door was opened. Barry found himself staring straight at the still bent nose of the knifeman Wayne. Their eyes met, and a look of surprise crossed Wayne's face, to be replaced by anger. But Barry turned, followed Michelle out of the door, and closed it. He didn't look back.

In the lift he said, "There was no way you could warn me that Wayne was there."

"No. But you were bound to meet sooner or later."

"That will make an interesting conversation with Ted. I'd like to be a fly on the wall in there now!"

When they were in the car Michelle asked, "What's your game then, Barry?"

"It's not a game. It's deadly serious."

"You're not going to start working for Mr Young are you? I don't want you going bad, like my dad."

"No chance of that. The fact is, Michelle, meeting you includes meeting Ted Young. You've seen he's interested in me, and clearly it's because of my accounting ability. You said yourself people regret saying no to him.

I want there to be a future for you, free of these crooks. There is no way they are going away on their own. So I'm going to play along, long enough to find out what their crooked business is. Long enough to get enough evidence to get them put away for a lot of years. Then you'll be free of them."

"We'll be free of them you mean."

"All three of us, yes."

"But that will be really dangerous."

"Maybe. I said before that Ted Young didn't scare me. He doesn't, in himself. But I am scared for you. And when someone is scared, in my book the best line of defence is attack. So, I need to get to a position where he really needs to be scared of me. But he mustn't know that yet."

"He's clever, Barry. And he can tell what people are thinking. He doesn't fool easily."

"I can believe that."

Barry was pretty sure that the sequence of events the previous day had worked in his favour. But even he was surprised the next morning to find Justin loitering outside Eagle Tower, waiting for him to arrive with Michelle. Justin waited till Michelle had gone in before speaking more than to acknowledge Barry's greeting.

"Well, you are a dark horse, mate."

"Really?"

"Yes. Dad wants you to come up to his place this evening."

"I think Michelle would be too tired for that."

"Yes. And Dad's noticed why that might be as well. But he wants you to come on your own. Be there at seven." And with that he was off.

*Chapter 21*

Steve rang Deborah from Gatwick Airport at seven thirty. A sleepy voice answered. "Not up yet then?" Steve chided.

"Overslept a bit. Which flight did you get?"

"Emirates, via Dubai. Look Debs, I think I'll head over to Monmouth first, to report to the Joneses, and Gwil Evans. I'm worried *The Independent* will publish before I've spoken to them. I don't want them to see it in the paper first."

"OK. But get back as soon as you can. We need to talk."

Steve was alarmed about this. "What's happened?"

"We had a couple of silent phone calls last night."

"Really? That is worrying. I'll try and be back as soon as possible."

Steve quickly discovered there was no station at Monmouth. Despite the early hour he phoned Gwil Evans. He was in luck. Gwil was off duty.

"Steve, good to hear from you. How have you got on?"

"I want to come and talk to you straight away. I've got quite a bit to report. I'm at Gatwick. But there doesn't appear to be a railway line through Monmouth."

"No. It was closed in the 1960s. Just before Beeching. I'll call the Joneses, and if they can come I suggest we meet in Newport. That's a big station, and not too far from here. While I'm ringing them, you find out train times."

It took Steve just over three hours to get to Newport. Gwil was on the platform to meet him. "Hi there, Steve. I've installed Mr and Mrs Jones in the Windsor Castle, down on Upper Dock Street. I would have offered to help with your bags, but you seem to travel light!"

"I had to abandon my main bag. It's probably been blown up in Nairobi Airport."

"That sounds like you've had an interesting time. Have you found out much?"

"Lots. But let's wait till we're all present."

Mr and Mrs Jones greeted Steve warmly. "You might not be so pleased when you see the bill I've run up," he warned them.

It took Steve a long time to recount his story, which continued over lunch. Gwil again ate twice as much as everyone else. When Steve had finished, there was a pause. Gwil spoke first. "You really should join the police."

"No thanks. And to be honest Gwil, nothing we did took any investigating prowess. They just are not investigating at all."

Mrs Jones was looking very worried. "I've a feeling you may have minimised the danger you were facing. Do you think you were really under threat?"

"Given that someone had killed Sylvia, who was the wife of a prominent politician, I'm pretty sure they would have been happy to kill me too. But that would have brought the international attention back on them, so they probably considered it better to try and scare me away. Once I'd missed that flight though, I think it would have been open season. I hope Giles and Kiboi will be OK."

"You shouldn't have taken the risk of missing the flight. We would never have forgiven ourselves if anything had happened to you."

"I knew that you'd feel like that. But I get especially irritated when threatened. Makes me even more likely to carry on. But Debs is going to be cross when I tell her the full details!"

"And will you be in danger now you're back here in Britain?"

"I wouldn't have thought so. This ship, the *Sea Empress*, sails to Rotterdam. It's a Dutch problem. I'm sure Gwil here will ensure the information gets passed on."

"Will do. So, you think Sylvia was involved in some sort of smuggling operation?"

"No. Not at all. But I think that somehow her husband was."

Mr Jones was doubtful. "You never met Patrick. I have no reason to believe he was anything other than completely honest. I know this may have made him an exception in Kenyan politics, but I have every confidence in him."

"In that case, he must somehow have been in the way of someone else's operation. But that doesn't tell us why Sylvia was killed."

"What sort of operation?"

"That I don't know. But I'm beginning to have a suspicion, although I'll keep that to myself just for the moment. I intend to do some more research here, and see if I can get any further. I'm hoping *The Independent* gives me at least a couple more days before they publish."

"We're very grateful for all you've done already. Don't feel under any obligation to do anything more."

"There's no way I can leave it alone now."

Deborah met Steve at Oxford station at six thirty. She hugged him for a long time. "I was really scared you wouldn't come back. Was it really dangerous?"

"I think so, yes. And they're not subtle. I'm really glad to be home. Where are the kids?"

"They're next door. What do you think about these silent phone calls?"

"I'm damned sure they are not a coincidence. Let's see if we get another one tonight. But I just want to get back home, and help get the kids to bed."

After the children were asleep, Steve gave Deborah the full story. "What do you propose to do now?" she asked.

"Well, I'm pretty tired, so I'm going to go to bed. I bet I'm not allowed to go straight to sleep, though."

"No."

"Then tomorrow, depending on whether we get any overnight calls, I'm going to go in to the department. I need to catch up on a couple of things. Then I'm going to do some searching on the internet. I just want to pin down as much as I can about the Dutch connection. Then the paper will have published, and the police can take over."

Steve was surprised, and relieved, that there was no disturbance during the night. "Perhaps it was just a wrong number," suggested Deborah.

"Perhaps."

"You don't think so?"

"No."

Steve had an office space at the Oxford University Zoology Department, which he used when he needed to access the library. In truth he could have worked from home today, but it was likely there he would be disturbed by phone calls. Here he could work on the internet in peace. He really needed to get back to his report, but he felt he needed to close off Sylvia's murder first.

Firstly he looked up the Heavenly Flower Export. There was little about this, except a link to a company in Rotterdam. Well that wasn't a surprise. So he turned his attention to the *Sea Empress*. This was less easy. There were several of them. But eventually he found what he was sure was the right one, sailing between Mombasa and Rotterdam.

The *Sea Empress* appeared to be a general cargo ship. It travelled round the Cape of Good Hope, so avoided Somali pirates. But there was one other detail. On the way to Rotterdam it stopped, twice. The first stop was Durban, which touted itself as 'the largest port in Africa'. The second was in Bristol.

So Steve went back to the Dutch company associated with the *Sea Empress*. It was called Euroimport BV. After much digging, he finally found what he was after, a link to a British company.

Satisfied with his morning's work, Steve decided to have a break, and to nip into town. He closed down the computer, and headed off towards the town centre. He walked quickly. But as he was turning from Broad Street into Cornmarket, he was almost knocked off his feet by someone barging into him from behind.

He regained his balance, and found himself staring into the face of a medium height, thick-set man. The man was staring straight into his face, and Steve realised he was under severe threat. But he wasn't just going to stand there and be intimidated. "So, are you just going to stare, or are you going to actually say something?"

But the man said nothing, and after a few seconds more turned and walked off, quickly being lost in the crowd. Steve didn't try to follow him. But stood where he was, gathering his composure. He decided not to go back to the Department, but instead caught the Park & Ride bus back to the Thornhill car park, where he had parked that morning.

He waited till the children were in bed before he talked to Deborah. She was very concerned. "I think we ought to call the police."

"That's what I'm thinking. But I'm not sure how easy it will be to get them to take any action. Let's wait till tomorrow. If there are any phone calls tonight, we'll definitely get the police involved."

But no sooner had he spoken these words than the phone rang. They looked at each other. Steve said, "I'll get it. I'm sure it's me they want to speak to."

He picked up the phone, and just said, "Hello?"

"Dr Smith?"

"And who am I speaking to?"

"Just shut up, and listen. I strongly suggest you stop interfering with matters that don't concern you." There was a pause, but Steve didn't fill the gap. "Do you understand me?"

"You're making yourself very clear."

"Good. And don't go to the police. Because if you do, very bad things will happen."

"Would you like to spell out how bad?"

"Just don't try and get fucking funny with me. You've got two children." Steve started to go cold. "Nice little school, Beckley. And your boy, Thomas, in Mrs Martin's class. With the nice red Spiderman lunchbox. And Jennifer, in Miss Platt's class. My Little Pony – a bit out of date isn't it? But you get my drift." And with that, the phone went dead.

Still holding the phone, Steve looked at Deborah. "What?" she asked.

"I've to leave off Sylvia's case. He told me not to go to the police. And they've just told me where the children go to school, their teachers' names, and described their lunchboxes."

"If they touch my children, I'll fucking kill them myself." Deborah's eyes were blazing.

"And I'd let you. But we'd better do something else. I won't call the police, but I will call George."

"But will they have tapped the phones?"

"I doubt it. But just in case, I'll use one they won't know about. Where's Jenny's emergency mobile?"

"In the kitchen drawer. It won't be charged up."

"Not a problem. I'll plug it into the charger."

Steve dialled the number. A woman answered. "Hello?"

"Hi Gill. It's Steve. Is George in?"

"Sure. I'll just get him."

A pause, then a man's voice. "Hi there Steve. How's the investigating going?"

"You'll see in *The Independent* in the next couple of days."

"Really?" The man was really surprised. "You mean you got some leads?"

"And more. But that's why I'm ringing. We've appear to have upset some people, and they've just phoned through some nasty threats to the children."

"I presume they told you not to go to the police?"

"Yes."

"So you're phoning me not in my position as a police officer?"

"Not exactly. I'm phoning you, because I think you might be able to set things in train without it looking like I've phoned the police."

"How did they threaten the children?"

"They knew all about where they went to school, and their teachers."

"Hmm. Not the brightest of threats."

"Why do you say that?"

"What day is it today?"

"Friday…….. Ah!"

"Yes. Saturday tomorrow. No school till Monday. Gives us quite a lot of time. I tell you what, I think it's about time I made a family visit to my cousin. I'm sure Gill will want to come as well, and it's some time since you've seen Julie. Shouldn't arouse any suspicion."

"That would be excellent. I can tell you about everything that's happened."

"And in the meantime I'll arrange some discrete protection for you. Nothing uniformed. You won't even know it's there. And we'll monitor your calls, just in case they ring again. So don't say anything embarrassing."

"Thanks very much George. Look forward to seeing you tomorrow. Just to be on the safe side, we'll just have something out of the freezer."

"Would be sensible. See you tomorrow."

## Chapter 22

Steve really needed an early night. The day's events had left him really tired. Deborah tried her best to persuade him to come to bed, but she could see his mind was elsewhere. The threats to his family had just bolstered his determination, so he sat down at his computer again.

The first thing he saw was that there was an e-mail from Giles. It said simply '*Get tomorrow's paper!*' There was no shop in Beckley, the nearest being in Stanton St John, a couple of miles away. Despite what he'd told George about staying in, Steve decided to go out first thing to get the paper.

He then followed up his lead about the British company that he'd found referred to earlier. It had the unprepossessing name of South West Imports. The only location given was a warehouse near Severn Beach, north of Avonmouth. Steve noted down the details, and had a good look on *Google Maps*. He printed out a couple of pages. Deciding that was enough, he went upstairs, hoping Deborah was still awake.

The following morning Steve was at the shop by half eight. He picked up a copy of *The Independent*. The headline made him smile. It read 'Murder investigation, Kenyan style'. Underneath was a large picture of Sylvia. In the bottom corner there was also a picture of Daniel Kipruto, in his full police uniform. Steve wondered how Giles had got hold of that.

He didn't read any of the paper there, but drove quickly back home. There was no evidence of anyone loitering around the house, but Steve was sure the police would be watching from somewhere.

Deborah was still in bed, but sat up when Steve tossed the paper on the bed. She looked at the front page. "Bloody hell. Someone's going to be fucking annoyed!"

"Probably. But they may be less interested in us now." He sat on the bed next to her, and they read together. Giles had no further information than what Steve had told him. That meant there was nothing to link the *Sea Empress* with Britain. Steve was pleased about that, because he had a plan that he wanted to talk through with George.

It was eleven o'clock when George's car pulled up outside. Steve had told Tom and Jenny that George and Gill were visiting, and that they were bringing Julie. The children couldn't quite get the concept of 'second cousin', and George and Gill were 'Uncle George' and 'Auntie Gill', but they were excited. Julie was only three, and Steve could tell she was going to get a lot of attention.

They sat in the lounge. Steve had been worried that Gill would be cross with him for getting George involved in something, but she thought it was a great joke. "Do you come looking for trouble Steve, or does it come looking for you?"

"A bit of both."

Rather than explain everything, Steve passed over the paper. George and Gill were quiet for some time. When they had finished George looked up. "It doesn't mention you."

"No. I asked Giles to try and keep my name out of it, and he's succeeded. Which is good, because I have a bit of a plan."

Deborah looked at him sharply. "You didn't say anything about a plan."

"Well, you didn't think I'd just let these people scare me into sitting here did you?"

"So what does your plan involve?"

"The first bit of it involves George and Gill agreeing to stay tonight."

Tom and Julie had clearly been listening in. "And can Julie stay as well?"

"She couldn't really go home on her own, could she?"

"Please Mummy, please Auntie Gill, can you stay, can you, can you?" This was repeated at length, in the irritating, but ultimately persuasive way that children have.

Deborah said, "That will be difficult for Auntie Gill and Uncle George. They won't have brought anything with them."

Gill laughed, for the second time that morning. "I think George may be quite used to Steve's plans. He told us to pack for the weekend, just in case! But I bet Steve's plan involves being out this evening."

"Probably all night," Steve admitted. "But just a bit of snooping. They may know where we live, but I think I know where they live."

"Who knows where we live Daddy?" asked Tom. This was the cue for Steve and George to disappear upstairs to Steve's study, to discuss the details of what Steve was planning.

After Steve had told George what he was proposing, George thought for a minute. Then he asked, "How far is Kidlington from here?"

"Kidlington. About six, maybe seven miles. What's at Kidlington?"

"I've got a friend there I'd like to call in to see on the way. Only for a moment. Is it much out of our way?"

"Not desperately."

"Show me on the map."

Steve fetched the road atlas. George studied it for a minute. "Right. We'll need to make sure we're not being followed. So firstly I suggest we take my car, not yours."

"What difference would that make?"

"We don't know exactly what type of people we're dealing with. So we can't eliminate the possibility that your car has had some sort of tracking device attached, although I think that's unlikely. Secondly, we'll take a little detour. So I suggest we head south down this road through Elsfield," George ran his finger over the map, "as far as the ring road, and then back up through Woodeaton. Two sides of a triangle."

"You think we'll be able to tell if we're being followed?"

"We probably won't. But someone will, and will let us know. If we are, we'll reconsider our options. But I wouldn't mind betting that this morning's paper will have taken some attention away from you. So what time shall we set off?"

"I reckon the drive will take us a couple of hours at most, so a few minutes out of the way won't matter. It may be best to have a bit of a drive past in daylight, then park up and have a closer look after dark. If we have lunch now we could set off before three."

"That would be sensible. I'll just make a few phone calls before lunch."

After eating Steve and George packed a few supplies, and headed off. George, directed by Steve, drove down through Elsfield village, slowing up through the traffic calming, then, just before the ring road, headed back up through Woodeaton. Steve was looking in the wing mirror, but could see nothing following. They turned towards Kidlington.

George's phone rang. "Hello? OK. Thanks. Leave us now and get back to position." He turned to Steve. "We're clean."

They turned left at Islip. George said, "Can you direct me to Oxford Road?"

"That's easy. It's the main road. At a guess I would say you're looking for the Thames Valley Police HQ."

"Quite right. And it wouldn't have done for anyone to know that we were calling in there. I just want to pick up some things that might come in useful."

"I get the feeling you're going to keep me in suspense, and not tell me what."

"That's right."

They pulled up outside the Police HQ, and George disappeared inside. He was gone about ten minutes, and reappeared with a largish rucksack, which he tossed on the back seat. Steve noted it was heavy. "OK, which way now?"

It took longer than Steve expected, but at five thirty they were driving north out of Avonmouth, along the A403. They passed various warehouses and industrial areas. After a couple of miles Steve said, "Just turn in left here, and pull up."

They were in a sort of lay-by, with a couple of roads going into an industrial area. "Is this it?"

"No. We're going to the Docks Industrial Area, a bit further on. But I've got a *Google Maps* printout that we should have a good look at first."

Steve got out the printout. At the scale Steve had printed the individual buildings were so large the map named them. "Our place isn't one of those marked on here, so we'll have to drive round. I know that's a bit of a risk, but the outside road seems to be a circle. I suggest we go left into Bank Road, and continue along..." Steve squinted at the map, trying to read the name, "....I think that's Greensplott Road. Then if we haven't seen what we are after, we turn right up Worthy Road, and then left back into Bank Road."

George took the map. He pointed to an area at the north east of the Industrial Area. "What do you think this is?"

"It looks like a bit of waste ground. Those look like bike tracks.

Probably a place the local kids ride their scrambling bikes."

"It could be a good place to park after dark. First of all let's drive past the entrance, to see if there's a board listing who's occupying the units. If so, no need to drive around. We can just do a drive past, and size the place up for later. If there is no board, I suggest we go past to start with, check out this place as a potential parking spot off the road, then go back for your drive around."

"OK. Let's do it. What's the place called?"

"South West Imports."

They turned round, and then right, back on to St Andrew's Road. After a roundabout the road bent right, and they passed the main entrance to the Industrial Area. There was no board at the entrance. What there was were two big red metal gates, currently open. There was also a security post. A bit further along was a second entrance, which Steve hadn't picked up from the printout, which led straight into Greensplott Road. Again this entrance had two big red gates, but these were closed.

Round the next bend, they took the opportunity to pull into an entrance. The buildings at the back had signs for a company called 'Smiths of Gloucester', but they clearly weren't open at the moment. From appearances it may even have been permanently closed.

"Do you think they close the big gates at the main entrance overnight?" asked Steve.

"Probably the left hand one. There was a barrier up next to that security guard post. It looked half the length of the entrance. I reckon any time now the guard will put the barrier down, and then check everyone coming in out of hours. Would be pretty standard."

"I didn't see anyone there."

"No. But I'll guarantee there would be someone. I suggest we go straight back in before he closes up. Otherwise we'll have to ask specifically for your South West Imports. And I'd rather not do that."

"No. It could rather show our hand."

George turned back right, and entered the industrial estate. In front of them, just after Bank Road headed off left, they saw what they had missed before, a board map of the units with a numbered key.

"Good-oh," said George. "I don't think we'll attract too much attention looking at this." He turned left into Bank Road, and pulled up. On the board the site was called the Chittening Industrial Estate, not the Docks Industrial Area, and it announced it was owned by the Bristol

Port Company.

There were over forty units marked. South West Imports was not named. "Pity," said George. "But we've got ten here not named. They're spread about a bit."

"I reckon there'll be a lot of turnover," added Steve. "This board was probably out of date before it was put up. Let's go back to Plan A, and drive round." Steve looked back towards the gate. "That's the third lorry that's come in while we've been standing here. This place is pretty busy."

Steve was right. The estate was very busy. All along Bank Road there were trailer units of articulated lorries parked. The vast majority of these were unmarked. In places it was not possible to see or work out the names of the companies that owned the units. "This is much harder than I expected," admitted Steve.

They carried on following Steve's route, along Greensplott Road, and then back up Worthy Road. With the number of trailers parked, and the number of lorries moving about, there was a great deal they just couldn't see from a drive through.

At the top of Worthy Road George stopped. "Left or right?"

"If anything I think right was more likely. And there was a small cluster of units in that top corner unnamed on the map."

"OK. But to be honest if we don't see anything this time, we'll have to ask the guard."

"Agreed. Otherwise it would be a wasted journey."

George turned right. As he approached the bend, a door opened in the facing unit. "Shit," Steve exclaimed.

"What's up?"

"Just drive on as normally as possible."

George followed the road round again. Steve looked straight on, but George kept half an eye on the two men who had emerged. They glanced at the car as it went past. But in his mirror he saw that one, then the other, turned and stared after the car.

"Bingo?" George asked.

"Yes. Did they pay us special attention?"

"I think so, yes. Do you know them?"

"The thick-set one is the character who assaulted me in Oxford. That's really going to stir things up."

"So, do you propose a change of plan?"

"Not necessarily. Let's go and check out that waste ground. Then if we head on up the main road there's a place up there called Severn Beach. Let's see if we can find a café, have something to eat, and discuss possibilities."

As they approached they saw that the guard was outside. He had, as George predicted, shut the further gate, and lowered the barrier. But as George approached, the barrier was raised. Steve wound down his window. "Thanks mate," he said.

The security guard was a large sikh, with a blue turban. "No problem, sir," he said, with a smile.

George turned left and headed up Chittening Road. "Why did you do that?" he asked.

"Because I'm a naturally friendly person. But also to see if we'd aroused any suspicion. And it was pretty clear we hadn't."

They continued up the road, and found the waste ground. It was exactly as Steve had suggested it would be, almost. George pulled in. "Shit," said Steve.

"And it was all going so well." The waste ground was very flat. There were well placed bushes to hide a car behind. And it bordered the exact part of the industrial estate they wanted to be in. But the entrance they were parked alongside had been blocked by a large soil bund, which Steve hadn't picked up from his printout.

"The annoying thing is that this just wouldn't stop bikers," Steve pointed out.

"It won't be to stop bikers. It'll be to stop travellers. But while we're parked here, let's have a good look."

George reached back into his bag, and pulled out a pair of binoculars. Steve was impressed. "I never thought of bringing those," he said.

"Well, as an ornithologist you should be ashamed of yourself."

George scanned across the waste ground for several minutes. "OK, this is looking good. There is a big fence to the right, but that seems to be round some sort of car park. Difficult to see with the trees, but I think it's got vans in it. There seems to be a gap between that and the edge of the first building. And surprisingly there doesn't appear to be a fence there. There's a lot of crap in the gap, pallets, a cement mixer, but we should be able to get through. But there is a dip before it, which might be a ditch, so that could be a problem, and then just a low pile of rubble."

"Can I have a look?" Steve took the binoculars and scanned across. Then he looked through them out of the windscreen.

"What have you seen?"

"You can see that big industrial complex just ahead on the right?"

"Well, I could hardly miss it, even with a few trees in the way."

"We've been sat here for several minutes, and nothing's been in or out. And there's no smoke coming out of anything. I reckon it's closed down. Let's go and have a look."

They drove on the couple of hundred yards to the entrance. A sign announced the complex as Sevalco Ltd. Opposite it was a flat area, with a sign saying it was 'Sevalco Visitors Car Park'. There were no visitors. George pulled in.

"This is no good," said George. It was just an open patch of land, with no cover, right next to the road.

"I was thinking more of hiding the car behind the buildings."

"That's a possibility, but I bet they've got security, either on site or calling frequently, to stop people stripping stuff. But what's that next door?"

There was a low building next to the plant entrance. "Columbian European Central Laboratory," read Steve. "Sounds like a cocaine factory."

"It's probably something to do with next door. But it's got a much better car park." This was definitely the case. There was a small car park in front of the building, sheltered behind a thick hedge. "It's probably got security as well, but they may well miss us. And if not, I am a policeman! I should be able to blag my way out."

Steve was looking back across the road. Two large pipes followed the north side of the ditch. But after a hundred yards or so they crossed over, just before the trees in front of the fenced car park. "I'm wondering if we could cross over those. Would be easier walking up the side of this ditch in the dark, rather than that waste ground. There could be lots of holes there that we wouldn't see in the dark."

"Crossing pipes in the dark wouldn't be easy. But there's something else up there. I'll just be a second." George walked briskly along the pipes, and returned within a minute. "There's a disused railway track also crosses behind the pipes. Definitely better."

"OK, I think we've seen enough. Shall we go and get something to eat?"

They continued up the road, and turned in to Severn Beach. Here though they were disappointed. They found Shirley's café, which was closed. Downs Bakery, also closed. Tubbies Burger Bar, closed. "I wouldn't have gone in if it was open!" said Steve. A small amusement arcade was also closed.

"What a dump," said George. "Shall we go back to Avonmouth?"

"You don't fancy the Rustic Caravan Park then? No? So let's go on."

They drove on a couple of miles, into Redwick. "That's more like it," said George. "The Queen's Head." It was set back from the road, but George pulled up next to the board. "Rump steak, chips and peas - £5.99. Bargain. And look, live football."

"Great," muttered Steve, with absolutely no enthusiasm.

"Don't be a misery. It'll be fine."

"That's what you say. I hope you've got strong teeth."

## Chapter 23

As Barry's car turned into the entrance of Barton Manor, the imposing wrought iron gates swung silently open. The impressive house was up an equally impressively long drive. Barry was conscious that his car, even though relatively new, was somewhat out of place next to the assorted Range Rovers and sports cars.

He parked, and crunched across the gravel to the front door. There would be no need to knock. One of the two men lounging outside would be sure to let him in. So, Barry thought, these two, plus Justin and Wayne. How many more?

As he expected, one of the men pushed the door open, and let him past. Not a word was spoken. He was not required even to give his name. Just inside the door, Justin was waiting. "He's in his study, but he's just on the phone. Shouldn't be more than five or ten minutes."

"OK. But rather than sitting around, why not give me a tour? This looks a very impressive spread."

"He'll be pleased you're interested. But it will just be a quick one. He doesn't like to be kept waiting."

The door to which Justin led him a few minutes later was at the end of a long corridor. Justin didn't knock, but just opened it to let him past. Barry entered. Justin didn't follow, but closed the door behind.

This was no proper study. It was clearly the former library. There were still many old books on the shelves, but Barry was certain they were never lifted down. At the far side was a large, presumably antique desk. This room contrasted markedly with the office in Eagle Tower, which was purely functional. As Michelle has suggested, the whole setup smelt of major wealth.

Ted looked up. "Sit down, Barry."

There was a large armchair in front of the desk. Barry saw several smaller chairs around the room, and presumed that the choice of this chair for him was in some way a mark of status. Barry sat down, or rather sank down.

"I'd offer you a drink, but you'll say you are driving."

"Happy to have a small whisky. One should be OK, and I'm only driving myself."

"Good man." Ted poured a glass, rather more than small. Barry took a sip. He was no expert, but he reckoned this was no cheap blend.

Ted fixed his eyes on Barry for a time. Barry held his gaze, steadily. Finally Ted spoke again. "Well, I seem to have seriously misjudged you."

"In what way?"

"Wayne has told me how his nose was broken."

"Dangerous business, threatening someone with a knife. Especially if you then try to stab them."

"That's not how he put it."

"No? But I bet you know which version is true."

"Yes. I'll ensure Justin gives him a good talking to about that. But I thought it would be worth doing some digging, to see the type of person I'm letting get close to my business."

"And what did you find?"

"Initially nothing. Clean as a whistle. Amazingly not even a speeding fine."

"You must have good contacts if you can find that much out about me. In the same Lodge as the Chief Inspector?"

Ted laughed. "No. But that would be cheaper."

"You said 'initially'."

"Yes. Someone picked up on some previous in the West Midlands. Seems you were quite a bad boy when you were young."

"I'm sure we were all a bit headstrong in our youth. And as you said, I have no criminal record."

"No. You clean your life up, and then have twenty blameless years of accountancy. You marry a lovely girl, who sadly dies a couple of years ago. But then you lie about knowing an injured woman you meet on a bus, move her in with you, and bang her up."

"I don't particularly like the way you put it, but in essence that's all correct."

"I bet Perkins don't know about your youthful exuberance."

So, thought Barry. We're getting to the point. But he was ready for this, and felt reasonably in control.

"Ted, don't bother trying to blackmail me. It won't work. I'm happy to give you my boss's number, so you can tell her everything. I've spent most of those twenty blameless years making them a shedload of money, and they're not likely to worry about me being a tearaway when I was young."

"You reckon?"

"Yes. And while I'm at it, I wouldn't bother threatening me either. You'll probably appreciate that I don't threaten easily. And before you get on to threatening Michelle, which I'm sure would be the next step, you'd better stop and think a bit."

Ted's eyes narrowed, and if anything they became even colder. Barry could see suppressed anger in the expression. He would need to tread very carefully now, but this was still all going according to plan. Ted spoke first.

"You are a fucking cocky bastard. Are you actually threatening me?"

"No. Not at all. But I think you're missing something really obvious."

"And what's that?"

"I'm almost disappointed, Ted. But I'll spell it out. As you pointed our, I'm a squeaky clean accountant. And you're a crook."

"What?"

"You're a crook. Quite big time too, according to Michelle. Did you think she wouldn't have told me? Her dad was your partner in crime, literally. So, knowing you're rather on the dark side, why am I sitting here in your study, drinking your whisky, and chewing the fat? It's much more likely to bugger my reputation that a misspent youth."

Some of the anger had disappeared from behind Ted's expression, and it had become more quizzical. This was clearly not how he expected the conversation to go. "All right, humour me."

"Happy to. As you have noted, I turned my life around. Married a beautiful, lovely woman. And we were blissfully happy. And then she died. And died fairly horribly. So now I'm past forty, kicked in the teeth by life, emotionally dead. So I start thinking, what did I get from turning my life around? Just an empty future.

Then suddenly life throws me some excitement. I pick up another beautiful woman, and she's got big criminal connections. And maybe I think well, fuck being Mr Nice. Maybe I need to get my own back on life, and teach it a lesson for a change."

Ted sat there for a bit, putting together what Barry had said. Finally he spoke. "I'm not happy about the way you describe my business activities, but I'll let that pass. But what really surprises me is that I've always thought I was a really good judge of people. Yet I've had you completely wrong. Twice."

"Twice?"

"Yes. First as Mr Clean. Mr Incorruptible. You've got skills that I need, but it wasn't obvious how I could get at them. And then suddenly I find you're a former thug, some sort of reformed delinquent, with real blackmail potential. But that was wrong as well, and all the while you were really just waiting for the opportunity to come after me."

"Come after you?" A slight feeing of unease passed across Barry, but he kept it out of his voice.

"Yes. I thought I needed to get you to work for me, and all the while you were sizing me up to get me to employ you."

Relief. "As I said, I could do with a bit of excitement. But as I see it, it wouldn't work if I left Perkins to come and work for you. As we have agreed, I have a squeaky clean reputation. If I leave Perkins and join your staff, that will be gone immediately. After all, it wasn't just Michelle who told me you were a........ what's another expression for crook? Told me you operated on the wrong side of the law. There was also a Detective Inspector at the hospital who made that pretty clear as well."

"Would that have been a DI Howell?"

"That would be him. So, instead of formally working for you, I could just do some stuff on the side. Stuff that you don't trust your Mr Johnston with, for whatever reason."

"Just supposing I was interested in making such an arrangement, we'd need to talk about payment."

"It might seem strange to you, Ted, but I'm not over worried about payment."

"No?" Ted seemed puzzled by this.

"No. Two reasons really. Firstly, if large unexplained sums of money start coming in to my account, it would be fairly obvious where they were coming from, and why. Secondly, as I said, I'm really just interested in some excitement at the moment. Money isn't particularly relevant. But maybe later on we can revisit that."

"You're certainly one of the strangest people I've ever dealt with. And you haven't at any stage asked me what business might need some careful accounting."

"No. Partly because I'm pretty sure I can guess from the name 'Gloucester Imports'. And partly because I'm sure you'll tell me when you need me to know."

As he turned out of the drive, Barry took the opportunity to take a deep breath. He knew that he had pushed Ted just about as far as it was possible without crossing the line. And he was also aware that now there was no turning back. He was in play, and whatever happened now would have to run its course.

Michelle was in bed when he got home. A fairly sleepy voice asked, "How did you get on?"

"It all went very much according to plan. But I'll have to sit and wait for him to make the next move."

"Come to bed then, and snuggle up. I was scared you wouldn't come back."

Barry didn't expect things to move particularly quickly, and he wasn't surprised when there had been no movement by the weekend. So he took the opportunity to ask Nick up to lunch.

Nick arrived at noon. Barry had asked him to bring someone if he wanted, but Nick was unaccompanied. "No-one on the horizon yet?"

"No. Would you expect me to replace Chris overnight? We were together for twenty years. Twice as long as you and Laura, and you took two years to date again."

Barry felt a touch guilty. "Sorry, Nick. A bit insensitive."

"No worries. And to be honest, running a bar is a pretty good way to meet new people. When I'm ready, I'm sure it won't be a problem. How's the expectant mum?"

"She's in the kitchen. Come in and say hello."

"Will do. But first, just tell me this. Can we talk about your current enterprise in front of her?"

"She knows what I'm up to. But she's agreed that the less she knows the better. In fact she said that herself. Then if Ted Young asks her anything, her ignorance won't have to be faked. I think she's a bit too genuine to lie easily. When we've eaten, she'll let us slip away."

In the lounge Michelle brought Nick a glass of red wine. "How did you know that's what I wanted?" he asked.

"It's what you were drinking at your party."

"Well remembered." Nick took a sip, and looked at the wall. The picture of Barry and Laura was still in place.

"How do you feel about that being there?"

"I wouldn't want it to be put away. It's a lovely picture, and Barry looks so good in it. And Laura was so beautiful. I would love to have known her."

After lunch, Barry took Nick in to the front room. "So," asked Nick. "Presumably you've got some sort of plan?"

"Only some sort at this stage."

"Before you get on to tell me that, you're clearly now messing big time with nasty people."

"That would be true."

"What have you done about security?"

"Security? What, like intruder alarms, that sort of thing?"

"Yes. Exactly that sort of thing."

"Don't tell me you've got a relative in the security industry?"

"Funnily enough….."

"Seriously though Nick, it's a good thought. But I'm pretty sure they'll be keeping an eye on what I'm up to. If I start cranking up the home security, they may ask awkward questions. I have taken some action. But I'm not telling you what!"

"It's up to you. But anyway, the offer's on the table. So, back to your plan."

"Well, I have a feeling it's fairly simple. They are an importing company, and I'm sure a significant chunk of what they do will be legitimate. But that will be a cover for some sort of illegal stuff."

"Any better idea yet what they might be bringing in?"

"No. But I still think drugs would be most likely. Michelle said they imported machinery. In terms of bulk and weight drugs could easily be lost amongst those."

"What about arms?"

"Why would they import those?"

"Why indeed? But when the machinery's arrived, with or without drugs, they'll have an empty container. No transport company likes moving an empty container. Call yourself an accountant?"

"Good point. I clearly hadn't thought this through fully. My plan is just to get in to their warehouse and see what they've got."

"Are you going to break in?"

"Possibly. Difficult though, since I don't know where it is. No, I'm hoping I'll get invited."

"Why do you think they'd invite you?"

"Because I'll need to know what I'm hiding in the accounts. Don't forget, if Ted takes me on, he's already revealed himself to a degree. So letting me see the stuff is not really worse than telling me what it is. And the bottom line is that I'm really easy to find if I do grass them up, and he knows I know that."

"But in that case whatever you find, you'll never be able to tell the police. You'll always be a target."

"Yes. I'll admit that's the real weakness in the plan. I have a vague idea what I might do, but I'll keep that to myself for the moment. Because you'll think it's crap."

"Well, if you develop your plan to the extent that you decide to carry it out, just give me a ring?"

"Why? Presumably you'll try and talk me out of it."

"Far from it. I want to come along."

"Really?" Barry was really surprised. "Why would you do that?"

"Because I'm single, and rather bored. And someone's got to watch your back."

*Chapter 24*

George said, "Before we eat, I'm going to make a couple of calls. You go in and see what it's like."

"I know what it will be like."

"Get me a pint of something reasonable."

It was a full twenty minutes later before George rejoined him. "Right, I'm starving. Have you ordered?"

They had a leisurely meal, only partly necessitated by the amount of chewing required. George said, "All the way down here you wouldn't tell me what your plan was. I have a feeling that's because you didn't really have a plan, but were waiting to see what the place looked like."

"That would be mostly true."

"So, now you've seen it, what do you propose? And I think I can guess."

"I think we go back after dark, and see if we can find a way in. Obviously it will depend on whether the chaps are still there or not."

"And how do you expect to get in? Do you think they'll have left a window open for you?"

"I doubt that. But I'm rather hoping you've got something in that rucksack that should help."

George smiled broadly. "You are a clever bastard! But I am worried about that chap recognising you. That's really going to put them on their guard."

"Is that what you were on the phone about?"

"Yes. Don't forget, I'm not a policeman while we nosing around here. And anyway I'm well out of my force area. But I've arranged some possible backup, just in case things go horribly wrong."

"Do they mind you interfering in their area?"

"Funnily enough, no. I had a long chat with a DI called Simon Howell. He's got a bit of an obsession with some seriously nasty locals. And he thinks our South West Imports may be connected with something they're involved in called Gloucester Imports. He's not got any evidence for that, just a hunch. He seemed to think we might flush his people out. He's Gloucestershire, but he's going to talk to Avon as well."

"If it's an obsession, he may not care too much about us. If something bad happened to us, it would give him his case!"

"Possibly. Anyway, it's nearly ten now. Are we happy that it's dark enough?"

"I think so, yes. Let's get moving."

George turned off his lights, and carefully pulled off the road into the Columbian Laboratory car park. No-one passing along the road would see the car.

"Ready?"

"As much as I'm ever going to be. I have to admit I'm a touch nervous."

George was sympathetic. "I don't blame you. But I bet part of that is excitement as much as fear."

"You may well be right. So are you going to distribute some goodies from your bag?"

"No. Not yet. I have got a couple of flashlights, but there's no way we can use them outside. And even inside we'll have to be really careful, because the light will be seen through the windows.

I suggest we go round outside both the small and the big building, and get an idea of the ways in, and, of course, the ways out. Then I suggest we concentrate on the storage units. I don't think we're too interested in the paperwork.

And make sure your mobile is turned off. We don't want any unexpected noises!"

George turned off the courtesy light, so it didn't come on when the doors opened, and they got out of the car. He put on the rucksack, and locked the car with the key rather than the remote, so it didn't make a noise. They had no problem following the pipes, and crossing over the railway track bridge. This brought them up to a large patch of trees. They pushed their way through, up to the car park fence. The car park was lit, presumably for security. There were four vans parked in it, but it was mostly empty.

"Right," whispered George. "If we get separated we meet in here. And you'd better put these on." He handed Steve a pair of surgical gloves. "Wouldn't be good to leave any fingerprints!"

They worked their way through towards the edge of the smaller building, keeping out of the car park lights. They stopped here and listened for a few minutes, but could hear nothing of concern.

George touched Steve's arm, and moved out from the cover. Steve followed close behind. They edged around the small building, noting where the doors were. At each corner they stopped and listened, before moving on. Still there was no sound.

They moved to the larger building. Edging along the first wall at the end they came to a large double door. Immediately they had a shock. One of the doors was fractionally open. Steve's immediate reaction was to hide somewhere, but George held him. He pointed to the lock.

Steve peered closely to see what George had spotted. He gasped. The door hadn't been unlocked, but broken open.

George carefully pulled off his bag, and got out one of the torches. Without turning it on he moved through the door, beckoning Steve to follow. Inside they pulled the door to behind them. George switched on his light. This had a cover on it, so it only produced a very low beam. They quickly scanned around. The building seemed to be divided into large sections, each presumably a separate storage area. This first bit seemed to just have a few bits of furniture. A passage continued directly off from the main door, and as far as they could judge, went the full length of the building.

They moved along. The next section also appeared to be furniture. Steve started to wonder if they were barking up the wrong tree. But the next one had some machinery, some large crates, and some large cupboards at the far end. When they tried these they were locked. George took his rucksack off again, and got out a set of what looked a little like keys. He examined the lock, then selected a key from the bunch. He opened one of the cupboards.

George grunted. Steve thought that whatever he had been expecting to find, he was disappointed. It was just papers, and some books. Maybe they were sensitive papers, but they had no time to look through them. George relocked the cupboard. He whispered to Steve, "We'll try and have a look in one of the crates on the way back."

There was a hum coming from the next area. The light picked out a set of large freezers. Steve moved quickly to open one up. George looked in. He was definitely disappointed this time, as he was faced with a freezer full of meat. But he was surprised to see Steve had his thumbs up.

As they approached the last storage area they started to pick up an unpleasant smell. This area was smaller than the other, and appeared to have been partly converted into rooms or offices. There were three doors. Two were open and one was closed. They moved to one of the open doors. Again George pointed at the lock; this door had also been broken open.

The smell now was really strong. There was a bucket in the corner of the room, and a quick look showed it contained human waste. There were three mattresses on the floor, and some scattered clothes, showing that someone had been living here. But the state of the door suggested they were not staying there of their own free will.

The second room with the open door was similar, but with a large crowbar lying on the floor. George opened the third door, but this one had no signs of recent occupation, although it had two beds in it.

George whispered, "I think we've seen enough."

Steve nodded. But then they both froze. It was only a slight noise, but it was a noise. They tried to pinpoint where it came from. There was another slight noise, which seemed to be coming from just above them. The torched picked out the foot of some stairs, leading behind the third room.

George motioned to Steve to stay where he was. Steve shook his head, and indicated he was following. George lifted off the rucksack, and pulled out a long object. Steve realised it was a crowbar. They moved up the stairs.

At the top was a door, also locked. George selected a key, and unlocked it. With the crowbar raised in his right hand, he opened the door with his left, and pushed it wide open. He shone the torch in.

Against the far wall, three people were staring back at them. A man was looking towards them, with an expression difficult to define, probably closest to defiance. Two small children were holding his legs, and staring out from behind.

George lowered the crowbar, completely taken aback. But Steve moved forward. "Patrick Murungaru?" he whispered.

Surprised, the man nodded. Then he said, "And who might you be?"

"My name's Steve Smith."

"Steve Smith? Sylvia has spoken to me about you."

"Well, no time for that now." Steve turned to George. "Let's get out. Come with us. Quickly, but very quietly. Do the children understand?" The reply was just a nod.

They moved down the stairs quickly, back through the building, and started out through the door. But as they went out they heard a car approaching. "Quick," said George, and they leapt into the scrub patch.

Steve said, "You get back to the car. Take Mr Murungaru and his children with you. Call your backup. I'll see what happens here. If necessary drive off. But get back soon."

Steve crouched down, ready to watch. But almost before he was ready he heard the sound of running, and he tensed as someone dived into the scrub within a few yards of him. Whoever it was lay there, panting slightly, and Steve relaxed.

The car pulled up in the car park. The man in front of Steve was now crouching up, watching what happened. Someone got out of the passenger side of the car, and moved to the driver's side. Steve recognised him immediately again as his assailant from Oxford. But now he had a gun in his hand.

The other occupants of the car were ordered out. The driver was a middle-aged man. From the back there emerged a young woman. She was dishevelled, and in tears.

The man was shouting at them. Shouting questions. "Where is he?" No answer. "Where is that fucker?" Again no answer. The man was smacked hard across his face. "Tell me, or you really will be sorry."

"There's no one here but me."

"Don't be so fucking stupid mate. OK, I'll try her." The girl was also smacked hard across the face. Steve noted that she barely responded, as though being smacked across her face was just her standard treatment.

Still the man would not answer the question. "OK mate, I'm sick of this." The gun was placed against the girl's head.

"It's the truth. There's no-one else but me."

"Suit yourself." He made to squeeze the trigger, but then stopped. "OK, get back in the car. In the back."

He roughly pushed the man to the back of the car, while keeping the gun on the woman. Shaking with fear, the two captives got back in the car.

The gunman pulled open one of the doors. "Open the window," he ordered. The back window was opened. He raised the gun again.

## Chapter 25

"Morning Linda."

"Morning Baz. Word of warning. Rebecca's here again."

"Again? And on a Friday? What's she after?"

"She said she's got a meeting in Gloucester, so thought she ought to call in."

"Very nice of her. But that's the third time in a fortnight. Do you think there's something odd going on?"

"Well Baz. She could think you've got your hand in the till. Or she could know you've got a new partner, and just wants to show you what you're missing."

"Linda!" Although amused, Barry was a bit shocked. He was fully aware that Rebecca had more than a bit of a thing going for him, and that this was fairly general gossip, but Linda had never articulated it so openly. "Where is she?"

"In the kitchen."

"No, I'm out now." Rebecca was now standing behind Linda. Barry had seen her coming, fortunately just too late to hear what Linda had said. But Linda turned beetroot red. Barry would have to reassure her later.

"Hi Becky. Linda was just saying it was good to see you again."

"Was she? After I've not been here for three months, I come three times in two weeks, and that's what she was saying?"

Linda was really speechless now. But Barry rescued her. He laughed. "No, what she really said was 'Is there a worry that someone's got their hand in the till?'"

Rebecca smiled. "Linda, you're a treasure. You're always watching out for Barry. What would he do without you? But don't worry, after today you probably won't see me for another three months. Barry, is your little meeting room free? I could do with a quick word."

"If it isn't, I'll kick out whoever's in there. Got to assert myself every so often. Otherwise they'll think I'm getting soft."

Settled inside the meeting room, Rebecca took a long look at Barry. "What's wrong?" he asked at last. "Am I growing an extra nose?"

"Not that I can tell. But I've just had a most interesting conversation in your kitchen."

"Really? Who with?"

"Chris was in there. And your new girl, I forget her name. The one you took on to handle the Dutch account."

"Phoebe."

"Phoebe. That's it. How sweet. Anyway, they were telling me this fantastic story about someone pulling a girl from a blazing car. Saving her life apparently."

"The stories they tell around here."

"And the amazing thing is, this hero is called Barry Clark. And he works in this office. Barry, is this true?"

"Substantially, yes."

"When did this happen?"

"Months ago now."

"But why didn't you tell me about this? But don't answer that, I know why. You're not the sort to shout about something like that. Pity really. It would make an excellent article in the newsletter."

"Don't you dare!"

Rebecca smiled. "What's it worth not to?" But then suddenly her face darkened. "This isn't connected in any way with the current business, is it?"

"It's completely connected. The girl is indeed the girl."

"But they said the girl you saved had lost her leg."

"Why would that matter?"

"Barry, I'm so sorry. That was deeply insensitive of me. It just slipped out. I wouldn't want you to think what I said was due to prejudice against anyone with a disability."

"It's OK Becky. I know you don't think that. But we can't help our natural reactions. Linda's met Michelle, and knows how we met. She let slip about the accident in the office, for which she's apologised many times! But the others have no idea about the connection between that and my new relationship.

But I'm guessing, given the suspicion you knew it would arouse, that you've got something important to talk to me about."

"Yes. I've had the police on the phone."

"All of them?"

"No. Just the one. A Detective Inspector, from Gloucestershire Police. I didn't want to talk about you on the phone, since I had no idea he was genuine and not just your new friends making enquiries, so I arranged for him to call and see me yesterday."

"Ah! I bet it's my old friend DI Howell."

"That's the one. Have you had a lot of dealings with him?"

"No. Just met him the once. At the hospital, the night Michelle was admitted. He was interested to know what my relationship was with this bunch of criminals. Since I had no idea they were a bunch of criminals, I think he was persuaded there was no relationship."

"He may have thought that then, but he's thinking differently now."

"That was always the danger. Why didn't you tell me before that he'd been in contact?"

"Because I have to think of the business. You know I trust you, and don't think I've changed my view. But I need to play this absolutely straight for Perkins, just on the one in a million chance I'm completely wrong about you."

"Quite right too. Absolute trust can be a dangerous thing. You see cases like that every day on the news. So, what did you tell him?"

"The truth. Up to a point. I told him you'd come to see me. You'd explained your new relationship, and the nature of the people that was bringing you into contact with. And that you would keep me completely informed if you came under any pressure to do anything illegal. I may have neglected to tell him that you were aiming to bring them down."

"I'm relieved you didn't say that. But why?"

"Well, despite what I said before, I'm rather enjoying getting into this murky world, and thinking like it's some sort of thriller. Even though he was a genuine policeman, how did I know that he wasn't a crooked one?"

"That was perfectly sensible thinking. From my conversation with Ted Young – he's the head baddie – they certainly have some police sources on the payroll."

"But there's one more thing. He referred to something in your past which meant to him that you might have a tendency to corruption."

"Ted Young's going to be really cross. That was his main hope for blackmail. And I'd already dashed that anyway. Did DI Howell say what it was?"

"No. He just left it hanging. But you seem to be suggesting there is something to it."

"Only to a degree. When I was young I was a bit of a tearaway. Well, quite a lot of a tearaway, although I was never convicted of anything. But I was there on the night my best friend was knifed to death in a street fight. It proved the incentive to get my life in order."

Rebecca took another long look at Barry. He wondered what was coming next, but he would never in a hundred years have guessed. "Everybody has a past Barry. Starting when I was eighteen I spent two years working as a prostitute. In Leeds. I've never told anyone that. Not even Bill. Not that he'd really care these days. He walked out two weeks ago. I think he's moved in with someone else."

It was Barry's turn to take a long look back. "It's a secret that's safe with me Becky. As you'd expect. And knowing that, I think a lot more of you, not less. Listen, I knew that it wasn't working between you and Bill, and I'm really sorry about that. But I get the impression that you think that's for the best."

"Probably, yes."

"And since we're well into open and honest territory here, whilst I shouldn't say it, I know you've got the screaming hots for me."

Rebecca blushed, almost as deeply as Linda earlier. "Is it that obvious?"

"Deep in the Amazon rain forest it's the only topic of conversation. If I was that sort of person I'd happily take advantage of the situation. You're a really attractive woman…"

"For my age."

"Which is actually rather less than my age. But I'm not that sort. And anyway I like you too much to treat you in that way. But like any man I'm perfectly happy to know you feel like that about me! I know you'd never even hint at abusing your position. And in any case I'd never consider anything you did as harassment."

"Thanks Barry. But I bet you know it's not just me. Half the women in the organisation would drop their knickers for you at the slightest encouragement. After Laura died, a lot of people were hoping that when you'd got over that, they might be back in with a chance. Awful thing to say, but true. And I would have fought my way to the front."

"In other circumstances Becky it could have been different. I've always kept you at arm's length. It's appropriate given our respective positions. But over the last few weeks I've got to know you better, and to a degree differently. If we'd talked like this before I met Michelle, who knows where it would have gone. But 'might have beens' are a waste of everyone's time and emotion. You've not seen a picture of Michelle, have you?"

"No. But I expect she's very good looking."

"It's funny, but I never carried a photo of Laura. Seemed an odd thing to do, since on any ordinary day I'd see her again in a few hours. And after she died I thought it would be just morbid to do it. But to Michelle that was very strange, and she insisted I put a photo of her in my wallet. Do you want to see it?"

"Go on then. Let me curse the opposition."

Barry handed over the photo. Rebecca's expression was an absolute picture. It was again some time before she spoke. "I'd better book myself in for plastic surgery. And buy a wig."

"Don't do that Becky. And I'm not with Michelle because she looks like Laura. Well, not directly anyway. But given the time we've been in here together, we should have got the gossip going nicely. So getting back to business, where do we go from here?"

"In summary, I think you're still just about in the clear, but I really don't think you've got time to sit back and wait for them to come and get you."

"No, I appreciate that. But in fact I've already upped the ante. I was summoned to see Ted, and rather proactively put my cards on the table."

"God, Barry. Wasn't that a risk?"

"It's all a risk now. But I clearly gave him the impression that I was quite keen to get involved in his business. Helped to bypass the blackmail and the threats. But if nothing happens in the next few days, I'll have to prod again."

"Well, just be careful. I won't come up here again for a bit. I need to pour a bucket of cold water over the rumour mill. If anything else happens, we'll arrange to meet somewhere else. They stood up. "You said that you wouldn't consider anything I did as harassment. Since there are no windows, will you kiss me, properly? I could do with that just now."

"So long as you don't consider it encouragement."

After she had gone, Barry realised that he was going to have to talk to Linda. So he was back in the meeting room.

"Is there something serious going on Baz?"

"Not for us. Look Linda, I'm going to have to let you in on a secret. And this time you can't let it slip in the office."

"What, that her husband's run off with another woman? Barry, that's last week's news. How did you miss that? And I thought she was confiding in you about that, which was why she'd turned up here so often."

"No. The other two times were just coincidence. But this time she deliberately came in to tell me."

"Just in case you were interested in taking up the vacancy?"

Barry smiled. "You can be quite evil sometimes, you know. But I wouldn't be surprised if there was something of that in it. So I showed her a picture of Michelle."

"How did she react to that?"

"She said she'd get plastic surgery."

"Ha! Proves it."

"Apparently I'm God's gift to women, and everyone's after me."

"Not quite everyone, matey boy. Shrink your head a bit."

"So, you can resist my charms?"

"Managing so far." Which wasn't completely true.

"Good. And I'm sure Brian's very relieved about that."

"He'd better be. So, that was all she came for, to update you on her revised status?"

"That, and to point out that Taunton are still ahead of us."

"Is that so? Well, I suppose I'd better get back to work then."

"You and me both."

Linda seemed assuaged by Barry's explanation, and the subject was let lie. But at lunchtime a call was put through to Barry. "It's a Mr Young," said Phoebe, transferring the call.

Barry expected it to be Ted, and was surprised to hear Justin on the other end. "Dad wants me to take you down to Avonmouth."

"Really? Why?" Barry got a feeling in his stomach. To some it would be fear, but for him it was excitement.

"We've got some storage there. He'd like me to show you around."

"OK. Sounds interesting. When do you want to go?"

"Be at Bristol Temple Meads at quarter past three. There's a direct train from Cheltenham just before half two."

This was all a bit of a rush. "What about getting Michelle home?"

"Dad's booked her a taxi."

"OK I'll….." The line had already gone dead.

Just to be sure, he rang Michelle. She confirmed the arrangement. In fact she'd booked the taxi herself. "Just be careful!" was all she said.

Justin met him at the ticket barrier. "I've got a car in the car park. Come on."

The car was a Vauxhall Corsa, not only not Justin's car, but also definitely not the type of car Barry expected Justin to be driving. Justin could see Barry's surprise. "This place at Avonmouth is nothing to do with us, as far as the authorities are concerned. So we only use hire cars to come here."

"I understand. Presumably you move around quite often?"

"Never in the same place more than a year or so. Usually much less. It's a bugger, but being a criminal is hard work." Justin smiled. "Probably harder than being legit."

The drive only took twenty minutes. They entered an industrial estate, and drove up to the top right hand corner. It was really busy, and Justin had to squeeze between two lorries to get into a small car and van park. "OK," he said. "Come and have a look round."

"I'm surprised you're trusting me enough to bring me here."

"Dad and I talked about it. I wasn't happy, but we've got a real problem now, so we're having to take a chance on you. But the bottom line is we know where you live, and if any difficulties arise we'll be knocking at your door. Although Dad said threats don't really work with you."

"He couldn't have forced me to work for him, no. But they may keep me on the straight and narrow, if that isn't entirely the wrong expression! So what's the urgent problem?"

"Paul Johnson's had a heart attack. He's in hospital. He's not going to die, as far as we can tell, but he'll be out of action for a bit. So, let me show you what we do."

He opened a door into a storage warehouse. Barry noticed that the lights were already on. The warehouse was in sections, the first of which seemed just to have furniture, completely filling it. "I'm no expert," said Barry, "but this doesn't seem to be any old tat."

"No. Old, but not tat. We export a lot of furniture. Mainly to the Middle East. But the people who are selling it don't want to pay any tax on it. So for your purposes 'old tat' is exactly what it is."

"Well, that should be easy enough. But I assume a lot of this is stolen to order?"

"Not by us. But we don't ask any questions."

"Any stolen stuff will have to have been cleaned somewhere along the way, whether you know about it or not. Your Mr Johnson will have created a company string to do it. I'll need to have a quick look at his books to be consistent with that."

"Of course. Take this." Justin passed Barry a cd. "It's nowhere near the full works, but Dad got Paul to put together enough to keep us going in case anything happened to him. Of course the 'anything' we expected was him getting arrested, not a heart attack."

Just at that moment, Barry heard something. It was a shout, or a cry, he wasn't sure which. But he acted as though he had heard nothing. "Is it just furniture you export?"

"No. But the furniture looks legit, so it's a good cover for a few other things. We do a lot of machinery as well." They were walking in to the next section. This had a few bits of machinery only. "We've just sent out a load. The ship went off Monday. Mostly agricultural machinery for East Africa."

"That sounds pretty legit as well. But what's in the crates?"

"The machinery is, yes. But well spotted. We also send out a lot of police equipment. The sort of stuff they use as standard in a number of countries, but which we've gone all virtuous about, so can't legally export. But some of that stuff we just transit from other countries."

"So what do you import?"

"Mostly stuff that doesn't end up here. Chemicals mainly. That's all clean, pretty much."

"I have to be honest and say I was expecting drugs."

"No. Dad thinks that's a mug's game. You can make a lot out of a shipment or two, but they'll catch up with you eventually, generally sooner rather than later. This stuff gives a more consistent income, with more security. But I'll show you the next one."

The next section was full of freezers. But before Justin opened one up, Barry became aware of people approaching from the end of the warehouse. He was surprised to see the Ndesandjo brothers, with Wayne.

"Hi there boys," Justin greeted them. "Everything to your satisfaction?"

Darweshi smiled, a broad smile. "Yes thank you. But we'd better get back."

"OK. I'll just walk you out." To Barry he added, "Wait here, and look through these freezers. Don't wander off."

As the party headed towards the exit, Barry opened the nearest freezer. It was full of meat. So was the second. But Barry wasn't interested in these. He peered round the corner, to see the four men just disappearing out of the door. He ran the short distance to the end, with a cold feeling as to what he was going to find.

There were three doors facing him. The first one was locked, but he looked through the window. There were mattresses on the floor, and there appeared to be two young women inside. One was lying on a mattress, the other leaning against the wall. Both were clearly crying.

The standing woman saw him, and shrank away. But she responded when Barry beckoned her over. "Who are you?" Barry asked.

"Olena." The accent was strongly Eastern European. "Who are you?"

"Barry. I'm not meant to be here. What's going on?"

"They keep us here. Make us have sex with men."

"Just now?"

"Yes. And before. Many times."

"How long have you been here?"

"Some days. Help us. Please help us……" She was crying again.

"How many of you?"

"Four, I think. We came on boat."

It was pretty clear why Justin hadn't wanted Barry to wander off. The Youngs had clearly decided that he was up for some criminal accountancy. But he was pretty sure they would reckon that forced prostitution was several steps too far for him, and that he might react adversely to it.

Barry couldn't risk loitering here any longer. He turned and ran back round to the freezers. Just as he turned in there, the door at the end opened. He quickly got a freezer open, and concentrated on getting his breath back. From behind him Justin said, "Seen enough?"

Barry gave a little pretend start. "I didn't hear you coming over the noise of these freezers! I presume this is the stuff to help the Ndesandjos and their countrymen get over their homesickness."

"A big part of it, yes. Anyway, let's get you back to Bristol. You'll have to get a train back to Cheltenham, while I drop off the hire car."

"No problem."

At the entrance to the trading estate the barrier was down. The security guard stepped out and looked in the car. He was a large sikh, with a broad smile. "Hello Mr Jones. Another new car?"

"Hi there Jas. Just borrowed it."

The barrier opened and Justin drove off. "Mr Jones," asked Barry.

"Best to keep a fake name nice and ordinary. Don't want to engage people in any unnecessary conversation. But since he's started to recognise me, it's time to move on. I'll tell Dad, and we'll get straight on with it."

## Chapter 26

As soon as he was home, Barry called Nick. "You said to call you when I'd finalised my plan. Well, I have. What are you doing tomorrow?"

"I was going to open up, as usual. But I can get someone to stand in. What are we going to do?"

By mutual agreement Barry didn't tell Michelle what he'd found out. But for the second day in a row Barry was arriving at Bristol Temple Meads, this time at eight twenty in the evening, and to be picked up by Nick. They had agreed that it was better to use Nick's car, since no-one should connect that with Barry.

"Just to be clear, we just park the car, break in to the warehouse, free the girls and drive off."

"Yes. I've got a crowbar. That's all it's going to need."

"But if it's that simple, people would be breaking in all the time."

"There is a security guard?"

"Just the one?"

"That's all I saw."

"OK. This is how it is. There will be security fencing. There will be security patrols, and there will be alarms in the warehouse to alert the baddies that other baddies are breaking in. And there will certainly be CCTV."

"Of course there will. So, we'll hide the car. I didn't notice a massive fence as we drove past, just something wooden with barbed wire on top. And I'm not spending time stealing stuff. I reckon the door will be off in less than a minute. I'll be down the building in thirty seconds. The two doors inside are really flimsy, and will be no trouble. I'll be back out in a minute. Adding in the time from where I break through the fence to the warehouse, I reckon I'm out in four minutes.

As to an alarm, where's that going to ring? The local police station? With all that stolen stuff inside? I suppose it might ring in with the guard, but more likely with the security company. They'll have to ring the guard to go and check. So if an alarm does go off when I break the main door, I'm out of the warehouse in three, which I reckon is quicker than they can react."

"You can be out in three minutes on your own. But you'll have some distressed girls, who aren't ready, and don't speak English. It'll take much longer. And I don't move that fast."

"No. That's why you'll be in the car. Ready for a quick getaway."

Nick didn't protest. If any thing he seemed a bit relieved. "Getting cold feet?" Barry asked.

"To be honest, yes. But I'm a bit happier now."

It was still partly light, so they drove past the industrial estate. "That looks a good place to park," said Nick. "'Smiths' something. Nice thick hedge I could pull up behind there."

"I was right about the fence. Looks like a crowbar will have no problems. Drive on another ten minutes, then turn round and we'll come back and park up. It should be pretty dark by then. Then we're off."

Twenty minutes later Nick pulled up behind the hedge, facing back out of the exit. He had turned the lights off a hundred yards before, and found the entrance in the fast fading light.  The car would not be visible from the road. Barry lifted a heavy crowbar off the back seat. "Ready?"

"No. But I never will be. Shall I keep the engine running?"

"No. That could attract attention. But keep watch on the fence, so as soon as we appear, get the doors open and the engine started. And before I open the door, turn off the courtesy light.

So, I'll ask again. Ready?"

"Yes. Go."

Barry ran diagonally across to the fence, jumping over concrete blocks set out to stop cars. When he reached it he found the fence to be thick planks about a foot wide, to about eight feet. He didn't look at the top. With his strength the bottom two planks splintered easily, but behind the gap these left were three strands of barbed wire. Barry grunted, but this was an eventuality for which he had prepared. He pulled some wire cutters from his pocket, and make short work of clearing these.

He crawled through the gap, and picked his way along the back of the building. This was slower progress than he expected, littered with broken pallets and other rubbish, making it much more difficult in the dark. He pulled a torch from his other pocket and shone it at the ground. This was better, but too dangerous for more than a few paces.

It would be quicker, but more dangerous along the road. He made a decision, and edged between two buildings, just pulling back as a lorry passed on the way to the exit. Even at this time on a Saturday night there was apparently some activity.

He took a chance, and ran down to the corner, turning quickly up to the warehouse. He rammed his crowbar into the gap between the doors. This barely made an impression, but it did make a big bang. Despite the noise, rather than delay, Barry hammered away, and within a minute had made a big enough gap to get purchase. From this point, with his strength, it was easy, and the lock splintered. No alarm rang.

Torch on in one hand, crowbar in the other, he ran the length of the building. The first door offered little resistance. He shone his torch in. Two very scared looking young women lay on beds staring into the light. Neither was Olena.

"Come on, hurry!" he commanded. Blank expressions stared back. "Come, quickly!" he tried again. Still nothing. He tried a different tack. "Olena?" he asked. A look of recognition crossed their faces. One pointed towards the next room.

Barry was out in a flash. The second door fell away. He shone his torch around. Only one bed was occupied, and the person there didn't move. Barry shook the figure, and it rolled over. Barry gasped. He could barely recognise her. It was probably Olena, but she had been so badly beaten, her mother would have difficulty recognising her. There was blood everywhere. Was she dead?

He shook her, and one eye twitched a bit. There was also a small grunt of pain. Barry couldn't wait any longer. He threw her over his shoulder, dumping the crowbar, but keeping hold of the torch. Back to the other door, both women were now up. Barry just made a sign for them to follow, and raced up the building. At the end he was pleased to see that they had followed. But it was also now he saw what he hadn't spotted before. The first section was almost empty. Justin had been true to his word, and they were moving immediately. There really was no time to lose.

Barry ran as quickly as he could back along the road. The two women were following, although he was sure they had no idea if this was making their situation better or worse. He found the same passage to edge between the buildings, and started working back towards the hole in the fence. Light though she was, he was starting to tire under Olena's weight.

At the hole he stopped. He flashed the light at the car, then turned it off. He lay Olena down, and, pushed one of the women towards the hole. "Go!" he instructed, kneeling next to the hole so he could watch. The woman crawled through, and ran to the car. Nick had seen the light and was already out, opening the doors.

After a slight pause the second woman started to crawl through. But a sound alerted Barry. A car was speeding in their direction. He tried to stop the woman. "Wait!" he said. But she was already through, and getting up to run. At that point the speeding car tore round the corner, and turned sharply in to their exit. The second woman stopped and turned back to Barry. "Quick," he said, beckoning her back. She did what he said, and in an instant was back through the hole.

Barry's heart was racing. What was going to happen? The car screeched to a stop, and Justin Young jumped out. And he was holding a gun. "Oh fuck!" said Barry, not realising he was actually saying the words.

Justin was pointing the gun at Nick. The woman was already in the back of the car. Justin ordered Nick back into the driver's seat, and he got in the passenger seat. It was clear to Barry that they would go back to the warehouse. He had to get there first to see what would happen, and to see what he could do.

"Wait here," he said, without even looking at the woman. Olena was still just lying there, clearly very badly injured. But at the moment there was nothing Barry could do for her. Despite the hazards, and without using the light, he was running back the way he had come. The lights of the car were already facing towards him. Keeping as close to the buildings as possible, so that parked lorries and trailers gave him cover, he sprinted to the end. At the fenced car park he made a split second decision, turned right, and threw himself into a patch of scrubby woodland, just as the car pulled in to the car park.

There was no time to regain his breath. He knelt up, and edged forwards so that only a thin bush was covering him. It was only now he realised that the tall fence was between him and the car, rendering him impotent.

He watched as Justin shouted at Nick and the girl, gun to their heads, and he winced as both were forcefully struck. When they were forced back into the car, Barry assumed that Justin would drive them off somewhere. But Justin raised his gun at the open window on Nick's side, and pulled the trigger. The retort stabbed into Barry's brain, as the bullet plunged into Nick's, followed a fraction of a second later by a second one as Justin shot the woman.

"No...!" Barry started to form the word, as he leapt up to his feet. But as he did so a hand grabbed him round the mouth and pulled him back down.

"There's nothing you can do," a voice hissed in his ear. "If you move, it will be us next."

Barry could tell the man holding him was much weaker than he was, and he tensed, ready to throw him off. But his brain was now moving quickly. He'd said "it will be us next", not "it will be you next". So he lay still. The hand was removed from his mouth, and, hard though it was to bear, Barry watched what happened next.

The girl had managed to half open her door before she was shot, and her body hung out of the car. Justin cursed, and shoved her back through the door. He then jumped in the front and drove off at speed.

A voice behind them, in a concerned whisper, said "Steve?"

"OK George."

The car had clearly turned left out of the estate, because it was now speeding along the road behind them. Steve was alarmed when it stopped by where their car was parked. There was a shouted exchange, and a door slammed shut. The car turned back the way it had come, and screeched to a halt again. More doors slammed, and then Steve got the impression that two cars sped off into the distance.

"Fuck, fuck, fuck," Barry could think of nothing else to say. He was beating his head against one of the bars of the fence.

"Who was he shooting at?" asked George.

"He shot two people in the car," Steve told him. "A man and a woman. Both in the head."

"Christ." George had his phone out. "We need backup now. Two people shot. No, bodies taken away so no need for an ambulance."

"There's an injured woman. Behind one of the warehouses." Barry regained a bit of composure.

"Change that. We need an ambulance. And a forensics team." George looked at Barry. "Who are you?"

"B....Brian."

"OK Brian. Who was shot?"

"The girl was East European. Forced into prostitution. There are two left, the injured one, and one other."

Steve interrupted. "George, where are the Murungarus?"

"Hiding in some bushes by the road. We were just about to cross over when someone lit a match by the car. So I hid them, and came back to tell you. That's when I heard the shots. Christ Steve, I never expected anything as bad as this."

"No. But here comes the cavalry." Sirens were wailing in the distance, but rapidly approaching. They turned to look in that direction.

"Who was the man who was shot?" George continued, turning back towards Barry. "Hey, he's gone!"

Steve looked round as well. Barry had indeed gone, as Steve and George were distracted by the approaching sirens. "Nothing we can do about him," said Steve. Let's get back to the Murungarus."

George shined a torch towards Steve. "Are you OK?"

"No. I've just seen two people murdered in cold blood, and I could do nothing to stop it. I feel physically sick."

George could tell Steve was telling the truth. He was pale, and shaking. "You need to sit down. I'll bring the others back here."

The sirens were loud now, and lights were racing up towards them through the estate. Steve took George's advice and sat down. He watched four police cars pull up, there was a pause before the doors opened, and a crowd of policemen piled out.

George was back with Patrick Murungaru and the children. "Wait here," George said. "I'll go down and make sure there's no shooting." He headed off and met the police. Steve watched as George showed his police ID, and then George turned, and waved them down. "Are you ready?" Steve asked Patrick.

"Yes, but the children are very scared."

"You carry your daughter, and, if he let's me I'll carry your son." They picked the children up and they walked out to join the police.

George had kept the police in a tight group, so as not to contaminate the scene. "This is DI Simon Howell," George introduced a plain clothes officer. "Before his Avon colleagues start rampaging around, we need to know which bits to secure."

Further vehicles were arriving. At the head was an ambulance. Steve said, "Two people were shot in the car park. The man shot them in the car, presumably to contain any blood. But the woman had got the door open, and half fell out, so there's bound to be blood on the ground. And I presume George has told you about the warehouse?"

"Yes. And he said something about another man here."

"Said his name was Brian."

"Brian what?"

"He didn't say. But he clearly knew the two people killed. He slipped away when our backs were turned. But he said there was an injured woman behind the warehouse. I presume he meant one that way." Steve pointed towards what he thought was the right direction, based on his and George's early look round.

"By injured, did he mean shot?"

"I don't know. But we were around for a bit and didn't hear any shots other than the two people being killed."

"OK. We're on it."

"And this is Patrick Murungaru and his family. They were being held hostage in the warehouse. You may remember his wife Sylvia was killed in Kenya."

Patrick interjected. "The children are very tired. Can we go somewhere where they can sleep?"

"I'm sorry Mr Murungaru. This is a murder investigation, and you're clearly a key witness, so we've going to have to interview you really soon. I'll get an officer to take you back to one of the vans, and see if we can get them comfortable there. But I'm afraid if you want them to stay near you, it will be some time before I can do any better."

"I understand. Given how much they've been through, a few more hours won't matter." A policeman led Patrick and the children away.

Behind them Steve could see the entrance to the car park was already taped off. More and more vehicles were arriving. Although the car park was already lit, large lights were being erected. A car pulled up right by the car park entrance, and a group in plain clothes appeared. "Forensics Team," said George.

Inspector Howell was keen to get going. He had two officers with notebooks ready. "Right Dr Smith, I want to get as much from you while it's fresh in your memory, then we'll get you back to HQ for more detailed questioning. I'm afraid you're going to have a long night."

"So I realise. After this first batch though I'd like to give my wife a ring, to say that George and I are OK. She'll be worrying."

"No problems. Do that first. But you'll have to stay where we can hear what you say. At the moment I don't know that you're not involved in anything criminal. Same for you George as well, for the moment."

"Understood," said George.

It was well gone midnight now, but Steve knew Deborah would still be awake. She answered the phone immediately. "Hello?"

"Hi Debs."

"Steve. God, Gill and I have been so worried. Are you and George both OK?"

"Yes. We're fine. And the good news is we've found the Murungarus. All well, or as well as could be expected."

"That's brilliant Steve. Get home as soon as possible, and tell us about it. We'll wait up."

"No, don't do that. The bad news is that we saw two people killed, and we're in the middle of a murder investigation. I've got to go and answer questions now."

Real concern entered Deborah's voice, "Fuck, Steve. Who was killed?"

"I don't know who they were. But I must go now."

"You're not under any suspicion, are you?"

"I don't think so. But I've got lots of questions to answer. I'll let you know when I can how things are going."

Steve rang off. "OK, ready."

"Right. I think I know what she asked. I'm not going to ask questions under caution. Not initially, anyway. But since I know why you were here, and that your actions were definitely the wrong side of legal, it could be embarrassing all round if it formed part of the official record!

George has told me he didn't see what happened, so describe to me what you saw. Start from when you left the building."

Steve gave as full an account as he could, and was happy he'd missed no significant detail. Inspector Howell clarified some points. "So, you knew the gunman?"

"I didn't know him as such. But he assaulted me in Oxford a couple of days ago. It was a threat, to stop me snooping around."

"Describe him."

Steve gave what he thought was a pretty reasonable description.

Inspector Howell smiled, a grim smile. "Do you know him? Steve asked.

"I sincerely hope so. We'll look at some pictures later. What about the other man, this Brian? Did you get a good view?"

"No. It was very dark. What about you, George?"

"No, not really."

"But one thing," Steve remembered. "He was maybe six foot, but well built. As I pulled him down I got the impression of someone very strong."

"But he didn't struggle?"

"No."

"We'll keep an eye out for him. He may have gone to the station."

"What station?"

"St Andrew's Road. It's back down the road a bit."

"We never saw it."

"No. It's set back and round a corner. The line just goes up to Severn Beach. But he'll be there a bit – there's only a couple of trains on a Sunday. I'll get someone to keep an eye on it to see if he shows up there. Now, did you get the number of the car?"

"No, and I'm not good on cars. I'd guess it was dark blue. Saloon of some sort. But we know there is CCTV in here, so that may pick up the number."

Behind them there was suddenly a great deal of activity. The ambulance crew had their stretcher out, and were moving with a group of police behind the warehouse. A policeman came up to report to Inspector Howell.

"They've found the woman, Sir. Alive. They'll take her straight off. We'll secure there as well."

George's radio crackled. "Inspector, Tom here. We're at the front gate. There's a security guard here. Been stabbed Sir. He's in a bad way, but we've got another ambulance coming."

"Thanks Tom. When he's out, secure it. Get Bert to send out another forensics team. And since we don't know what else might have gone on, let's get a big crowd in to search the place thoroughly."

"OK Sir. Right on it."

"Well, let's go and look in this warehouse. Where did you break in?"

"We didn't," said George. "Someone already had."

They took the Inspector through the broken door. A gloved policeman accompanied them to minimise further fingerprint disturbance. They passed the first couple of sections. "Antique furniture," said George. "Presumably stolen. Next section, the same."

In the third section George waved towards the cupboards at the back. "In those we've got antique books and manuscripts."

"So, they are basically exporting stolen goods?"

"Not entirely. We didn't look in the crates, so as to what's in there, your guess is as good as mine. But my guess is arms. And this next section," they were looking at the freezers, "just has meat in it."

"Not any old meat," said Steve. "It's bushmeat."

"What's that?"

"Meat from game animals. Presumably going to expat African communities. But trade in bushmeat is against wildlife protection law. It's also banned because of the danger of introducing diseases like Foot and Mouth."

At the end they looked at the three small rooms. The crowbar was still lying on the floor of the second one. "That won't have your fingerprints on it, will it?" asked the Inspector.

"No. It was there when we came in. And I used a key on the other doors."

"That's helpful. We may be in the clear."

"The Murungarus were upstairs," George told him. "But I have a feeling these downstairs rooms were used for something very nasty."

"Yes, I reckon you're right. Your friend Brian said the injured woman was Eastern European. I reckon they imported girls as prostitutes, and it was here they, to put it crudely, broke them in. Then they'd move them on."

"God, that's terrible," said Steve. "Does that really happen here?"

"Probably a lot. But the girls get moved all over Europe. Some are probably sold on to the Middle East. It's modern slavery."

"Brian said there were two more, so three with the one that was killed. So there's one more around somewhere. She must be in a terrible state."

"We'll find her. But for now I'll get you back to HQ. I want you to check some photos before I let you get some sleep."

George said, "I've got my car just out the back. Can you get one of your chaps to drive us back in that?"

"Makes sense."

"Sorry George," said Steve. "Didn't you say that someone by the car lit a match, which was how you knew someone was there? Could there be some evidence there?"

"Steve, I've told you before you should join the police. You'd better send us back in one of yours Simon, and get the forensics on mine."

The Inspector was smiling, if a bit grimly. "It's been a long night already for you, George. I'll have them show you the pictures as soon as you get there, and then you can get some sleep. But I've got a lot to do here, and I'm sure the press will be turning up any minute."

## Chapter 27

It was only a twenty minute drive back to Avon and Somerset Police HQ in Portishead, but Steve was asleep as soon as they set off. It was a struggle having to wake up when they arrived. They were led into an interview room, and provided with cups of strong coffee.

A policewoman brought in a laptop. She clicked a tape recorder on. "I'm going to show you some photos. Let me know if you recognise anyone. She clicked on the first picture. "No," said Steve. The next few had a similar response, although they were closer in appearance. But then, "Yes, that's him."

The policewoman smiled. "DI Howell said it would be him."

"So why did you show me the others?"

"Standard procedure. For the record, positive ID at picture number eleven. Justin Young." She turned off the tape recorder. "I'll let you get some sleep now. I'm afraid it will be in one of the cells. But it won't be locked! Your friend Mr Murungaru and his children are already in the next one. The Inspector relented and let them come back for some shuteye. But you'll all be interviewed again in the morning."

It was a good job Steve was tired, because the cell bed was far from comfortable. He sincerely hoped that DI Howell wouldn't decide to charge him with anything, with the risk of further nights here. But despite his tiredness, he took an age to get to sleep. He couldn't move the picture of the moment the two people were shot from his mind.

At eight o'clock he and George were woken up, and taken in to the canteen for breakfast. Both were very hungry, and were grateful that policemen were fed well. Then they were back in the interview room.

DI Howell had been up all night, but he was still looking pretty fresh.

That could partly be explained by Steve's identification the previous night. "I've been after the Youngs for a long time, and this is something they won't get out of so easily. My Gloucestershire colleagues are raiding some properties as we speak, so with a bit of luck we'll bring Mr Young in shortly."

Steve thought for a moment. "There's one more thing."

"What's that?"

"Your Mr Young would fit the description I was given in Kenya of the man who shot Sylvia Murungaru. You should perhaps show Patrick the picture as well. But probably not when the children are there."

"I'll get on with that as soon as I've brought you up to speed. Firstly, the security guard is in intensive care. He's critical, but stable. Lucky for him he's a big chap, with a lot of blood to spare."

"Is he a sikh?"

"Yes." The Inspector seemed surprised. "Did you know him?"

"I spoke to him. He was very friendly. Let's hope he makes it."

"The interesting thing is that he was stabbed, whereas your two were shot. Knife work is not Justin's M.O., to coin a phrase. But we do have a good idea whose it might be. And we picked up a fag end from by your car, so we're hopeful for a fingerprint for confirmation. So now we're looking for a second suspect as well.

The CCTV tapes have of course gone, presumably why the guard was stabbed, so we have no further leads on the car at present. But we'll trawl through pictures from all the local traffic cameras, and I reckon we'll pin this down pretty quickly. We've got the accurate time they set off from George's phone call, and we know in which direction they headed.

The injured girl is not in danger, but she took the most appalling beating. She's conscious. Name of Olena, from Ukraine. And we were right about forced prostitution. We picked up the second girl hiding in the back of a trailer. She doesn't speak English, so we're getting in a translator. Olena told us that they'd just moved one girl on. Olena tried to stop them, which is why they beat her.

Also the forensics team found some blood and other tissue where you indicated in the car park. They've got a tent up now, but I reckon they won't take too long there.

I've had the Foreign Office on the phone about Mr Murungaru. They want him released immediately into protective custody. He suggested going to Monmouth to stay with the parents-in-law, but there is concern that they are quite elderly. The children could well have emotional difficulties that they might struggle with."

"I'll talk to him," said Steve. "They could come home with me for a day or two, before we make more permanent arrangements."

"They're actually next door. Let's go and talk to them. Then I'll bring Mr Murungaru in here, and show him the photo."

Patrick Murungaru and his children were sitting with a policewoman. The children were busy with some colouring books that had been provided. Patrick rose when they entered. "Dr Smith, I would like to thank you and your friend for our rescue."

"This is my cousin, George. We were very pleased, although also very surprised, to find you. It just hadn't entered our minds that you might be there. We just thought we'd be identifying the criminal activity these characters were up to. I can't begin to imagine how much of an ordeal you've been through."

Extra chairs were brought in for them all to sit. Patrick sat silent for a bit. Then he said, "We will talk about that at another time. But I haven't introduced my children. This is my daughter Alice," the girl looked up briefly, but then got back on with her colouring. "And this is my son," he paused, "Stephen."

"Stephen?" Steve repeated.

"Yes. Sylvia wanted to name him after an old friend. I think he can carry the name with pride."

Steve didn't know what to say. George said, "Not often I see you speechless Steve!"

Regaining his composure, Steve suggested to Patrick that his family returned to Beckley with Steve and George. "I'll make a few phone calls. Patrick, I'll leave you to phone your parents-in-law, but I'll ring someone to arrange for them to be driven over if they want. We can get them put up at a guest house very close by. How soon will you let us leave?"

DI Howell thought for a bit. "We'll definitely want to interview you again in the near future. But we've got enough to go on for the moment, so any time really."

"Excellent."

"But just before you go, could I ask Mr Murungaru, to come next door with me for a moment."

Steve knew that Deborah would have no problem putting up visitors, so first he phoned Gwil Evans. "Hi there Gwil, Steve Smith here."

"Steve. Good to hear from you. Any developments?"

"Well, I've just been standing in a room with Patrick Murungaru, and his children are sitting by me at the moment, if you class that as a development."

There was an expletive from the other end of the phone. "Where are you? And do the Joneses know?"

"Patrick's just about to phone them. Just give him ten minutes before you ring them. Can you get off work, and drive them over to Oxfordshire? We'll get accommodation for them and you, and tell you the full story later. But if you need any help getting off work, I can get the Foreign Office to request it!"

Steve was just about to ring Deborah when Patrick came back in the room. He had a grim expression on his face. Steve caught his eye, and asked the question just with a slight inclination of the head. Patrick nodded. Steve said, "You'd better phone the parents-in-law. All sorts of arrangements are being made."

Then it was Deborah's turn for a phone call. "Hi Debs."

"Hi Steve. How are you?"

"I can't begin to explain on the phone. Elation at finding Patrick and the children, but I can't get the picture of those people being murdered in cold blood out of my mind."

"Don't take this wrong, but you're going to need to see someone. So don't go all manly about it. Are you likely to be able to come home soon?"

"Yes. We'll set off any time now. But we're going to have visitors."

"You're bringing them back with you?"

"Yes. I hope that's OK?"

"We'll cope."

"And can you book a double and a single at Lower House as well? Double for Mr and Mrs Jones, and a single for Gwil Evans – though you'd better tell them he's a big chap, and may need a double on his own."

"Party time, is it?"

"I think it deserves one, don't you?"

But George and Steve didn't drive Patrick and his family back. Instead they followed a very smart people carrier, with two policemen to drive it. It was lunchtime when they arrived. Already waiting for them was an official from the Foreign Office named, to Steve's great amusement, Humphrey Twistleton-Smythe. Steve whispered to George, "You couldn't make it up!"

Rather than catering for a large party, Deborah had booked a table at the Abingdon Arms. The two policemen politely declined the offer to stay, and headed back to Portishead. Gwil Evans arrived with Mr and Mrs Jones soon after the others, and there was an emotional reunion. Everyone allowed the family a bit of private time, before they all moved off for lunch.

With five children and nine adults it quickly became a very jolly group, and, to his credit, Mr Twistleton-Smythe played his full part in that. He was quickly abbreviated to Mr T-S, because no-one really dared to try 'Humph'. Tom and Jenny were fascinated by Alice and Stephen, which did at least give Julie a bit of a break. "Daddy," Jenny asked, "why has Stephen got the same name as you?"

After lunch Patrick and Mr T-S had a long private conversation, most of which remained unreported to the rest. Mr and Mrs Jones enjoyed playing with their grandchildren, with the 'help' of Tom and Jenny. With Julie having a nap upstairs, Steve and George recounted the events of the last twenty four hours to Deborah and Gill. There were no smiles in this discussion.

Deborah could see that Steve had been seriously affected by what he had seen, and that they would need to talk at length about it. This was going to stay with him for a long time. Steve knew it himself. But for now he, and the rest of them, needed to keep up an appearance. And there was real joy about the safe recovery of Patrick and the children.

Much later, when Mr T-S had left, and all the children were not only in bed, but also asleep, there was time for deeper reflection.

Gill asked the question that many of them thought of, but couldn't bring themselves to articulate. "Why did they kill Sylvia?"

"They'd taken us at gunpoint, and loaded us in the back of the truck. The white man for no real reason slapped Stephen. Sylvia was furious, and went at him."

"Sounds like Sylvia," said Steve, and her mother nodded as well.

"Yes. She caught the side of his face, left a big scratch down his cheek. Probably from her engagement ring. He just stepped back, and shot her. Then we were just locked in with her body, while they drove off. You can't imagine what that was like for the children." They could all imagine what it was like for Patrick as well. "God knows how much later, they opened the back, just took her out, and I presume dumped her by the side of the road. They were only gone a matter of seconds.

But as they drove off they crashed into something. We were thrown about badly in the back, and we were all bruised, but luckily nothing worse. When they drove off it was fairly slowly, and they seemed to be having some trouble steering. We stopped somewhere, and they got a mechanic of some sort to work on the truck. Part of it they threw in the back with us."

"Apparently they hit a zebra as they drove off. It was this that set off the train of events that led up to us finding you. Sylvia was found by a local policeman called Daniel Kipruto. Against orders he did some fine detective work, which led directly to us finding you."

"When I return to Kenya I will go to thank him."

"You may wish to do more than that. He's in hiding, having just escaped with his family, and nothing else, before they burnt his house down. We managed to find him, and get all his information."

"You have been to Kenya?"

"Yes. Mr Jones...."

"No need for such formality, Steve" Mr Jones said. "It's Christopher."

"Sorry. Christopher and Marjory........"

"Well remembered!" said Mrs Jones.

"Christopher and Marjory asked if I'd go and snoop round a bit. Your 'friends' are not subtle, and tend to leave burnt out buildings and bodies around. But for some reason these aren't clues in Kenya. Officer Kipruto was helped by a friend, who was murdered as well."

"So many people have suffered for this."

"Maybe," said Steve. "But you are not to blame for that."

"When I return to Kenya I will make sure the Officer Kipruto is properly rewarded."

"I think you'll find that he just wants his house back, and the chance to become a detective."

"If that's what he wants, I'm sure I'll be able to arrange for him to have it."

Steve wanted to confirm his suspicions were correct. "I've assumed that this was all about bushmeat."

"Yes, that is true."

"So what is this bushmeat, then?" Gill asked, "and why's it important enough to kill people for?"

"Bushmeat is the meat from wild animals. Many of our rural people still, to a greater or lesser degree, hunt to supplement their diet. They have no licence to do this of course, so it is against the law. But small scale local hunting for food is by and large tolerated.

But when people move to cities, or abroad, they come to miss their traditional foods. This is not the need of poor people to eat, but of rich people who can pay to have their desires fulfilled. And this ability to pay fuels poaching, on a much larger scale, and organised crime starts to join in.

I became aware that a number of my ministerial colleagues were not only turning a blind eye to illegal trade, but were actively participating in it. What you have seen in that warehouse is only part of the story. There are other export routes as well. I am aware that westerners think Kenya is corrupt, and I cannot argue otherwise. But these people were enriching themselves, by raping our environment. I am Minister for Trade, but I also have responsibility for the environment. I was not going to stand idly by!"

Gill clearly felt it was her job to ask all the difficult questions. "So why didn't they just kill all of you?"

"Mr T-S asked me the same question. I am sure the reason is that my family is very influential. If I had been killed, or was believed to be dead, that influence would have come into play, and would have proved very damaging to my enemies. But they knew I wasn't dead, and that I was effectively a hostage. If my family had tried to take any action, they knew another one of us, or all of us, would have died."

"So, some people in Kenya knew you were still alive?"

"Of course."

Gill then raised a subject that Deborah would have wished left closed. "Has anyone any idea who the two people were who were killed? And who that Brian is?"

George gave her a look, but then answered, "There was no further information on that when we left."

Steve was looking pensive, but then said, "I'm sure his name wasn't Brian, and he just gave us a false name, but I bet his real name began with a 'B'."

"Why do you say that?"

"When I asked him his name he sort of stuttered and said 'B....Brian'. Thinking back I reckon he was going to give his real name, but changed part way through."

"Why?"

"For the same reason he slipped off like that. Because he was somehow involved in what was going on, and didn't want the police to know he had been there."

George appeared quite cross with himself. "You're right Steve. That was important information. We'll pass it in the morning."

"If you do, there's one other snippet you and I had also forgotten in the heat of the moment that you should add."

"What's that?"

"That he was a brummie."

"Fuck, yes. Sorry," he said, looking at the Joneses. "But that would indeed have been useful. I suppose I could ring in now, but I'll wait till the morning and speak to Simon directly."

Finally they retired to bed. Steve asked George, "Are your friends watching over us?"

"A mouse couldn't get in. But we won't notice a thing."

After much complex discussion, beds were found for everyone. With Julie in with George and Gill, the other four children were all in a room together; the adults were surprised and pleased that Alice and Tom had relaxed enough to be separate from their father. But their door was left open, in case the night brought any terrors. Patrick had refused to countenance displacing Steve and Deborah, and was in the box room.

Deborah and Steve held each other tight. "Do you want to go straight to sleep?" Deborah asked. There was no answer from Steve. She became aware that he was sobbing. She said nothing for a bit, and just held him tight. Finally she said, "I fucking hope nothing like this ever happens to us again."

## Chapter 28

The approaching sirens had distracted the other two. Barry took his chance. He stepped back, avoided a couple of depressions, and then, crouching to reduce his silhouette, he moved quickly across the open space to the road. He crossed, and, realising he needed to be off the road, climbed over the fence. He headed north, but almost immediately came up against a deep drainage ditch, running perpendicular to the road, almost due east.

This seemed to run in as good a direction as any, and the ground was quite easy to walk over. After a bit the ditch bent round to the right, and he hit a lane. This he crossed, and continued along the ditch. But very quickly the ditch branched, and he was forced south. He didn't like this direction, but at the corner of the field he picked up a footpath, which soon took him south east. But after crossing a couple of further fields, he reached an abrupt end.

The footpath had been severed by a motorway. He guessed, correctly, that it was the M49. And he realised that there would also be the M5 to follow. He decided to turn right, striking off south. This turned out to be a reasonable choice, as he ended up on a small lane, which crossed over the motorway, alongside a railway line.

He moved quickly along this past a caravan park, before it hit a larger road in a small village called Hallen. Here he turned south again, and was very pleased to fairly soon pass under what must be the M5.

Now he had to make a choice. It was clear he had to get into Bristol, and pick up a train. He thought he'd head for Temple Meads. Here he could easily mix in and lose himself amongst a crowd. Whilst he wasn't completely sure where he was at the moment, he had a reasonably good idea. He must be quite close to Filton Airfield and his old stamping ground of Filton. Nearby would be the big shopping centre at Cribb's Causeway. From here on in there would be no easy hiding place, and he could be easily spotted by police driving up the road.

Instead he decided to get off the road and keep under cover till morning. Then he could move about more freely when there were other people about. So, just off the motorway, he followed a sign for a footpath up Oakhill Lane, and very quickly entered some woodland.

Just inside the wood he stepped off the path, behind some trees. Here he just threw himself down on the ground. His mind was numb, paralysed by the picture of Nick being shot. He couldn't clear the image from his mind. With his eyes shut it was replaying in front of him over and over again.

But slowly he regained some composure, and thought processes started to take over again. Initially these were even worse than the images. He realised that for the second time in his life, his best friend had been killed in front of him. And for the second time in his life he had left the scene, so not given the police the name of his best friend's killer. Was life just repeating itself?

No. Definitely not. For one thing, this time he would talk to the police. Just not yet. First, he had to secure Michelle's safety. And he already had an idea how to do this. But he knew that at the moment she was alone, and vulnerable. Justin Young had known he was involved. What was it he was shouting at Nick? 'Where is that fucker?' That must be referring to him. Even now Justin Young could be heading to his house. He needed to phone Michelle and warn her, to tell her to get away.

But it made no sense. Justin hadn't seen him, and had no reason to know the connection between Nick and himself. And yet it was clear Justin was looking for a hidden car. Why would he be doing that? And who were the other two men, one of whom had also witnessed the killings? George and Steve, apparently. Their behaviour, and the call for backup, made it quite clear they were police. But why were they hiding in the bushes.?

It gradually became clear to Barry that 'the other fucker' was probably not him, but one of these other two. Presumably Justin had rumbled the surveillance, without their knowing it. He was therefore on the lookout for a vehicle, and had assumed Nick was one of the surveillance team. The 'other fucker' would then have been the other one. It was just bad luck that this was the night Barry and Nick had made their move. Whilst this wasn't exactly how it was, it wasn't a million miles from the actual position.

This meant that Justin believed he had the body of a plain-clothes police officer, plus one of the imported girls. But the Youngs had good connections in the police, and a quick check of the number plate would tell them their mistake. And you wouldn't need to be Mastermind to realise Nick's car wasn't a police vehicle anyway. It would then probably be a reasonably short step to link Nick to Barry.

If this theory was true, and, for his and Michelle's sake it had to be, how much time had they got? A bit longer. Maybe a day or so. So if he went to the police as soon as possible, would Michelle's safety be guaranteed? Ted clearly indicated that he had contacts in the police, so probably not. Anything he did would need to be done from distance.

Barry's trail of logical thought was being subsumed by another thought, which had started as a seed, but was growing to overwhelm the logic. He wanted revenge. Nick would be avenged, and that was that. He realised that if he was overwhelmed by this feeling, all logic would go out of the window. It would take him over. But he knew that he would have to service it at some stage.

Having worked through his thoughts, to a degree, he was suddenly very tired. So he just slept where he was.

He was woken by the sound of people talking. It was broad daylight. He stood up and hid behind a tree as two women walked past along the footpath, with a black labrador on a lead. He looked at his watch. It was gone eight thirty. Shit. How many trains had he missed? But then he realised it was Sunday, and there might not be many trains. He needed to get moving.

As he walked he decided on reflection that Temple Meads was too far, and that he might as well just pick up a train at Filton Abbey Wood. This was definitely his old stamping ground, and on a Sunday all the trains from Bristol to Worcester would stop here. He reckoned it was maybe three to four miles or so, so walking at a good speed he should be there in well less than a couple of hours, if he didn't get lost.

But he needed to phone Michelle. This he had been putting off, because he didn't know what to say. He didn't know how to break the news to her that Nick was dead. So he decided the best policy was to lie.

Michelle answered immediately, making it clear that she'd been sitting by the phone. "Barry, where are you? What's happened? Is everything all right?"

"Hi Michelle. I'm sorry I didn't ring earlier. We've had an interesting night. I'll tell you about it when I'm back. But Nick's buggered his car I'm afraid, so I'm walking to the station. And I don't think there'll be many trains on a Sunday. I may not be back till mid afternoon."

Michelle sounded relieved. He hated fooling her like this. "OK Barry, I'll see you later. You'll be hungry when you get in."

"Very. See you as soon as possible. Bye." He had to end the conversation quickly, before he gave something away.

He headed towards Bristol, and pretty soon was in Henbury. This was more familiar, and he knew that he would soon be in areas that he knew well. He continued east until he reached Filton Golf Course. Now it was a simple job to work through back streets to the station. He was there in less than an hour and a half.

But his self congratulations were short lived. It was ten o'clock. There was no timetable at the station, so he phoned rail enquiries. The next train wasn't till eleven forty two. That was a long time to be sitting on a station on any occasion, and specifically when the police might be looking for you.

Barry knew there were a number of fast food outlets on Filton Avenue, but he couldn't remember any cafés. But it was worth a try. As Michelle had suggested, he was very hungry.

He was right, there were no cafés. But just past the Bulldog he came to Guimaraes Portuguese Restaurant, which was just opening. Whilst he didn't fancy shredded cod, or any of the other specialities (which he was probably too early for anyway), he was pleased to see they also did a full English breakfast. That he was certainly ready for.

As he sat there, he firmed up the idea that had come to him earlier. He was definitely going to talk to the police, but from a safe distance. He and Michelle would only return, if at all, when he believed it was safe to do so. And he must put all thoughts of any physical revenge away. It would not be fair on Michelle to do anything else.

He was back at the station in reasonable time for the train. But at Bristol Parkway he had to change, for a replacement bus service. He realised he shouldn't be surprised about engineering works on a Sunday, but this was eating into the time he needed to make arrangements.

At Gloucester he was back on a train, but it was half two before he was at Worcester Shrub Hill. From here he got a taxi home. Michelle greeted him as though she'd thought she would have never seen him again.

"Is Nick OK?"

Barry knew he was going to have to keep up his pretence for a bit. "Yes. But he's going to keep a low profile for a bit. We stirred things up a touch."

"What happened?"

"When I went to the warehouse on Friday I found out that the main business was smuggling. Which wasn't at all surprising. But I also found they were importing women for prostitution."

"That's not nice."

"No, it wouldn't be even if the women were willing. But these ones weren't. They'd either been kidnapped, or lured along with the offer of some sort of job. But they were forced into prostitution. They'd only been there a few days, but had been repeatedly raped. While I was there a couple of African brothers had been given a free go. You'll remember them, the Ndesandjo brothers. I'm assuming this is just to get them used to it, before they have to start earning."

"Barry that's horrible. I never knew such things happened." She was starting to cry. "And Mr Young and Justin are involved in this?"

"Not involved. They are running it. But to them it's just a sideline. Anyway we rescued some girls. But it turned out the police had been watching the place as well, so we headed off. That's when Nick damaged his car."

"So Mr Young will be arrested? And Justin?"

"Probably, but not straight away. Not Ted anyway. It will probably take them a few days to link him to this. And in that time they'll have linked Nick's car to him, and then to me. And then we'll be in danger even if Ted is arrested. Especially if he's arrested. So we're going to disappear for a bit."

"Disappear? Where to? And what about your job?"

"The job should be OK. My boss Rebecca is aware of what was going on. I had to tell her just in case Perkins found out about my connection with the Youngs, and didn't like it. And where to? We're going to visit my sister."

"Your sister. But she's in Australia."

"Yes. That should be far enough. I reckon a month out there, and it should be safe for us to return."

"But you don't get on."

"Let's hope she and I can put the past behind us."

"When do you propose leaving?"

"As soon as possible. Hopefully tomorrow."

"Tomorrow?" Michelle was wide eyed. "You've got to get tickets and things like that. And won't we need one of those things that let you in the country?"

"A visa? I'm hoping we can get one when we arrive. If not, we'll have to turn round and come home!" A sudden thought occurred to him. "You have got a passport, haven't you?"

"Yes. We went to Spain when we got married. Some place with lots of hotels and a nice beach. It was hot, but a bit boring."

"Well, Australia may be hot, although it's winter there. I've never been, but I don't expect it to be boring. Although boring might be quite good at the moment."

The first thing Barry did was to look up visa requirements. He was very pleased to see that you could do this on line, and the visa would come through almost immediately. Then, with fears for his credit card limit, he went to the British Airways website. Here he was pleasantly surprised. He could get two return tickets for tomorrow, with returns a month later, and have change from £2,000. There were several flights to choose between, so he booked the one at noon. With the details of the flights he then got the visas. It was that simple.

"We'll have missed the shops," he said to Michelle. "So no chance to buy new clothes. Can you manage on a combination of yours and Laura's?"

"Well, I can't get into many of Laura's any more. They were bought for someone a bit smaller than me anyway, and now I'm very much bigger than me. I have bought a couple of very unsexy pairs of elasticated trousers, which will do for a start. But I suspect they'll have shops in Australia, so I'll get more there."

"That's good. We'll have to get some Australian dollars at a *Bureau de Change* at the airport. The exchange rate will be terrible, but we've no choice. And we'll have to leave no later than about half six in the morning, to be sure to have enough time to check in. So we ought to pack now."

"Well that won't take long. Then you look like you need an early night."

"That's true. The bit of sleep I had last night was on the ground in a wood."

"Let's go now. Then we can make sure you're properly tired."

Barry was restless. He had been tired, and after he'd made love to Michelle he did drop off to sleep embarrassingly quickly. But it was light sleep, and now he was half awake. Had something woken him? It was still dark, and his alarm was set for five thirty. Maybe it was just that his brain was too active to allow deep sleep. That was probably it.

No it wasn't. There was a noise. Just a slight noise, but not a sound he would have expected. He slipped out of bed, and reached underneath to pull something out. Then, naked, he pulled open the bedroom door.

In the small amount of light filtering through the landing curtain from the street light outside, he was aware of a figure on the stairs in front of him. But a movement to his left distracted him. He pushed hard with his left hand, and something solid was shoved backwards, a searing pain shooting through his left arm. But he had to ignore that.

The figure on the stairs was now on the top step. Barry took his baseball bat in both hands, and rammed it forcefully into the middle of the shape. There was a grunt, and a bundle fell back down the stairs.

Barry flicked on the landing light. To his left a man was regaining his balance, just along the landing. In his hand was a knife, and the blade was covered in blood. The man made to move swiftly towards Barry. But there was just enough room on the landing for Barry to get a full swing of the bat. He caught his assailant full on the neck. There was a horrible crack, and the man's head bent right over sideways. He dropped in a pile on the ground.

Without a second look, Barry started down the stairs. He was aware that this was particularly dangerous, but his measured tread was from determination, not fear. From behind he heard Michelle calling. "Barry. Barry. What's going on?" He didn't reply, but continued down. He'd already seen his target.

Justin Young was sitting with his back against the front door. One of his legs was bent at an impossible angle. Blood was seeping from his mouth, suggesting that the blow from the bat had caused significant internal injury. He looked blankly as Barry approached. There was no sign of the gun.

Barry held Justin's gaze briefly. Justin said nothing. Barry said, "I watched you shoot my best friend in cold blood. So this is all you deserve." With that, and with the full force of a single swing of the bat, he smashed Justin's skull.

There was a scream from upstairs. Michelle had managed to get her prosthesis on, probably taking longer than usual by trying to hurry. She was looking at the body on the landing. "That's Wayne. Isn't it?"

"Was Wayne, yes."

"Is Justin here?"

"Yes, downstairs."

"How is he?"

"Well, I'm sorry to inform you that you're now officially a widow."

Sobbing, Michelle fell into Barry's arms. There she saw the blood, flowing freely from his left arm. "Barry, you need to get to hospital."

"No time for that. We'll have to bandage it up."

"Let me see." There was a long, deep incision. Fortunately blood was not pumping out, so no artery had been hit. But it clearly needed stitches.

"If we strap it really tightly, it should stop the flow. There's a first aid kit in the car. I bought one after your accident! But we'll try and stop the blood first."

Between them they improvised a bandage from a tea-towel, which greatly reduced, but didn't quite stop the flow. "We'll have to cancel the trip," Michelle said.

"No we won't. But we'll have to think what we do. What's the time?"

"I don't know, and you've not got a watch on. Or anything."

"I'll get dressed. Whatever time it is, we wouldn't get back to sleep now. And I'll get the first aid kit so we can make a better job of this." The tea-towel wasn't really doing the business.

"How can you be so calm? You've been in a terrible fight. You're injured. And you've killed two people. How can you be so cold?"

"Quite easily. Because I didn't tell you the truth yesterday. Nick's not OK. He's dead."

"Dead?" Michelle was aghast.

"Yes. Justin shot him in cold blood, right in front of me. He didn't know I was there. I was watching from behind a fence. He shot one of the girls too. So as far as I'm concerned he deserved to die. Before he killed anyone else."

"Why didn't you tell me this yesterday?"

"Because it would upset you. And I realised we had to get away. I would have told you when we got to Australia."

"So what do we do now?"

"We both get dressed, and have a think."

When he was dressed, Barry decided the first thing to do was to move the bodies. He started with Justin, dragging him towards the dining room. As he moved him, he saw the gun underneath. Justin must have had it in his hand as he came up the stairs, presumably dropping it as he lifted himself to a sitting position by the door. Barry realised he was lucky it didn't go off when he forced Justin down the stairs.

It seemed likely to Barry that it was Wayne's job to kill them, with his knife. That would be mostly silent. Justin would only have used his gun if something unexpected had happened. But the 'something unexpected' had happened too quickly even for that.

Having moved Justin, Barry picked up the cd Justin had given him from the table where he'd dropped it. Thinking it would give someone some interesting reading, he slipped it into Justin's trouser pocket. Then, back in the hall, he picked up the gun before Michelle could see it. He took this out to his car, and hid it in the glove compartment.

Back inside, he had to get Wayne down from the landing. Wayne's death had been instantaneous; the knife was still in his hand. A sardonic smile passed Barry's lips when he recognised it as the same knife Wayne had tried to stab him with before. Unceremoniously Barry grabbed both of Wayne's legs, and pulled him down the stairs, Wayne's head bumping down each step. It was a sickening sight, with the neck broken, but Michelle stayed in the kitchen so she didn't have to see.

That done, Barry wiped down the worst of the blood. This wasn't to hide evidence, but to stop it spreading any further. Then he had a shower, keeping the bandaged arm out, and got out clean clothes. The bandage was already quite bloody, so before he dressed he got Michelle to help redo it. He put a lot of padding in it, and this was more successful at reducing the flow.

"Aren't you worried about losing too much blood?"

"I'm a big chap. I've got plenty to spare. What time is it?"

"About half past four. It will be light soon. After all that's happened, are you hungry?"

"Not really. But it would probably be good for me to force some breakfast down."

As they munched unenthusiastically, Barry decided to tell Michelle what he'd formulated. "There's going to have to be a change of plan, and I'm going to need you to do exactly what I say."

"That doesn't sound good. Aren't we going any more?"

"You are. I'm not."

"Michelle was wide eyed. "Barry, I can't go without you. I've never travelled on my own. I'd be scared."

"I know that. But it's very easy. Once you're on the plane, you only have to get off once, in Singapore, while they put some more fuel in. You'll all go and sit in one place in the terminal, so you shouldn't be able to get lost. When we check in, we'll ask for them to keep an eye on you, because of your disability. I'm sure they'll make sure they don't lose you."

"But what happens when I arrive? I don't know your sister. How's she going to know I'm coming?"

"I probably wouldn't recognise her either. But I've got an e-mail address for her. So I'll send her your flight details, and your photo, so she knows who to look for."

"But what happens if she isn't there?"

"Just go to an information desk and ask them to help. After all, they all speak English. Sort of."

"But what will you be doing?"

"I'll be talking to the police. The trouble is, if I run away they may reach all sorts of conclusions, and take a lot of convincing that I was acting in self defence." This was true. They would certainly take a dim view of the way Justin had been finished off. "So once you are on the plane, I'll go and do that."

"So why can't I stay here?"

"Because even if our friend Mr Young senior is arrested, I'm sure he's got a lot of very unpleasant associates. When he finds out his son and heir is dead, he might be pissed off. And if I'm helping the police with their inquiries, you'd be very vulnerable. And that's my baby as well as yours."

"The way you put it makes sense. But it still doesn't seem right."

"But it is. Now let's sort out here, make sure we've got your passport, and get the stuff in the car and go. It will do no harm to leave a bit earlier. But before we go I'd better phone in sick. The Ansaphone will be on, so I won't have to talk to anyone. And it will stop them worrying, or coming looking for me."

*Chapter 29*

At the check-in desk Barry had his story ready.

"Hello there. Sydney?" the check-in attendant asked.

"Yes. But just my wife. I'm meant to be travelling with her, but some urgent business has come up. I'm going to have to rebook for later in the week."

"Do you want to do that now, Mr Young?" The man was looking at Michelle's passport. Barry hadn't thought of that. But Michelle covered well.

"I use my maiden name."

"Yes," continued Barry. "You'll see on the booking that I'm Barry Clark."

"Sorry sir," the man apologised. "But I can rebook you if you'd like."

Barry pretended to think for a second, then said, "I'm not sure at the moment if it will be Wednesday or Thursday, so best to do it later."

"No problem. Just the one bag?"

"Yes. And my wife hasn't travelled much, so she's very worried she might get lost, especially at Singapore. You'll see she's pregnant. And she had a serious accident recently, and has an artificial leg. So I was hoping you could keep a look out for her."

"Certainly Mr Clark. And I'll see if I can get her a better seat as well."

Once checked in they sat down for a last brief conversation. "OK," Barry said. "You've got a thousand dollars, which is about £650. And you've got your credit card. That should cover you for emergencies."

"I did like being your wife, if only briefly."

"We can make it more permanent later, if you want."

Michelle started crying. "But Barry, am I ever going to see you again?"

"I sincerely hope so. But I suspect the police won't let me join you for a bit. It may be a couple of weeks, or possibly not till you're back. But by then everything should be sorted. Let's move you through now, because I'd rather talk to the police before they break in and find what we've left behind."

At security there was barely a queue. Just outside they held each other tight. Michelle kissed Barry, and then walked through. She didn't look back, but Barry knew this was because she was crying.

As soon as she was out of sight, Barry turned and walked quickly back to the car park. He had lots to do, and it was already nine o'clock.

Before he'd left home, he had packed a number of items in the car, making sure Michelle didn't see them. There was no way he could go back to the house now; one side or the other could well be waiting for him there. He also couldn't go to Cheltenham, in case someone from the office saw him. He didn't want the hassle of going in to a big town, like Reading or Oxford. Instead he decided to travel back via the M4, and cut across into Cirencester. This would be a reasonably convenient place for what he needed to do.

It was well before eleven when he arrived in Cirencester. By asking, he found all the shops he wanted, although he needed extra directions to find the Countrywide store, out on the Driffield road.

With the car suitably loaded, he drove back into Cirencester, and parked up. Walking through town there appeared to be an abundance of solicitors. He chose one at random, and stepped in.

When he had finished there, he went into the library. He logged on to a computer, plugged in a USB stick, and drafted an e-mail.

*Molly*

*There is a lady called Michelle Young arriving tomorrow (Tuesday) at Sydney Airport, 7.20pm local time, flight BA7372. Please meet her. See attached photo. The baby she is carrying is your niece or nephew.*

*Barry*

He attached a photo of Michelle off the data stick. Then he hovered over the send button, but paused and added:

*I'm sorry that we never made up.*

He pressed send, and logged off. Undecided where to go next, he picked up an Ordnance Survey map at a newsagent. Back in his car he looked for a likely nearby quiet place. He thought the Cotswold Water Park looked promising. Somewhere amongst all those lakes there should be a quiet dead end. He found something that looked promising, just west of Somerford Keynes. He set off immediately, parked up, and set to work.

It was gone five when he was finished. That gave him quite a bit of time to fill. But he had one call he wanted to make, and it was in the wrong direction.

Just before six he pulled up outside a cottage on the outskirts of Wotton-under-Edge. It was an attractive cottage, well kept, and with a pretty garden. Barry was pleased to see a car parked on the drive. He knocked on the front door.

A woman answered. She was dressed as though she had just come in from work. But in her hand was a glass of red wine.

"Drinking alone, Becky?"

The woman looked very surprised to see him. "Barry. They told me you'd called in sick today. What are you doing here?"

"I've come to hand in my notice. I felt I owed it to you to do it in person."

"Your notice? Has something happened?"

"Virtually everything has happened. I'm going to have to disappear for a bit, or even more than a bit."

"Is Michelle with you?" Rebecca was looking towards the car.

"No. She's on a plane to Australia."

"To Australia? Well, if you're hiding, you'd better come in. You can tell me all about it. That's if you can spare the time."

"Thanks Becky. Perhaps I could join you in a drink."

Barry stepped inside. He'd been here just the once before, and he had been pleased to have remembered the way. It was all very nice, and very tidy. He sat in the lounge, which was open plan with the kitchen. Rebecca handed him a glass, quite a big one he noted. "Do you mind if I go upstairs and get out of these clothes? I like to put the office behind me when I get in."

"What, are you going to slip into something more comfortable?"

She smiled. "Yes. But not specially for you, but because I always do. But I'll still be decent, so don't worry."

Normally Barry in a strange house would have been up, looking through books and cds to get a feel for the person whose house he was in. But tonight he just sat sipping his wine. He was tired. It had been a long day, following the long day before. And this one wasn't over yet. So he just looked around, admiring everything. The beautiful furniture, the neat bookshelves, the thick pile rug. He kicked his shoes off, and let his feet feel the softness.

Rebecca returned. She was now wearing a very fetching print satin dressing gown. "Is this too provocative?"

Barry stood up. "I'm not sure it's the ideal garment to wear in the presence of someone you manage. And I bet you've got nothing on underneath."

"But you've handed in your notice. At least verbally. So I don't manage you any more. Have you got it in writing?"

"No. But if you've got a pen and paper, I'll do that for you."

"Later. But for now consider it done." She parted her robe.

"Shame I hadn't put money on it," Barry commented.

Rebecca put her arms round him, and kissed him. Barry didn't resist. This seemed to surprise her. She pulled back and looked at him. "What about Michelle?" she asked.

"In the scheme of things, it should be me asking that question. But you'll notice I'm not. Michelle will never know."

A look of real concern crossed Rebecca's face. "Barry, what are you going to do?"

"If we can finish what we've just started, I'll tell you. Then you can feed me a bit, because I've just realised I've not eaten today. Then if there's time we can have another go."

He undid her robe, and let it slip off her shoulders. He ran his hands over her body, and she shivered under his touch. Then they kissed again, long, passionate kisses. Then Rebecca said, "This isn't fair. You need to catch up." She started to undress him. But when she took his shirt off, she saw the bandage, already well stained again with blood.

"What's happened to you Barry?"

"I got knifed."

"Let me have a look. I'm a trained first aider."

"You can do it afterwards. I'm not going to die in the next half hour."

They sank into the rug, bodies wrapped around each other. When they were exhausted they lay there, Rebecca on top of Barry, looking in his eyes. "Was I OK?"

"I may need another go to be sure. But it was a lot better than my quarterly reviews. I think some of your professional tricks came in to play."

"It's a funny thing, but having been a prostitute, I thought I could never really enjoy sex for pleasure."

"But if it was always like that, Bill's made a big mistake."

"Maybe. But, like so many before me, I've been traded for a younger model. The sex clearly wasn't enough. So, tell me what's happened."

"I'll tell you a bit, but not everything. It's a funny thing in a way. Do you remember when I told you I'd had a difficult adolescence, you said that everybody had a past?"

"Yes. And then told you mine."

"Quite. But the funny thing is that you were the second person to say that to me. The first was your policeman friend, Inspector Howell. And then he said that sometimes it can come back to haunt you. Well, in a big way it has."

"I don't think mine will. I'm a bit too old to go back on the game."

"The people I'm dealing with are also involved in prostitution. They've been bringing in Eastern European girls. But they aren't willing, like you. They've been tricked into coming. When they get here they are locked up in a warehouse, repeatedly raped, then put out for hire."

"God, Barry. That's awful. Have you gone to the police?"

"The police know."

"I can't imagine what that must be like for them. I was never forced. It was just a career choice for me."

"Why do you say that?"

"Because it was. The idea came from an off the cuff remark from a short-term boyfriend. He said I could make a lot of money doing it. Obviously I dumped him like a shot. But I thought about it, and thought I might as well give it a go. I think I was terribly oversexed as a teenager.

"And did you make a lot of money out of it?"

"Not as much as I could have, but a pretty tidy sum, yes. It helped that I was never into drugs, like so many of the girls."

"Why did you stop?"

"Occasional assault was an occupational hazard. But I was badly beaten by one chap, who stole that night's earnings. So I called it a day.

Used the money I'd made to support myself through college. And to be honest I've never missed it. But let's have a look at that arm."

Barry sat on a kitchen chair, while Rebecca removed the bandage. "Whoever put this on would benefit from a few lessons." She looked at the exposed wound, and whistled. "Christ Barry. You're lucky it didn't hit anything more important. It definitely needs stitches. But presumably you won't be getting those just yet?"

"No. Can you bandage it up so it stops bleeding?"

"I think so. But promise me that as soon as you've finished what you're doing, you'll go to hospital."

"I promise."

"What happened to whoever stabbed you?"

"Don't ask."

Rebecca rustled up a light tea, and they sat and ate it at the kitchen table. She laughed.

"What's so funny?"

"I don't think Bill and I ever sat here eating naked, like this. I wish you could stay with me Barry. I've always wanted you to."

"I know. But you're a lovely looking woman, Becky. And, for a manager, you're a really nice person. I'm sure you'll hook up with someone decent soon."

"Maybe. But it's a shame it won't be you."

"Well, it will be again in a minute. But not after that."

At nine o'clock Barry carefully lifted Rebecca's head off his chest, and started to get dressed. She opened her eyes. "Are you off now?" she said, sleepily.

"Yes. Don't get up. I'll take this picture of you away with me."

"Will I ever see you again?"

"Maybe. But it's been great to know you Becky."

"Especially tonight?"

"Hard to argue with that." He knelt down beside her, and kissed her one last time. "Goodbye," he said.

"Goodbye Barry. Good luck."

As Barry closed the front door, Rebecca got up, picked up the phone, and dialled 999.

It was later than Barry had meant it to be, and he still had about an hour's drive. And, with the wine he'd drunk, he was probably over the limit. But losing his licence wasn't a particular worry at the moment, and he didn't particularly care about speeding tickets. So it was actually only fifty minutes later that he pulled into a quiet layby. It was almost dark, which was in itself a bonus.

He took out his phone, pulled a card out of his wallet, and dialled the number on it. He was disappointed when it went to voicemail, but he left a message. "Hello Inspector Howell. I was hoping to speak to you, but hey ho. It's Barry Clark here. I would remind you who I am, but I suspect you'll be remembering me already. I don't know if your chaps have been round to my house yet, or if they have, whether they went in or not. But if they haven't yet, I would recommend it. To make it easier for you, I've left a key under the mat. I know that's not advisable, but it will save you from causing any unnecessary damage.

You warned me against getting involved with the Youngs, and I have to say that was sound advice. But you should also have warned them about getting involved with me."

He gathered his various bits together, and threw his rucksack across his shoulder. It was surprisingly heavy, but not a problem. Across the road he was faced with a Cotswold stone wall. This didn't present much of a barrier, but in crossing it he dislodged a couple of coping stones. Idly he wondered if that would set off some alarm or other, but he didn't pause to worry about it.

Using a variety of shrubs, plus a low wall, he zigzagged towards the house, always with some cover. At the closest point he was only a couple of metres away from the patio doors. Here he stopped, and waited.

He didn't have to wait too long. After five minutes two men appeared round the side of the building. They were clearly on guard duty, most obviously because they were both openly holding guns. But they clearly weren't fully committed to the task, and just idly glanced at the patio doors as they went past.

As the men passed the next corner, Barry was at the doors. He reckoned he'd get a good five to ten minutes before they came round again, provided he made little noise. But it was short work with his new crowbar to prize open the door, and the glass remained intact. He stepped inside, and pulled the door to.

From here it was a short step to Ted Young's study. There were no guards in the house, presumably because they were confident they'd stop any intruder outside. This was an operation that had got a bit sloppy, Barry thought.

He could hear voices from the study. It wasn't Ted on the telephone. There were people in the room with him. He lay the crowbar down, and swung the rucksack off his back, holding it is his left hand. With his right hand he turned the handle, and pushed the door open.

As he stepped through the door, he pulled out Justin's gun. Ted was sitting at his desk. There were three other men present, all strangers to Barry. They all looked at him as he entered, and there was some movement. Barry pointed his gun in their general direction. "Please don't bother to get up. Except you, Ted. Come round here and join the others. Then I can see your hands as well."

Ted was looking at him with daggers in his eyes. "What the fuck do you want, you piece of shit?"

"I'm the piece of shit with the gun, and if you don't come round now, you'll be the corpse behind the desk. Get moving."

Ted decided it was better to obey. He came round and sat on an empty chair with the other three. They looked between Ted and Barry, and the gun. Barry could see they were all thinking about how they could take him. He glanced around the room, and noted that it wasn't quite as tidy as the last time he'd been here.

"I bet I'm not the only unexpected visitor you've had recently. Looks like the police have given the place a good working over. Anyway, you look surprised to see me Ted. Is there a reason for that?"

"Fuck you. Where's Justin?"

"Hasn't he called?" Ted didn't answer. "Well, since you ask, I left him at my house. Maybe he was a bit too dead to ring."

"What?"

"You heard me. You made the mistake of sending him and Wayne to kill Michelle and me. I took exception to that."

"You're fucking dead, mate. Even if you kill me, you'll be tracked down. You and your cripple whore."

"That's not a nice way to talk to a man with a gun. And you other three, what's this? A gathering of the clans? Ted's partners in crime? As far as I can see this is a bonus. You've chosen a bad night to call round.

I can see you working out that if you rush me, I won't be able to shoot you all. You're right. But I'd get a couple of you. And I'd fancy my chances against the survivors with my bare hands. So, down to business."

"What business? We're not dealing with you. In a couple of minutes the guards will realise someone's broken in. I'll make sure they don't kill you. Not quickly, anyway."

"Nothing but threats, Ted." Barry put the rucksack down in front of the seated men. "So it's my turn. You'll remember, Ted, that when you looked into my history, you saw I'd turned my life around. Gone to college, got a degree, remember?"

"So fucking what?"

"Did you find out what degree?"

"I don't give a fucking shit."

"You will do. Because it was in Chemistry. And if there's one thing any chemist knows, it's that if you know the right things to buy, you can mix up a crude but effective explosive on your kitchen table. Or in my case, in the boot of my car. And there's quite a lot of it in that rucksack."

All the men immediately shifted their gaze to the rucksack.

"That's right. Give it a good look. But I have a bit of a problem. To make it go bang, you need a detonator of some sort. Usually some sort of electrical circuit I suppose, to make a spark. But I'm no good at Physics. I didn't have the time to research it. So, I've got a big bag of explosives, and no trigger. Sad isn't it."

There was a bit of shifting in the seats, with maybe a slight look of relief.

"I wouldn't get carried away yet."

"So, what are we waiting for?"

"We're waiting for something to happen. Then I'm going to try an experiment."

"What are we waiting to happen?"

In the distance Barry could make out the sound of sirens. Then there was a loud shout from outside. "This, I think."

Running footsteps approached the door, and it was thrown open. The two guards pushed their way into the room, guns at the ready.

"So let's see," said Barry.

He pointed Justin's gun at the rucksack, and pulled the trigger.

## About the author

Peter Holmes is still working in nature conservation. That means he is committed to the environmental cause, or he didn't sell enough copies of his first novel.